DEAR DIARY

BRONWYN STUART

CONTENTS

1

"I beg your pardon?" I can't believe what I'm hearing. Sure, they're speaking clear English but had my three bestest friends in the whole world really just declared I'm going to die? Alone? Surrounded by hungry cats?

"We don't mean it like that, Imelda," Candice says, her ice-cold hand on my arm in a gesture so sickly patronizing that I fight the impulse to swat her away. My stomach churns and my head spins, the reasonably affordable white wine turns to vinegar in my mouth.

"How long has it been since you had a boyfriend?" Amy asks.

Before I have a chance to reply or defend myself Jess decides to join the ambush and fires off a shot of her own. "Forget boyfriends, how long since you had really good sex?"

What the hell am I supposed to say to that? A few answers pop into my head but most of them include telling my usually well-meaning friends to go to hell.

The worst thing about this moment in time? I can't remember my last sexual partner (or didn't want to). The last time there was a steady boyfriend in my picture was probably college and even then it didn't last long. The relationship or the sex.

"I get sex," I lie. I also wonder how we stumbled into this Imelda bashing.

The others see straight through it with a chorus of, "Sure you do's" and a softly muttered, "Your own hands don't count".

Damn it. I have to escape but with my dignity intact. Either that or go the whole hog and let the floor swallow me. "If you will excuse me, I actually have to get ready for a date right now. I thought you'd all be gone by eight."

I push my chair back, dumping Harry the ginger tom unceremoniously onto the floor, but then I realize they aren't leaving. There they sit, at *my* dining table, drinking too much of *my* wine. I have nowhere to go and they aren't buying any of the crap I'm selling. Can I kick my friends out? Do I have the lady cojones? Should I at least take the bottle away? They do not need any more liquid courage.

I'd like to drown in the stuff.

"Date?" Candice asks suspiciously, eyes narrowed. "On a Monday night?

"Yep. I'm meeting him after he gets off work. Late." *Gulp*.

"And who is he?" Jess's eyes bore into mine with all the power of a hammer drill. She's small but she's intimidating.

"Just a guy I met, uh, on Tinder."

Jess shakes her head and clucks her tongue. At least her tone is gentle when she says, "Imelda, Tinder is not for you."

"Name?" Amy lays her hand on the table like I'll just drop it in her palm.

I gulp again. They're not stupid. But I am. I sit back down and bang my head against the tabletop. To cap off the cat-lady prediction perfectly, Harry jumps back on my lap and lies his fluffy butt down like he has total ownership of my thighs.

"You *seriously* need to get laid," Candice says, all snooty, her pert little nose in the air as she leans back in her chair and bends a long, elegant elbow over the backrest. "It's not just a guy thing, you know. Women need sexual release just as much as men do. Maybe more."

Just because she gets it on with a different hot guy every week does not mean she has to rub my face in it. Candice is a knockout at 5"11, bleached to perfection, great boobs and an even better ass. All my friends are hot. How the hell had I stayed the same from our school days and they'd morphed into supermodel candidates? Jess has this red, curly hair that's always shiny and beautiful, a hint of an Irish accent and a body that curves in all the right places.

And then there's Amy. If ever the call went out for a poster girl for Pixies R Us, she'd nail the brief. Her brown hair is cut short and spiky, her eyes are the shapes of perfect almonds and her face is small and oval. Of all of my friends, she is the most attractive by far.

Then there's me. Imelda Mahari. My great, great, great, great, great grandfather fled a cargo ship from Europe a century or two ago and even after generations of smooth, pale babies, I bear the mark of my mixed heritage in my slightly olive skin and light-brown eyes. My brothers taunted me endlessly about being adopted and as a kid and I hated it. I hated being different. It would have been okay if I looked kind of intriguing or alluring but my average height, my average body and my average personality means I stand out but not for any truly great reasons and not to anyone truly great either.

One time during a particularly nasty battle over the TV remote, my brother called me a throwback. At first I thought it meant to be thrown back, like you would a fish that didn't quite meet the guidelines on the big sign on the end of the jetty at the beach. I called him a poo-poo head or something equally childish over it. Later that night I'd looked it up in the dictionary by torchlight under my blankets after everyone else had gone to sleep and there I was 'a reversion to an earlier ancestral characteristic'. The next ten years of my life saw me trying to at least blend in, if not fit in.

"Earth to Mellow," Amy calls, waving a hand in front of my face.

And there's the crux of it. The bane of my existence. Who the hell has the nickname *Mellow*? It makes me sound fat, frumpy and squishy. Or buzzed. All are as bad as each other.

"I'm here," I mumble against the table top. All eyes are on me and I can't meet a single set of them.

"You don't have a date do you?" Jess asks. At least she tries to sound nice about it, I guess.

I shake my head, mortified when hot tears sting the back of my eyes.

"Why'd you lie about it?" Candice makes the question sound more like an accusation and if I didn't know her blunt nature better, I'd tell her to get out.

"You guys sit here and tell me I'm going to die alone, asking me stupid questions. What'd you think I'd to do?" That's right, Mellow. Get angry with your friends for trying to help. Getting defensive is something I'm really good at after a lifetime of trying to please everyone.

Harry lets out a long meow when my fingers tighten around his back. He's the kind of perpetually hungry cat who would take the first bite if I did wind up dead on the floor and wasn't found for a few days.

"Aw, honey, I'm sorry." Amy squeezes my other hand but she doesn't take any of it back. None of them do.

My anger deflates just as quickly as it blew up. It's not my friends' fault I'm a loser who sits at home on the weekend feeling sorry for myself.

Instead of getting out there and living.

My nickname should be Wallow. Misery makes for good company. I pick up the wine and hold the neck over my now empty glass. Why even bother measuring it out? If they keep at me, I'm going to need to drink it from the bottle to block out the harsh, ugly truth.

Confidence is something my friends all have. In spades. They throw it around and it takes them places. Literally. Europe for modelling, America for a conference, Japan for a world fair. I have to work so hard to start conversations and even harder to keep them going. I don't talk unless I'm spoken to. I don't meet new people unless it's at work. I'm the kid who hung out in the folds of her mother's skirts for a decade, anything to hide under. Shy doesn't even begin to describe the earliest years of my childhood.

I need this wine.

They don't.

"Don't you miss sex?" Candice asks. Her voice is softer now, less judgmental, not as harsh.

I've never said the words out loud before but the frustration gets to me before my brain can catch up. I brace myself and later mentally blame the alcohol. "I don't even really like sex."

Three sets of beautiful eyes stare hard. Jess's glass is halfway to her lips and Amy is about to start dealing the bright red cards with the intricate, timeless design on the back but her hands stop mid-air.

Candice coughs. Just once. And one simple word follows. "What?"

"I've just never really enjoyed it the way everyone says you're supposed to." To be truly honest with myself, I think there's something wrong with me. Traditionally women talk about orgasms like they have firecrackers going off inside. Books speak of reaching mountainous heights with toe-curling moans and sometimes even screams as stars explode around them. I like the intimacy, the connection. But I don't love the actual sex. I just don't get the hype.

"Oh honey, I think you might be doing it wrong," Jess tells me.

"How many guys have you been with?" Amy asks. "Three? Four?"

"A few," I admit with my head back down on the hard timber. I hear Amy dealing the cards next to my ear but my heart isn't in it tonight.

I was raised in a super conservative household on top of being the shy kid. According to my parents, I'm not married so therefore should technically still be a virgin. I don't personally believe I'll go to hell but it's hard to shake that kind of upbringing. I snort and my breath fogs against the tabletop. I lost my virginity at nineteen with a boy three houses down who I'd known all my life. When all my friends were playing Russian roulette with getting pregnant in high school, I had braces, head gear and a deep shame of everything I was at that time. I couldn't talk to boys and the only time they talked to me was to make fun. So, finally, at nineteen, I gave in. The sex had been painful and awkward and it had taken me an entire year before I got naked with the next guy. Luke had never looked me in the eye again after that day which made family parties unbearable. His parents and my mother are best friends and hang out a lot. They still live on the same street. They think we had a fight and that's why we can't stand to be in the same room as each other.

My phone rings and I almost for a second believe there is a god and he's saving me from this shitty situation.

"Hello," I mumble into my cell. I should have let the call go to message bank but I need a distraction. I need a second to gather my thoughts and my answers.

"Imelda, we have a problem."

Groan. It's the way these calls always start. "What is it, Denni?"

"A bus load of pensioners arrived unannounced and want the full package."

"Do you have the rooms?"

"Yeah, but..."

"But what? Give them rooms, sort out breakfasts and I'll come in early tomorrow and fix the paperwork."

"Excellent, thanks Imelda, you're the best."

Am I? Now I'd have to get up at four am instead of five thirty to do something Denni could have if he tried with more than half a brain. Running nightshift at a hotel doesn't have to be very hard. You'd think he'd have picked up a clue somewhere along the way. This is why I'm in the situation I now face. A sexless existence and being eaten by my cats one day. Because I love my job. It's what I'm good at. It's what I love to do. It's all I do. Day in, day out. On call twenty-four-seven even though it's only supposed to be for events. Everyone knows I run that place. I come from a long line of conscientious over-achievers and take pride in what I do. I love a challenge. At least I did. Now a part of me thinks I'm bored and over-worked but I don't let it show. It's just a phase. A rut. I'm probably just restless on account of never having had a real orgasm.

God, tomorrow is only Wednesday. Hump day. And I'd just made mine worse by prolonging the agony.

Denni had already gone but I still held the cell to my ear so I put it back down with a thunk before I can act on the urge to beat myself to death with it.

"What are you going to do?" Candice asks before I even sit back down.

I pick up my cards from the table's glossy surface and ignore the face of the king who also stares at me with an accusing frown. It's tradition that we meet every second Monday night for a few rounds of cards. I stare at my hand, a chilly glare for the king, and think about it. In the last half an hour my carefully built, fragile little glass existence had fallen from the pedestal it rested on and smashed into a million pieces. Don't get me wrong, I knew it teetered and had for a while. I do get kind of lonely sometimes but I'm building a career and being the good girl my mother consistently scares me into being. While Matilda, Misty, Harry and Fluffy are great housemates, three cats and a Japanese fighting fish just aren't enough. I have to stop putting it off. I have to shake things up and it has to start here and now.

"I'm going to put myself out there," I say. "Maybe even get laid, find out what all the fuss is about." As I speak, I put my perfect hand down to a chorus of groans.

Full house.

I'm not sure how but I'm going to win in this. There's never been a personal goal I haven't achieved. I tell myself this won't be any different.

2

All the way to work on the train before the sun is up the next day, I make a dozen plans in my head but discount them all. Each one gets more ridiculous than the last and involves less and less clothing. It's really the only way I'm going to see any action. Unless the guy is blind. Or just plain desperate.

I know sex isn't going to solve all my problems and putting it out there really goes against my character to date but it's a start and the glaringly obvious right now is I need to start somewhere. Anywhere. I've realized there's this tension that rides with me every second of the day and I want to send it packing. I want to lower my shoulders, take a deep breath and relax.

Which is easier said than done!

Smoothing my plain black skirt over my average thighs, I stare down at my comfy black shoes with the sensible heels. I'm boring. Seriously staid and predictable and sexless. But, I reason with myself, I am going to work and work isn't sexy or exciting. It's fulfilling and

I take pride in it but I never associate any of my day-to-day actions with sexy or sex because I'm a professional.

I take a minute to get nosy and look around at the other women heading to work unbelievably early. There's only about fifteen and a few wear the same boring office crap I have on but a couple are different. One woman a few bums down wears a pair of red Mary-Janes, the strap snug over her unstockinged foot and a heel that would have me at the podiatrists getting fitted for some sort of brace so I can walk again. Her skirt is black like mine, only it's tight and has a long, elegant split up the side. Her black knit sweater pulls in at her waist with a wide belt the same shiny red as her shoes. I want to ask her what she does for a job but it doesn't matter. She looks great and still professional. Real estate agent, I decide in my head.

One thought snags me. If I'm at the podiatrist's office getting my feet fixed from wearing painful shoes, maybe I can ask him out on a date? At least he would've already seen my un-peddied nails and the corn on my little toe. Ugh. Depression begins to dig its ugly claws in. I'm just not cut out for this.

The train stops with a shudder, the doors swish open and yet another ridiculously well-dressed woman steps on, the man at her shoulder helping to make sure she doesn't overbalance. They both laugh about something and as they sit opposite me, I feel a stab of jealousy so sharp, it could slice through my heart and come out the other side.

It's like there's a restless ticking in me that must have started last night because it certainly wasn't there yesterday. I know it's not my biological clock. I have a cousin with three kids and they're loud and dirty and cry every time there's a family get together. I don't want kids. At least not yet. The urgency of my ticking clock must be more about relationships. I don't want to still be waking up alone when I'm fifty or sixty. I'd love to have someone to talk about my day with, to make coffee for in the mornings and watch movies with at night. I want the kind of relationship you see on TV shows. The ones with the happily ever after, not the ones where the character ends up dead on the floor for two weeks.

Right now I take paperwork home and do that at night. I drink wine and tick boxes and argue with my cats when they play with my pens and try to steal my paper clips.

I sip coffee from my well-used travel cup meant to save the environment and look away from the insensible heels, the short skirts, the business shirts that are in some cases a size too small, the buttons straining over boobs better than mine. Before I know it my pity-party has played out all the way to my stop. My sensible shoes carry me over the uneven footpath all the way to the hotel where I spend the best hours of my life and then into the lobby. Those same shoes, complete with practical rubber soles, make no sound as I dejectedly make my way to the concierge desk to clock in for another day of same-same and check the notes from the night shift.

Minutes go by as my stumpy nails tap a rhythm on the marble countertop, but no one comes out. Where the hell is Denni? It's early but he should be here. Rounding the desk, I use my electronic swipe card to let myself in through the door to the room where we hold luggage for people checking out and I stop short, the remnants of my cold coffee splash around in the cup.

There's Denni, black, monogrammed slacks bunched around his ankles as he pounds into one of the room attendants he has up against the only wall that isn't shelved. Petite legs are wrapped around his waist and dainty little navy heels hang from curled toes as she groans, "Denni, oh Denni, harder, harder, do it to me, tiger."

Shame heats my cheeks when a fire licks to life inside me at the view. Denni is a sleaze-ball and I am not turned on by what I'm seeing, which is a whole lot of ass cheek and white legs.

Startled eyes meet mine below perfectly plucked eyebrows but then the face curves into a smile and a wink heavy with dark mascara is thrown in my direction.

I back out of the room without a word. The situation is already beyond embarrassing and I don't want to make it worse by throwing up on the floor.

You're probably shocked and thinking Denni should be fired. He's not just inept, he's also sleeping with half the cleaning staff, on the job. But. This isn't the first time I've walked in on staff banging other staff and I don't personally care what they're doing, I just don't want to see it first thing in the morning. Susan from HR would have her workload doubled or even tripled if she knew even a bit of what went on behind closed doors around the hotel and no one wanted to do that to her when retirement is only months away.

My chin droops lower than usual as I back out of the luggage hold and make my way to my office. I flick the lights on, drop my boring, non-descript handbag on the beige carpet and throw my travel cup in the bin. I will never be able to hold that cup in my hand again without Denni's bare ass popping into my mind.

The handwriting on memos on the smooth surface of my desk blur together as I sit and I wait and I think.

And think.

And think.

Why can't it be that easy for me? Why can't one of my business clients lose control while on a tour of the conference rooms and back me up against a wall? Why? Because I'm not hot or confident or good at throwing out signals of the sexual kind. There's nothing about me to catch the eye. I'm a wallflower. A nerd. I fit squarely into a square hole made just for square people like me. On the phone guys flirt with me and women laugh at my jokes. I'm everyone's best friend while I sort travel plans or confirm conference seating or wedding check lists. But when it comes to the face-to-face stuff, I'm the doormat who takes care of it. I don't think I've ever once got a second glance at work. I'm virtually invisible until there's a problem.

"Morning," Denni sings as he sticks his head into my office, his smile more brilliant than the midday sun.

"Morning." I try to smile back but I'm still so grossed out. I can't tell if it's from the mental image in my head or if it's my body's reaction to seeing the real thing up close and personal for the first time in forever that turns my stomach.

"It's going to be a glorious day."

"Maybe for you," I mutter under my breath.

He hears and comes back with, "What's up, luv?"

It's another thing I can't stand about Denni besides his laziness and now the image of his bare ass. I want to scream *you're not British, you're a half-Asian straight guy under thirty-five! Stop calling me luv!* But I stay quiet. I always stay quiet. My mother raised me to have excellent manners and always be polite.

'You don't need to have an answer for everything, Imelda', she would say daily during my high school years.

"Come on," Denni pleads. "You can tell me. Maybe I can help?"

The image of his naked ass pops into my head again and I want to gag. Again. I don't need his kind of help. But before I can stop myself, my mouth opens and I blurt out a question. "How do you do it?"

"Do what?"

"How do you manage to have sex with so many women so often?"

His laugh becomes nervous and his attention darts around the room like someone might be watching or listening. Now he cares about discretion? "What?"

My question does border on the insulting so I rephrase. "You and Stephanie...just now... you were just...um...well she's really attractive. I don't mean that you're not but she's barely worked here a month and already you're... You know. Is it a pick-up line or something?"

"Nope." He's not even embarrassed that I know. He goes all cocky and sure as he struts the rest of the way into my office and perches on the edge of my desk.

"Are you going to tell me?" I'm not sure I even want to know all that bad.

"Are you going to dob me in?"

I give him my best are-you-dumb look. "I'd have to try to prove it and that does not interest me at all. I just want to know how you do it."

"I could show you?" He wriggles his thick black eyebrows and the gag is back.

"Umm, no thanks," I say, carefully, slowly, definitively. All of this probably fits very neatly under the banner of sexual harassment but I remember Susan in HR and how old and slow she is, that it would be my word against his and everyone loves Denni.

"What's this all about anyway?" he finally asks.

"Nothing."

"Tell me, otherwise I'm going to ask a lot more questions and we don't want to go there, do we?"

I meet his eyes, gulp, try to swallow past the sudden desert in my mouth. "I need to have sex."

Denni throws his head back and roars with laughter. I prickle and anger heats my insides.

"Are you serious?" he asks, after wiping his eyes with his forearms.

"Yeah." I sigh. Can I take it all back? I shouldn't have said anything.

"Just do it then."

So much easier said than done. "I can't."

"Why not? You're not that bad looking and you're nice too."

"Gee thanks," I reply with more than a hint of sarcasm. "If you're trying to boost my self-esteem, it's totally working."

"Have you tried Tinder? Plenty of Fish? Bumble, Hinge or OKCupid? They're easy."

I recall Jess saying Tinder isn't for me. I know a bit about dating apps and I don't want to do it like that. I don't want to waste weeks messaging with a guy who's stolen an image from the internet and is pretending to be someone else. "I'd like to meet someone the old fashion way." Face-to-face. No surprises.

Denni rolls his eyes like I'm a lost cause already but then I can literally see a thought tip into his tiny mind. "What you need is a makeover."

Shallow much? "I doubt that's going to help."

"Stand up," Denni commands with a swish of his metro hand.

I shake my head and roll my eyes but I stand anyway. He rounds the desk and walks around my body. When his hand shoots out to grab my butt, I want to punch him in the face. I sidestep instead. "Sexual harassment," I warn him but we both know it's an empty threat.

He chuckles. "You have a good body, Imelda. Why do you hide it?"

"I do not." Is my first reaction. But I've had this argument with myself today already. I look like the professional I want to portray. *I look boring and maid-like.*

"Your skirt is about five years old isn't it?"

"No," I scoff. But really, how the hell am I supposed to know how old my skirt is?

Denni just glares at me, his brows high up his forehead until the skin wrinkles. He nods in my direction. "Exactly."

"So what? I don't get time to shop. Sue me."

"What do you wear when you're not here?" he asks.

"I don't know, the usual."

His brows rise higher. I don't know how that's possible.

"Jeans, sweaters, t-shirts when I'm at home. I dress up when I go out."

"In what?"

I'm involved in the Spanish inquisition with a dude who'd been having sex in a coat room only thirty minutes before. What is my world coming to?

"Do you even own a sexy dress?" he asks, either unaware or uncaring of my inner turmoil. "What about underwear? Make-up?"

"I am not going to tell you what kind of underwear I own."

"Alright but tell me what you've got on right now. Briefs or a g? Bra or no bra?"

I groan and sink back down in my chair. Damn. He's right. I'd gone from twenty-seven to fifty-eight in the space of a few years.

"Briefs, huh."

My forehead slams on the desk a few times. It makes me feel a little better but only marginally. At this rate I'll likely give myself brain damage before I get in bed with someone.

"What am I going to do?"

"Go shopping for starters. Seconds, where do you hang out?"

"Nowhere in particular."

"You don't have a local bar or club you like to go to?"

"I don't have time," I point out.

"Make time. How are you going to meet someone the old-fashioned way if you don't go out?"

Maybe if he shared some of my workload, I would have more hours in the day for potential fun. I want to shake him until he gets it but I keep my hands to myself. I'm not a touchy person which is also part of the problem. Remember my super conservative family? Not the hugging or emotional displays of any kind type.

"Lunchtime today, go shopping. Take a little longer and buy yourself a hot new outfit. Then when you finish work, find a nice bar or club and have a drink."

"On my own?"

"Sure. Hopefully you won't be alone for long. Imelda." He drops to his knees on the thick carpet next to me and meets my dry eyes with his suddenly serious ones. "There are thousands of guys in this city walking around with hard-on's you could hang a wet towel from. You just need to find one who is half-way decent and drop a few unsubtle hints. If you have no luck, go back tomorrow and the day after and the day after. This is the twenty first century and you're a grown woman, if you want to get laid, go out and do it!"

He's right. My sexual destiny is firmly in my own hands (well, not literally) and I'm the only one who can end this drought. Only, I'm blushing just thinking about hard-ons. I'm a good girl. A good, God-fearing, don't-step-on-spiders-outside kinda girl. But I also haven't had me any fun in forever. Years have gone by and I'd left my sexuality and femininity in a box when I picked up my career. I have to get it back. I have to have sex even if just to prove to myself that I can. And who's going to know? Besides me and the guy, no one else has to know. Certainly not my parents or even my friends if it's bad.

Even as I think the thought, the funk closes over me, tries suck me back into the land of no fun and no men and no happiness. I always ask myself what my parents would say when I'm in a position of right or wrong. My father would be mortified and my mother would wring her hands, her cheeks would become bright pink and I'd have to change the subject. I don't like anyone's intense displeasure and that's all I'd get from my family in this case. But the path to marriage for me, and possibly future grandchildren for them, has to start somewhere. In order to settle down I first have to get out there and meet some people. Take some carefully calculated risks. Because at the end of the day, I think I want to settle down. It's what comes next in life. Career, relationship, marriage, houses, babies (maybe). Possibly a dog after all of that. No more cats.

I roll my shoulders, shake the funk free and smile. "I'm going to do it. I'm going to find myself a guy and I'm going to get laid." I want to throw in a few other smutty doing words but I don't want Denni getting any ideas. Any more than he probably already has.

He gets to his feet, looks at me and smiles. He rubs his hands together and says, "My work here is done."

Cocky, arrogant, son of a bitch, but he knew exactly what to say to me in my moment of doubt. In my mind I forgive him for the image I don't want in my head and thank him for his straightforward—even insulting—advice.

At lunch I'm going to shop and then after work, chat up a hotty with a hard-on.

3

I nearly chicken out and that's putting it mildly. After a lunch-time shopping trip, I finish with the unannounced busload of pensioners and I take off from the hotel an hour early, a couple of brightly colored bags in my hands. I wasn't going to put on the dress I bought with no intention of ever actually wearing, but after an unfortunate—and well-timed—disaster with a senior holding a glass of orange juice, I have no alternative.

So here I am, already dressed better than I started the day, about to enter a little bar I found on Google Maps, only a few streets from my apartment complex called *Johnnie's*. My little black dress would serve better in a strip club and my newly purchased, not-even-washed-yet G-string is already disappearing to parts unseen. A strappy pair of stilettos picked up on my way home compliments the dress and I like them. I like how I look.

What I don't like is how I feel.

My nerves are shot and I'm lightheaded with anxiety. I keep telling myself I don't actually have to talk to anyone if I don't want. Order a drink. Drink it. Leave.

What the hell am I doing? My palms sweat and my insides churn.

I can't walk into a place dressed the way I am and expect to remain intact. I'm already too nervous. What I need is a halfway outfit so I can ease into this. Not boring and predictable, but not what I have on. I've overdone it and the thought sours in my stomach already burning with the unknown.

Avoiding the avid stares of a couple who push past me into the dim abyss, I turn on my new heel and practically run home. It only takes a few minutes to strip off, an hour to find something more decent to wear, a half an hour to feed three cats who won't let me leave my apartment while they're hungry, and a few more minutes before I'm once again standing outside the polished timber and embossed glass doors.

My 'going-out' skinny jeans feel better, more familiar, but I still have on the nice little strappy diamante-stuck heels and my plain charcoal knit molds to my curves in a way I'm fairly happy with. Not so dressy to say I'm in the wrong place but more casual and looking for fun.

Pasting on a bright smile I push the door open and make my grand entrance.

No one pays any attention. Of course they don't.

My smile slips a little as I cross to the bar and sit on a stool.

"What can I getcha?" the barman asks, flicking his little towel back over his shoulder after wiping the stainless steel near my elbows.

Hmm. Tough question. It really has been a long time since I'd drank at a bar. Should I order something strong with no ice? A cocktail? Wine?

"Hello?" the bartender waves his hand in front of my face. "Do you need another minute?"

"I'll have a martini," I respond with what I hope is a warm smile. Yeah. Something I've never had before.

"What kind?"

Were there so many? "Apple." I think that's what they drink on *Sex and The City* isn't it? I watched it in secret as a teen and always envied Samantha for her confidence. What I really want to do is take my phone out and search for drinks people order to say, 'I'm single, horny and hopeless! Come and get me!' Oh, and also call up a friend and ask them to hold my hand. The full extent of my complete terror makes the room spin and I clench my hands into fists beneath the edge of the bar. I suppress the nervous laughter wanting to bubble up to embarrass me. I don't reach for my phone. I can do this. I'm a grown woman, an adult, a decision making, empowered feminist. Who just happens to be looking for a guy. Is that irony or something else?

"Sure thing."

I watch as he picks up a bottle of something, grabs a cocktail glass from under the bar and starts to make my drink. This guy has to be over six foot, and built, but he handles the shaker and the glass like they're precious. He ignores me as he effortlessly places it on a coaster, takes the twenty I hold out and then goes to serve someone else.

Expensive drink. I turn on the stool and glance over the patrons as though I'm here every night and I'm waiting for someone. I cross my knees and attempt to look relaxed.

I'm not.

My heart races. There's no question about it. Everything I've done over the course of the day has been building up to this moment where my morals and inhibitions would go with the wind and I'd take a stranger home to my bed. Slutty with a capital S, but for some reason it doesn't bother me as much as it should. There is only so far a good girl persona can take you and I'd fought hard to leave my crippling shyness behind after high school. Tonight, I didn't have to be the good girl with the good job and career highlights. I want more. I deserve more.

I want to be someone different and here, where no one knows me, I can at least give it a go.

The spark that had come to life inside me this morning wouldn't go away and I still hadn't worked out if it was welcome or a nuisance. It's like my libido had been sleeping but Denni's sexcapades had woken it up. Nuisance, I decide with a nod.

On the other hand, I deserve sex. I work hard, pay my taxes, keep my nose clean. Why can't I have one night to be someone different? Gain a little confidence back. Maybe if I can find my sexy, I can start the real, and hopefully short, process of finding Mr. Right. Then I won't become a cat lady and a meal for the starving little fur-balls. Maybe my Mr. Right is such an awesome stand-up guy that he actually saves me from dying in the first place? Heimlich maneuver or some shit like that? I keep up my perusal of the patrons with renewed determination.

Not much to choose from but hopefully as the night wears on more guys will get thirsty. They have to walk past me to get to the bar and I can make eye contact, say hello, start a conversation about the weather.

Not the case.

I'm avoided like the plague. Three apple martini's later, which taste more like dirty mother vinegar in a glass, I'm not happy. Is it my vibe? Am I giving off desperate and dateless signals? Am I really just too safe and boring and unattractive that they give me a wide berth?

I have to do something. Denni said there were men out there. Maybe they're as nervous and shy as me and need someone else to make the first move? Maybe they're at a different bar?

Fortifying what's left of my nerves needs one more drink but the bartender is talking to a much older, Italian guy a few stools away from me. As I wait, I listen. I don't mean to be nosy but I can't help hearing their conversation.

"Obviously the judge didn't throw you in the slammer then 'ey Niko?"

Niko—the barman—replies to the other man's ribbing. "Nah but I have to do some stupid stuff over the next few months to show that my anger is under control."

"Is it?" the other guy asks.

"It has to be. I'm not doing time over that asshole. Now I have to write in a diary every night. A friggin diary, man. It's making me angrier. And girly. Only chicks write in diaries. And what does he get for picking the fight, eh? Nothing!"

I want to laugh. The look on his face is gold and his tone too. I'm intrigued as to what he'd done to deserve the punishment and why he isn't in the 'slammer'.

He sees me looking and comes right over with a sarcastic smile creasing his features. He knows I've been listening in on his private conversation and I should be ashamed but I'm not. "Another martini?" His tone isn't nice.

I smile the best one I can find since I'm getting a little tipsy. "They really aren't very good. Can you make me something that tastes better?'

"You don't get out much do you?" he asks as he stares at me with one dark brow raised. I wonder what he sees. "Get stood up?"

I deflect with a giggle. "Not much and no." Where had that come from? I couldn't remember the last time I'd giggled but the idea of this brute of a man lying in bed at night with his 'dear diary' was funnier with the alcohol warming me up. "I've just had a rough day and needed a drink or three."

He eyes me with a wariness that's almost insulting but then asks, "What do you like?"

"What do you mean?"

"Sweet, sour, salty?"

"Sweet." *I think.*

"How about sex on the beach?"

"I beg your pardon?" My heart gives one thump against my ribs and then seems to stop altogether. Am I being hit on? Was the wariness actually interest? I flutter my eyelashes just a little but then he shakes his head and walks away.

If there's a color for idiot, my cheeks turn that burning shade. He goes to an icy machine I hadn't noticed resting on one corner of the bar and fills a deep, dessert looking glass. The kind that would come with chocolate mousse and ice cream at your favorite cafe.

When he comes back toward me, he sets the glass down and indicates it with a nod. He's waiting for me to try it. He doesn't want to have sex on the beach. It's what the cocktail is called. I almost groan out loud. I really am bad at this stuff. And I'm getting quite drunk.

"Thanks." I sigh and toy with the black straw, unable to make eye contact again. I ignore everyone behind me in the bar and sip the new drink while staring at the scratches on the timber's surface. This drink is much nicer than the other one but I don't need it. This was a huge mistake and I'm dejected in a way I didn't think I could be.

Maybe some women just aren't cut out to be confident, sexy go-getters? Maybe I am doomed to live out my days with my cats?

If I don't die of embarrassment first.

· ♥ · ♥ · ♥ · ♥ · ♥ ·

Nick's diary.

First Entry.

~~This sucks.~~

~~It's an unfair waste of time.~~

I am not going to write dear diary and I absolutely flat out refuse to tell anything other than the mundane, every day crap. According to the terms of my suspended sentence I have to call you something. I'm going to call you Freddy. My dad had a dog called Freddy. Chewed everything in sight. Got under everyone's feet. Barked at air. Annoying as hell.

So,

Dear Freddy,

~~*Today I woke up, had a shower, went to work and then went home.*~~

This morning I woke up, had a shower and then went to work. Like every other day I poured drinks, made small talk and got hit on.

Judge Battle-axe would want more than all of that, Nick thought, throwing the pen down. She'd warned him to take this seriously or wind up in jail. He breathed deep, flexed his fingers and then picked the pen up again.

Mostly it was the same old regulars, only there was this new chick who came in and ordered an apple martini. Lucky I had the booze to pull that one off but they stink like sweetened rotting apples and by the look on her pretty little face, taste just as bad.

Pretty little face? What did that come from?

Poor little thing. She doesn't get out much and no one wanted a bar of her. Probably out making friends and had to go home to her lonely existence and curl up alone. A country girl in the big smoke if ever I saw one.

The words kept coming but he felt bad. He should have been nicer to her. After all, he was curled up alone too. Damn this diary thing. Already making him feel. He didn't want to feel. He wanted to be left alone.

The end.

He added one more for good measure.

Goodnight.

4

Why am I such a loser? I roll over in bed and groan into the pre-dawn darkness. My stomach burns like the inside of an erupting volcano and I only drank a few of those awful cocktails. I open my eyes and come face to furry face with a serial killer. Misty is sitting on my pillow probably contemplating actual murder and we both know she's a winner in this one of her nine lives. I'm reluctant to move my feet because Harry likes to pretend he's Mike Tyson first thing in the morning and bite me if I make any sudden moves. The heavy lump at my side tells me Matilda is snuggling in for a long day of doing nothing.

This is my life.

Matilda is sort of mine but the other two cats are strays. Mostly well-behaved strays which means at some time, somewhere, some- one had loved them. Not anymore. I live on the ground floor of an apartment block that backs onto a childcare centre with only a dark, dank alley in between. It's the stuff of nightmares at night, the alley, not the centre, and during the day it attracts all manner of four-legged creature, mostly rats. Cats really like chasing rats. Assholes really like dumping their unwanted cats in alleys too. Bastards.

I'm distracted which is nice. It's what cats do. But I have to get out of bed. Today is going to be difficult but even harder would be to go back to the bar and have another crack at breaking the drought.

There are plenty of bars in the city. I know that fact better than a lot after walking past a majority of them on my way home from work. Pity I'd never had the courage to go in. And that's what I need now. Courage. Some women wish they had bigger boobs or better hair, I just wish I had more courage to step out of my comfort zone.

I get up, shower, dress in my same old boring clothes, take one look in the mirror and strip back down to nothing. If I'm going to change my life and stop being a dateless loser, it has to start with underwear.

Cringing at what I'll discover as I open my rarely-sees-the-light lingerie drawer, I peek in and breathe a sigh of relief when nothing nasty jumps out and attacks me. I have to find something sexy without being too over the top. I'm a blusher and I can't afford to have red cheeks all day. Someone will think I'm sick with a fever. I need something I can be comfortable in during the day but then feel good in when I hit the bar again (without running home to change).

By the time I find a black lacy pair of French panties and a matching bra, I'm running out of time. Throwing my closet doors wide I do a quick scan of endless black and charcoal but I can't find anything different from what I always wear. Then I remember the clothes my sister gave me when she'd had her boobs done.

"I can't wear half of this stuff anymore, Mellow, you may as well have it all."

A little bit of jealousy had settled in me as I'd stared at my baby sister that day, with her pale, flawless skin and enormous, perky, perfect boobs. I resented the fact I was getting second-hand clothes while she got expensive enhancements so I'd chucked it in the back of the wardrobe without opening the box.

Rummaging in, nearly getting lost in the mess, my hands close around the cardboard and I pull, twist, swear and finally get it free. Standing there in my undies, huffing stray frizz out of my eyes, feeling more self-conscious than ever despite being on my own in my apartment, I rip the tape off and open the top wide.

Lucky there isn't too much jammed in otherwise I'd have to plug in the iron and muck around. Then I'll be late to work and it isn't worth the hassle.

Reaching in, I pull out a fitted burgundy business dress. Perfect. I don't bother looking for anything else in the box but I do close the lid. Cats love boxes. Cats love peeing in boxes.

Pulling the dress over my head, I struggle a bit when I realize the zip is still done up. Swearing some more, I take it off, unzip the bloody thing and put it back on. This time, the satin lining floats over my skin and when I zip it under my armpit, the knit fabric molds to my curves like a glove. I hope it looks all right because I'm out of time to change. I don't even bother checking my reflection as I slip on the new heels from yesterday, run a brush through my hair and then with my handbag in hand, fly out of my building and practically jog all the way to the train platform.

It's only a few minutes after eight when I flick on the light in my office and sink down in the chair behind my desk with a dramatic sigh. I made it in one piece. No one laughed at my clothes, and I hadn't stacked it in the shoes despite running like someone who didn't even know how to walk. A good start.

"Good morning." Denni pokes his head into my office, his smile bigger than yesterday. The image of his butt flashes through my brain and ruins any reply I might come up with. I'd bet money in that moment that he'd been having sex in the coatroom again.

I roll my eyes.

"Any luck last night?" he asks, looking me up and down. "Nice dress by the way," he says before I have the chance to answer.

"No." I can't help the groan as it passes my lips to settle like the martinis in my stomach. Badly.

"What happened?" Denni sits opposite me, leans forward, his hands clasped together between his navy-clad knees, waiting for me to the spill the beans.

"Nothing happened. That's the miserable point."

"What did you do? What did you wear? Where did you go?"

"Just a little bar down the way from my place. I wore nice jeans and a nice top. I drank martinis and... Well, that's about it." I was not going to tell him of my abject humiliation.

"There's your problem." Denni smacks his forehead like he'd just fit the last piece to my silly puzzle. "You looked nice."

"What's wrong with looking nice?"

"Nothing if you want a nice guy. But you don't."

I don't? "I don't?"

"No. You want a guy who's going to bend you over the hood of his Mercedes and make you forget your own name for fifteen heavenly minutes."

My jaw drops. Is that what I want? My insides heat as a mental image drops into my mind. I would never have guessed.

"Don't look at me like that," he says, shaking his head. "A nice guy will not cure what ails you. You need a guy who's going to give no mercy, bang your brains out and then disappear. A bad boy but without the prison term under his belt."

"Hang on, why do I want him to disappear?" This whole conversation is becoming alarmingly one sided and I haven't agreed with him about anything. All I can do is repeat his questions like a dumb ass. I did think of the bartender though when Denni said, *prison term.*

"Are you looking for sex or a boyfriend?"

"Can't I look for both?"

"Have you been hiding under a rock?" Denni asks, his black eyes wide and disbelieving. The look on his face reminds me of a teacher impatiently trying to make sense of a four-year old's ramblings.

I nod and hope it's the right answer.

"You can't have re-entry sex with a potential boyfriend."

"What? C'mon and be serious for a minute. You're confusing me."

"Okay, okay." He raises his hands in defeat, it's still patronizing. "You can't have sex on the first night, after so long, with a potential boyfriend. The guy is going to crow to all his mates the next day in graphic detail, and I do mean graphic. No guy will think about a future with a girl if he's told all his mates how she takes it."

"Do guys do that?" I'm dumbfounded. I'd discovered more on the dos and don'ts of dating in one morning than I'd heard in my entire life. A slow burn begins to rise in the back of my throat and I wonder if the martinis are about to make a reappearance.

"We do." He said it like it was, in fact, something to brag about.

"All right then," I nod, slowly. Rally my thoughts. Should I be taking notes? "Let's say I'm looking for sex and not a boyfriend. What happens if he calls me after. . . You know."

"He won't."

"But what if he does?"

"Booty call. He wants to have sex with you again."

"Do I?"

"You're getting ahead of yourself, luv. Find the man first. Work the details later."

I nod again. There is so much to process. So many tiny details I'd neglected in my planning and I'm a planner, a details person. *Damn.*

"Anyway. That's me. I'll see you tomorrow morning and you better have a smile on your dial."

"Sure, no worries." I nod for the third time but inside I'm reeling.

The rest of my morning is spent pondering the 'details' as I supervise set up for a conference coming to town. This one is a wound conference for nurses and health professionals. The posters make my stomach roll more uncomfortably than when I'd woken up. There are infected cuts, abrasions, boiling sores and lots of other super gross images.

Leaving the icky stuff far behind, I make a few calls from my office, have a light lunch, carbs to settle my tummy, set up another boardroom for an afternoon AGM and then it's suddenly five o'clock. Why is it that when you want time to slow down and give you a break, it speeds up and slams into the back of your head.

At least I hadn't thought about the bar much or my shockingly embarrassing effort at picking up. God, I hadn't even talked to anyone other than the bartender. I have to try harder tonight. I have to actually approach someone and have a conversation. Leaving won't be an option until I achieve at least that much.

With that resolution firmly in my mind, I pack up, turn the light off and leave my office. On the way through the foyer, the hotel manager catches my eye. I call him the manager but it's a loose position description since he does no actual managing. Mr. Rodney likes to bark orders but after he leaves the room, we reassign jobs based on who can get them done rather than who he thinks will, or should, do the work.

"Ms. Mahari. Leaving early today are we?" The way he says Ms is buzzy, as though he doesn't like the sound in his own mouth.

We call him Mr. Rodney because he likes to use our family names on us. He thinks it gives him some sort of professional control but it doesn't. "My contract is nine to five with the occasional Saturday for weddings." We both know this but every now and then I feel the need to drop in a reminder. It's my fault really. I never leave before six and work most Saturdays with the occasional Sunday morning to avoid church invitations from my family.

He harrumphs like he's coming down with strep and turns on his shiny black heels and stalks off to annoy someone else. Usually I'm civil and polite and I know I was all of those things just now but tension makes my teeth clench. I put in so much overtime it's not even funny but the whole hotel notices when I leave on time or take my full lunch hour.

With every stop, with every clickety turn the train takes on the tracks, my confidence diminishes and my anger rises. By the time I get off one stop early so I can walk to the bar instead of home, my tummy is roiling again and my palms and fingertips are damp.

You can do it, you can do it. I keep repeating the mantra over and over but I don't believe it. It's a hollow thought and flees as soon I push through the doors to the bar and sit down before I fall down.

"Back again?" The guy, Niko, gives me a fake half smile and waits for me to order my first nightmare in a glass. Earlier in the afternoon I called to the hotel bar and asked one of the waiters what the most popular cocktail is. General consensus is a Fruit Tingle. Sweet and potent despite the name. And if sweet isn't my cup of tea then a gin and tonic or vodka and lime is what I want. Apparently.

"Do you know what a Fruit Tingle is?" I ask hesitantly, my elbows on the polished bar, my chin in my hands.

"Do you?" he counters, staring at me with a strange kind of intensity.

I shake my head. I'm always at a loss for words in these kinds of awkward situations and I've done so much head shaking in the last few days, my neck is getting sore. But Jesus, this guy has a pair of eyes on him I hadn't noticed the night before. Frank Sinatra eyes to boot. They are the deepest blue I've ever stared into. Gerard Butler's shoulders, Michael Buble's thick brown hair.

"What are you doing here, honey?" He puts his towel down on the bar and leans against it.

So many answers spring to life on my tongue but none of them are any of his business. I ignore his ruggedly handsome, smooth rugby looks and do the only thing I can.

I lie.

"I just moved here and I don't know anyone. I was hoping a bar was a good a place as any to socialize, you know, meet some like-minded people."

His pause and the answering shrug says he doesn't believe a word I've said but is happy to go along with the lie for now. Why am I so bad at hiding the truth? It doesn't even have to be an outright lie and my cheeks heat and I'm sure my skin is blotchy and flushed. To try to keep up the pretense I stick my hand out and introduce myself. "My name's Imelda."

"Seriously?" He stares at my hand like I'm holding dog shit in it. I'm not sure if he's questioning my name, the fact I'm introducing myself or my personal hygiene so I nod.

"Nick." His reply is curt but he does take the risk and shake my hand quickly and firmly. There's an 'ooh-ahh' from down the other end of the bar followed by raucous laughter.

I know I'm definitely blushing now as I pull away, the heat of his rough hand enclosed within my fist.

One of the guys from down the bar comes up and sits next to me. He orders a beer and as soon as Nick turns his back, introduces himself. "I'm Mikey."

"Imelda." I shake his hand but I don't like the way it feels in mine. To start with, it's smooth, damp and cold from holding a beer. Like a slimy, wet fish.

"Why don't you come on down and shoot a game of pool with us."

"Us?" I look further down to where his mates crowd around a pool table I'd missed last night. In fact, I'd missed heaps last night. This place is actually kind of nice. It's certainly bigger than it looks from the street.

"Me and the boys. We shoot a mean game."

"Uh, maybe later. I don't shoot so well."

"What have I told you about making nice with my customers, Mikey?" Nick comes back over and puts his beer on the bar, far away from where I sit.

"I can't seem to remember, Nick."

Nick leans in real close and gives him a menacing glare. "I can give you a refresher."

I feel like I'm watching one of those movies where the bar guy pulls a sawed-off shot gun out and threatens the drunk to get him to leave off, whereby the drunk comes back later and torches the place.

"I'm going, I'm going." Mikey gives me a wink and then says, "If you change your mind you know where to find me."

"Sure," I nod and break eye contact. I have no wish to spend my night with a bunch of boozy idiots.

"He's not the type you want to make friends with, honey."

I stare at Nick across the Wild Turkey bar mat. Is he seriously giving me friendship advice? We've only just met. Then it occurs to me. He is probably the best judge of the bar's patrons. He can tell me who is boyfriend material and who might be good for a fun night. He'd certainly told me who wasn't.

"Maybe you can point out someone who is?" It's worth a try.

Once again that skeptical look is back in the narrowing of his baby blues. "I'm just the bartender."

"How long have you worked here, Nick?"

"Going on ten years."

"Then there's no one better to tell me who to avoid."

"I don't know..." His skepticism changes to suspicion in a heart-beat.

"Look you don't have to set me up with any guys or anything. Just guide me away from the losers, yeah?"

He still doesn't look too wild about the idea but nods before walking away.

Excellent. An ally.

For the rest of the night, I float around the room, spend time at the bar, in a booth against the wall to eat some chunky seasoned wedges and then back at the bar. No one approaches me. I'm starting to feel quite defeated when Nick stands in front of me and clears his throat loudly.

I look up and almost laugh at his face. Now he's turning red and shifting around uncomfortably. I wait for him to say something.

"There's a guy over there. Comes in every week on a Monday. I can't vouch for his character but he seems all right to me. No red flags or anything. I don't think."

"Thanks, Nick." I give him a smile of appreciation but he's already walking away. Again. I wonder if he ever stands still?

I study my quarry for a few minutes while I try to strike up the courage to go over. I promised myself that I would at least approach one eligible looking guy tonight. If my pounding heart can take it. I have to remember I'm running a marathon and I'm not even half done, the finish line still miles down the road.

I square my shoulders, smooth down my burgundy dress, pick up what's left of my drink and go over to the booth he's sitting at. About halfway there I don't know what to say. I nearly freak out but then a hundred cheesy catchphrases and sayings and pick up lines flash through my mind and I'm pretty sure I can come up with something.

"Hi there," I say, my friendliest smile still in place. I slide into the booth across from him. I don't need an invitation. If the guy doesn't want company, he can say so and I can go.

"Hi." His smile is nice, friendly. Even white teeth, blond hair you could run your hands through and eyes that crinkle at the corners meaning he laughs. I like that.

"Come here much?" I ask, then realize just how extra cheesy that one is.

He laughs and shakes his head, his hand crossing the table. "I'm Ian."

"Imelda." I shake it and don't get any immediate bad vibes so I relax back into the seat, the leather shifting with me.

"What's a nice girl like you doing in a bar like this?" Ian asks.

God, we must watch the same corny movies. I don't miss the derisive note in his tone as he looks around the bar either. It doesn't take a genius to figure out Ian doesn't want to be here.

"I'm new in town. Just out to meet some people." I recycle the same story I've given Nick but I also want an out just in case this guy is a weirdo.

"Where did you move from?" An inevitable question but one I haven't prepared for.

"Adelaide."

"Really, you sound like a Queenslander to me."

"My family spent a lot of time moving around." God, I'm such a liar. Lucky I wasn't there to find an actual boyfriend. Relationships could not and should never be started with lies.

"What do you do?" he asks next. Typical small talk but I'm having a one-sided conversation. I don't love it.

"I work at the Hilton. Events coordinator. You?"

"Bit of this, bit of that."

I nod slowly and contemplate the deliberately vague reply, all the while drinking half my Fruit Tingle down in one long suck on the softening paper straw. The silence grows awkward but what else can I expect?

"I'm going to grab another beer." Ian stands up and without asking if I want anything, he makes for the bar but then switches direction and walks out the door.

Well, there it is. My heart stops beating and sinks quicker than a rock in a pond. I'm repulsive.

I let my head fall and bang hard on the table. Not only is that a big fat rejection, it's an I-can't-get-out-of-here-fast-enough rejection. He could have just told me he wanted to drink alone. I bang my head again.

"It can't be that bad." A deep, rumbly voice surprises me from the seat Ian had just fled.

"It is," I say without looking up. If I lift my head, another one might flee into the night.

"Why don't you let me buy you a drink and you can tell me about it."

That gets my attention. I lift my face and meet the eyes of one hell of a hotty. His wide mouth curves up into a smile that goes all the way to his eyes and beyond.

He waves towards Nick who seems to chuckle and shake his head.

"I'm Imelda." Better to get the intro out of the way before he runs out.

"Matt."

This time when I hold my hand out, he takes it in his and before my very eyes, lifts it to his mouth and kisses my knuckle. Heat starts a slow burn in my abdomen and quickly spreads outward making me shift in my seat.

"So, Imelda, was that your boyfriend?"

"Who?" I'm having trouble thinking as his deep green eyes twinkle with pure mischief.

"The guy who just walked out of here looking a little lost. Did you break up with him or something?"

"Oh, Ian? We were having a chat but that's it."

"Not your boyfriend?"

"Not my boyfriend." This is much better. Straight to the heart of it. I look Matt over and decide he's certainly not boyfriend material with his dimples and way too smooth charm. Big tick for him already. He's been here before and done this before. I can tell. He's oozing confidence and in-it-for-a-fuck energy.

Lucky for me.

"So what brings you to *Johnnie's*?"

I shrug. "Just here to meet someone."

"Who?" he asks. He's being nosy and direct but it doesn't bother me much.

I smile and tilt my head to the side. "I don't know yet."

Matt starts to laugh but then Nick is standing there, blocking out the light as he thunks a beer on the table in front of Matt and another Fruit Tingle for me. Instead of leaving like he should, since he's interrupting an important moment in my getting laid quest, he looks at me, intently. More intently than he had earlier at the bar.

"Remember that conversation we had earlier?" he says.

I nod and my joy takes an uneasy dip.

"Well, this is one those things you wanted a heads-up on."

"Sure, thanks," I mumble, doubt creeping in on my new-found confidence.

I know what he's saying but he has to be wrong. Surely he's wrong. But why would he say something if Matt isn't bad news?

And is he bad, bad or just not boyfriend material? In my book, there's a difference. There has to be.

"What was that all about?" Matt askes as his suddenly cranky gaze breaks from Nick's retreating form to stare back at me.

"Nothing." Now what am I supposed to do? I've already had one rejection for the night. One word to this guy and I know the drought will be over, I'll be satisfied and I can tell my friends I'd finally done it.

"I've never seen you in here before," he continues, chasing away the tense silence.

"This is only my second time."

"You live around here?"

That's an uncomfortable question. Putting this together with Nick's weird warning makes my head ache. Suddenly it all seems complicated. Like a good idea at the time until later when you realize you should have run in the opposite direction. "Will you excuse me for a minute?"

"Hurry back." Now, instead of twinkling eyes and charisma, all I notice is sleazy and almost scary. I cannot do this.

Making my way to the powder room, I try to signal Nick with my eyes. I need more information. He gets the hint and follows me right into the bathroom.

"What's wrong with him?" I ask after making sure the solitary stall is empty.

"Nothing. If you like 'em married."

That blows the wind out of my sails. Completely thrown, I lean against the cool tiled wall. Damn, talk about a spanner.

"I take it married doesn't appeal to you?"

"Not even a little bit," I snap. His abrasive tone rubs me up the wrong way.

"You want to tell me what's really going on? I like to know what people are doing in my bar. I'm getting a bad vibe or something from you and I'm not usually far off the mark."

I let my thoughts run wild for a second. *He* is in the ladies room with *me* and he's the one with a bad feeling? "I need to find a guy," I finally admit, quietly, desperately.

"Why here?"

"Why anywhere?" I turn around and put my forehead against the cold wall, rolling it on the tiles to try to dispel the heat in my skin.

"You better not be a hooker."

I turn around so quick he actually takes a step back. Fury replaces humiliation. "I beg your pardon."

He raises both his hands. "I think it's a perfectly reasonable question since you're in my bar looking for a man."

"I said I wanted to find someone, I didn't say I was going to solicit the patrons."

"So you are a hooker."

"If you say that to me one more time, I swear to God I'm going to slap you. The correct term is sex worker and that's not me."

"Tell me the truth then."

The urge to scream fills me and I feel mildly violent. I wanted to swear and throw something and then claw this guy's Frank Sinatra eyes out. How dare he? "Do I seriously look like a sex worker? Honestly? Is that the vibe you're getting from me?"

"No, you don't." He must have guessed just how angry I'm getting because he backs off and his voice drops low like he's trying to calm a child.

The gesture makes me angrier. "How dare you accuse me of anything? You're a bartender for God's sake. Why I'm here has nothing to do with you as long as I'm buying drinks and having a good time."

"That's where you're wrong sweetheart. My bar, my rules."

"I'll speak to the manager then."

"That's me."

"The owner?"

"You got him."

I stare for a full minute, nothing else to say. Nick can't be much older than me and he owns a city bar? I shake my head. It doesn't matter. Why am I having this fight with him, in the female restroom? Why aren't I out there sitting with Matt and enjoying some male attention.

Oh, that's right. He's married.

"How do you know Matt's married anyway?"

"He's my brother-in-law."

· ❤ · ❤ · ❤ · ❤ · ❤ ·

Dear Freddy.

What a night. I've been so bored lately but now I'm almost buzzing. Same patrons, same problems, until she walks back in.

I ended this night in the most bizarre way. Having a shouting match in the girls toilet with the patron I thought was a helpless newb but turns out to be a hooker and then isn't. She tells me she's looking for a man and then I tell her to take a hike and she gets all insulted.

Turns out she's looking for a man all right, for what, she wouldn't tell me. Stormed off in a huff, grabbed her bag and left in a tizzy. I had to physically stop Matt from following after her. It was the best part of the night, but Freddy, you don't want to know about that.

5

"You look like hell," Denni comments helpfully as he places a coffee on the desk in front of me early the next morning.

"Thanks." The steaming cup feels great between my fingers despite the fact my body is pretty warm already. Complete humiliation tends to have that effect.

"Big night?"

"Not the way it should've been," I say with a sigh. I don't want to be having this conversation. Thank God my girlfriends have no idea what I'm up too. Telling them would be mortifying. At least I only have to see Denni at work for an hour as he finishes the night shift.

"Did you at least talk to anyone?" he asks.

"Yeah, but it didn't make a difference. I still went home alone."

"So, what happened with the one you did talk to?"

"The first one actually got up and left." Denni laughs. I scowl. "Turns out the other guy, who was hot by the way, super-hot, is married."

Tears stream down Denni's face and he holds his stomach like he's going to bust a stitch.

"It's not that funny," I grate out through clenched teeth.

His laughter turns to giggles as he says, "It really is."

"There should be a handbook for this kind of stuff," I grumble.

"If it was that easy, there would be no single people anywhere. We would all be living in boring marital bliss and I wouldn't be nailing the housekeeping ladies."

Even I have to chuckle at that. I will never believe there are people in the world who don't want to find their soul mate. Who doesn't want to settle down and have babies and live happily ever after? I'd settle for the companionship at this stage. If I had a two-bed flat, I'd get a housemate. *Must love cats*, the ad would read.

"Are you going back again?" Denni's voice startles me out of my musings.

"I really don't know. On the one hand, I think I've failed at what I set out to achieve. On the other hand, I'm really pissed off that no one thinks I'm one night stand material. Or any material for that matter."

"Honey, dressed like that, you aren't."

"But why should I have to become someone else to try to impress? Why can't I just be me?" It should be enough. I should be enough. I think that's what depresses me more than anything. No one wants me for me and it sucks.

"You aren't trying to be you. If you were being you, you wouldn't be in that bar in the first place."

He has half a point.

"What you need is some girlie advice. Someone who can give you a few female pointers on picking up."

That would of course involve admitting to one of my friends just how desperate and hopeless I'd become. And I don't think I'm quite ready for that.

"Are you sure?" I ask. "Can't you just tell me what you're looking for when you go out to pick up?" I do not want to emulate the kind of girl he's into but anything is better than what I've come up with so far.

"Honey, I don't do the chasing so I got nothin' for ya. I can tell you what I like."

Ew. Not what I want to hear but could it hurt? I hope not. "Go on. But easy on the details."

"Well, I have to say I'm a boobs man. A great set, nice cleavage, maybe a hint of lace. When you lean over, I want to know it's not all padding. And your ass! You have a great ass, show it off more! Buy a pair of pants one size too small and shake it like you mean it!"

"You're getting carried away down the bottom end of the pool," I point out to possibly the world's shallowest guy. "What about personality? It can't be all about appearances."

"It's *all* about looks with a one-nighter. Why would I want to bag the wallflower when her beautiful friend is just as desperate? You're desperate too. You need to glam it up a bit, show off your assets."

His leery smile offends me. His complete lack of depth makes me feel sick. I don't ever want someone like Denni. Is it possible to need a shower after a conversation because I'm feeling icky.

Hours after Denni has gone home to sleep (or dream about nailing the ladies) I'm still thinking about what he'd said. I have cleavage. I could show it. When I think about the dress from yesterday, even the pant suit I have on today—courtesy of the sister box—it isn't very enticing. I did decide to wear a red lace bra and matching undies so I feel the power under the surface. I feel sexy on the inside. I need to bring that to the outside. Let it loose just a little at a time.

On the way home, I shed my jacket and to the bemused glances from those sitting near me, I undo the first few buttons of my shirt and roll the long white sleeves to just below my elbows. Pulling the bobby pins from my hair, I let the brown down and gave it a flick.

Right. Casual. That's about as much as I can do without taking it all off and painting a target on my upper thighs which at this moment is quite a tempting thought. There's a guy a few seats down sitting opposite who is flat out staring at my boobs now that my cleavage is on display.

I test the new feelings, lick my lips and lean my head back, making sure my chest juts out a little more, close my eyes and rest my hands on the flat of my tummy. I can feel his gaze, and a few others, and have to resist the urge to smile and crow. Maybe tonight I can actually pull this off. If it's about confidence, mine is rising. I'm far enough along that I'm pretty sure I can fake what I don't have. Maybe.

Just as I'm ready to start the action plan, my cell rings. After I dig it out of the receipts, tissues and bits of crap from my handbag, I punch the button o the private number and hold it to my ear.

"Imelda Mahari."

"Mellow, how you going?"

"Hey, Amy." I'm happy to hear from her, I am, but I don't want to tell any lies and she will inevitably have questions.

"Just wondering what you're doing tonight. I'm thinking of catching a movie."

"Sorry, I sort of have plans." I can tell instantly that she doesn't believe me in the silence from her end so I try to cover it up by asking a question of my own. "Amy, can I ask you something?"

"Sure." She's apprehensive. Good.

"What do you do if you see a guy you like but you don't know how to get his attention?'

"Ooh, did you meet someone? About time!"

I am not prepared to lie to my best friend so I grab part of the truth and twist it into some form of self-serving vagueness. "Well, I haven't met him yet. Just a really nice looking guy I keep running into around the neighborhood."

"That's great, Mels. Well, I would make him notice me."

"Yeah, but how?"

She's quiet for a minute and then with a sigh gives me an answer I can't use. "I don't know. I've never really been faced with that problem. I just go up and start talking."

"About what?" I know she doesn't mean to sound egotistical, just honest, but my jealous streak gnaws at me.

"The weather, sports. Whatever. If he's out jogging, I ask him how it's going. If he has a briefcase, I ask him about work. If he has a tattoo, I ask him about that."

"I get it, thanks, Amy."

"Anytime, and Mels?"

"Yeah?"

"Be careful okay. There are guys out there who only want one thing. If you're not prepared to give it to them, don't dive in. Test the waters first."

Sage advice. "Thanks Amy, I'll let you know how I get on."

"Be yourself and he will love you."

"Yeah, thanks. Seeya."

"Bye."

Be yourself. Yeah right. That's what has me in this mess in the first place. Denni says don't be yourself and Amy says the opposite. Who the hell should I be if I can't be either of those? Should I split my personality so there's a third option?

I snort. I have to find the first two before trekking out for any more.

All too soon I'm standing outside *Johnnie's*, peeking in through the windows, suddenly too scared to go in and get rejected again. I wonder how much I can take before my pride shatters and my heart goes into hiding.

I give myself a shake. My heart does not have a place in any of this. I'm not out to fall in love. God, that is last thing I need right now. I don't have the time for my cats let alone a boyfriend. I want to try to move up the corporate ladder, land a job somewhere like Hawaii or better still Dubai, somewhere I don't have to pay taxes and can horde my earnings into a tidy little nest egg.

It's only a matter of time before my biological clock does decide to strike up a rhythm. I think I still have a few good years left. Twenty seven is nowhere near old. I'm in the prime of my life. Woman hit their sexual peak in their thirties and I have to find out what the fuss is before I get there. I can't lie awake for an entire decade and wonder what I'm missing out on. Maybe that's why this drought is suddenly so much harder to bear. I'm clinically supposed to be in the 'making it like rabbits' part of my life but for some reason that bus left without me.

"Are you going in?"

I come back to the now and I'm shocked to see a sandy haired guy holding the door open for me. I look around to make sure he's actually talking to me and that he's alone, no significant other at his back.

Yes and yes.

"Sure am." As I precede the stranger into the slightly brighter interior, I wonder what is off. There's something different about it all tonight but I can't put my finger on it. My attention snaps back to the guy I was planning to stalk all the way to the bar.

No runners. No briefcase and no visible tattoos. That leaves the weather.

I take a seat on a high stool, drop my handbag at my feet and turn to stare at the guy. Only, he's already staring at me.

Delicious anticipation trickles through me and I hope this one won't run when we shake hands and he hears my name. For some unknown reason it scares people. Either that or Ian had an ex with the same name? Maybe it was his mom's name and it left him queasy?

"Can I get you a drink..." he waits for my name.

I nod and my hand shoots out between us. "Mel."

"What can I get you, Mel?" He shakes my hand but doesn't offer his name in return.

"Something yummy with heaps of liquor in it." I flash him a smile and I'm grateful not to have had to bring up the weather.

Sitting there, waiting for the still stranger to order my drink, I'm aware of the cooler air touching my cleavage. Of the hair standing up on my arms as the air conditioner blasts the room with ice and the fact that every time I move, the lace of my bra shifts across my nipples.

I'm feeling strangely exhilarated now that I've warned my heart to stay out of what might happen in my pants. Maybe I've finally found that person in the middle, the girl who wants to have fun and the woman who isn't scared to go out and find it.

The cocktail that lands in front of me tonight is a milky one and not served by Nick. She's young, the girl behind the bar, probably early twenties, midriff bare and a stud in her nose. I sniff the drink to make sure it isn't coconut, I hate coconut but I'll drink it because a handsome someone bought it for me. Satisfied with the coffee like smell, I take a cautious sip and forget about the gorgeous girl behind the bar.

"Hmm." I can't stop the groan escaping my lips. This is my kind of drink.

"I'm guessing you needed that?" the stranger asks, a half smile lifting his full lips.

"You have no idea." I laugh. The alcohol warms me right along with this guy's killer smile. Add the exhilaration and I'm feeling kind of free. Maybe third time's the charm after all?

"I'm Roger."

"Well, thanks for the drink, Roger. Just what the doctor ordered."

"Rough day?" he asks.

"No, just a long week." That's when I realize it's Friday. The weekend is here and I have no plans. If things go well with Roger, I could be looking at a full two days in bed not just one night.

I smile again.

As if reading my mind, he asks, "Any special plans for the weekend?"

"Nope. You?" I'm still not getting any better at small talk but I'm careful to not babble too. I give away too much when I babble. I'm sticking to closed questions that require a yes or a no, not the openers that elicit a book full of answers that reveal too much.

"Not yet." The hint of meaning in his words isn't lost on me. I'm slow in social situations but I'm not stupid.

"It's going to be nice." Ah, the weather. *Good one, Mellow.* What is wrong with me?

"Back again, Imelda?" Nick gives me a wink as he glides past, hands full of beers.

Great. Now I'm on a first name basis with the guy serving the drinks. I hope it doesn't turn Roger off.

"Do you want to go sit somewhere more comfortable?" I dare to ask him, fluttering my eyelashes with what I hope is the right amount of flirt.

"Sure thing. I'll get us another round."

I'm surprised to find I've nearly polished off the cocktail. It's better than I thought so I'll have to be careful. I don't want to get so drunk I'll hurl at the first hurdle.

As I settle into the nearest booth, I keep my eyes on Roger's broad back, adjust my top so it will open just a little if I lean forward, and plaster a provocative smile on my face. I have to take charge and realize that Mr. Right Now isn't going to walk up out of nowhere and take me to bed. It's going to take an invitation and maybe a few not so subtle hints to spell out exactly what I want.

Just as I begin to wonder what's taking so long, he flashes me another one of those killer smiles. Out of the corner of my eye, I notice Nick shake his head but I ignore him for the moment.

Roger slides into the booth next to me. He's so close the heat from his thigh burns through my slacks and his spicy cologne is like a spark to my sexy side.

"Not to trout out a bad line, but what's a girl like you doing in a place like this?" he asks.

It is a bad line. Does every man use it? I pick up my drink, find the straw with my tongue and flick it into my mouth. Roger's eyes drop to where my lips wrap around the little piece of striped paper. I let it slide from my mouth, leaving a little of the coffee cocktail on my bottom lip.

"You got a little..." When his thumb touches my lip to wipe away the moisture, I trap his wrist in my grip and lick the leftover cocktail. I don't know where the hell the move comes from but his eyes darken instantly. He moves closer so our legs touch firmly instead of out of innocence. I'm not cold anymore.

"Thanks," I say, my voice hitting a new level of husky.

"You're welcome."

Our moment, the one where my world tilts and the forgotten place between my legs aches to be touched, the moment I want to strip my clothes off and lay naked on the table with Roger on top of me, is ruined by, "You done with this?"

I tear my gaze from Roger's and put as much hostility into my glare as I can. "Go away, Nick."

"Can I take your glass?" he enunciates slowly.

"I'm not done with it." The damn thing is still half full. What the hell is he playing at this time?

"My mistake," he shrugs.

He stalks off, the thump-thump of his footsteps heavy on the polished timber floor. I don't know I'm holding my breath until it leaves my body in an angry rush. So much for the guy being a help.

"He seems a little territorial," Roger comments, the moment more than broken as he leans away from me and swigs beer from the bottle. "Something going on between you?"

"I don't even know the guy."

"He sure knows you."

There's innuendo in his voice this time too but it isn't seductive. Nick should have pissed on my leg while he was here. He has no right to be so possessive over me. I've asked for his help in pointing out the bad eggs, not in putting off perfectly good ones.

"Forget about him," I reply, switching my attention back to where it had been.

"How long have you known Nick?"

Great. "I don't know him. I only came in here for the first time a few days ago."

"Yet he knows your name."

Bloody hell. "Are we going to talk about the bar guy all night?" I ask. I try not to let any frustration taint my question but it's hard. Roger and I were about to go somewhere I hadn't been before and I'm eager to try to get back.

Roger shrugs and the gesture makes me think he isn't going to drop it completely but he does seem content to leave it be for a minute.

"Tell me a little about yourself, Roger."

"Not much to tell," he shrugs again. I ignore it.

"What do you do for a living?"

"I'm in Law Enforcement."

"Cool, a cop?" No wonder Roger is built. He probably works out daily to stay in shape for such a physically demanding job.

"Something like that. You?"

Ignoring also the vague answers, I decide to share. "I'm the Function Coordinator at the Hilton."

"That sounds interesting. What kind of functions?"

"Weddings, conferences, meetings, that kind of thing."

"You must speak to some movers and shakers with a job like that."

Ah. There's the open question. He wants me to do the talking but I'm not a motor-mouth. I also don't want to share my life story with a guy I won't be seeing again. In the space of a few minutes, we went from nearly hot and heavy to talking about careers and I want to go back to hot. And less talk.

I lean in closer. I'm absolutely being slutty now but this dude is hot and I'm hurting. "Some," I nod. "But I'm not really the talking type. More the doing kind."

"Really?" Roger breathes, closing the distance again.

The minute his lips touch mine, everything else drops away. My worries about never having sex again. My friends and their unhelpful jibes. All I can picture is two days in bed with a hot guy who tastes like beer and heaven.

I open my mouth and dip my tongue into his, running it along the line of his teeth, gasping when he nips my bottom lip. The fingers on one hand spear through his hair and with the other I cup his cheek to keep him where he is. He grabs my ass and pulls me closer so I'm practically sitting on his lap.

The kiss goes on and on and on until my head spins from the lack of oxygen. When I come up for air, I keep my eyes shut for a second to savor it. I'm a bit scared of breaking the spell, scared that Roger will flee.

"That was incredible," he whispers against my neck while he catches his breath.

I open my heavy lids real slow. I don't want to look into his mesmerizing gaze to see if he's teasing or lying. What I do see when our eyes lock takes what little breath I have left. He isn't making it up. He liked it.

Licking my lips, I nod. That was...awesome. Sure, the butterflies in my stomach that I know should be there somewhere didn't take flight, but that was some kiss and I'm turned on.

It's crunch time.

And I start to doubt myself.

Can I really ask this guy to come home with me? Can I take my clothes off in front of a perfect stranger and let him into my bed? Possibly my heart?

This is me. The terrified girl. The unsure woman. It doesn't matter how many faces I pretend to have, this is me. And in this space, I'm not sure I like her...

6

It's just sex. Millions of people do this every day. One night stands, holiday flings, office romances and affairs. Sex happens between strangers everywhere, every minute. Why do I have to overthink it? I should thank my lucky stars and take my piece of the action.

I need to regroup. Maybe have a shot or two since the cocktails aren't providing me with enough courage to open my mouth and say the words my libido wants me to. "I'm going to go powder my nose."

Roger nods. Sinking back into the worn leather, he salutes me with his bottle of beer.

Damn, but the man can smile.

A few minutes later, my business taken care of, I'm freshening up, examining my reflection in the mirror. Nick had no right to call me a hooker. I wasn't asking anyone to buy me drinks or pay for sex. I'll pretty much give it away for the right guy.

Lobbing my wet hand towel into the waste basket, I'm filled with anticipation and it makes me a little breathless and whole lot of hot.

I pull open the door but stop when I hear loud voices. Two men arguing about something and one of them is really pissed.

"You can't get her involved."

Ah, so Nick is the angry one. Well, good. It's about time someone rubbed him up the wrong way. I'm about to mind my own business but the muttered words in reply are odd.

"She isn't involved. I'm off duty the second I observed you not breaking any of the rules of your sentencing conditions."

"She's vulnerable and you're using her."

"Using her for what?" the other voice asks.

"To get at me."

A laugh echoes along the corridor. Intrigued, I move closer, tip-toeing along the floor boards. Someone is playing games with Nick? The strangely morbid, narcissistic side of me wants to know who. Maybe I can use the info when the time comes to get him to back off.

"She doesn't know you."

"Said that did she?" All the anger falls away from Nick's voice and he becomes tauntingly cocky.

"Are you telling me she lied?"

As I creep around the corner, I see it's Roger fighting with Nick. I nearly snort out loud. Law enforcement, my ass! Why hadn't he said he was there as a spy? I probably would have told him about the ladies room episode. Now all the questions about how well I know Nick make sense. The guy grilled me for information. Son of a bitch.

"It's her story to tell," Nick shrugs.

Why are they talking about me? Once again Nick goes above and beyond to scare the guys away.

"Well, I'm not touching your criminal leftovers."

"You looked like you were getting pretty cozy with her."

Roger exhales. "She's pretty in a way, and she's hot for it."

Nick growls and his hands clench into fists. If he hits the guy because of me, he'll go to jail. I can't let that happen even if there is the possibility he's an asshole too.

I step out into the light and strike a supermodel-at-the-end-of-a-catwalk-pose. "There you are, Roger." Anger pitches my voice lower than usual.

"Nick and I were just having a chat."

"Hmm." I nod and take another step. "Are you done?"

"I reckon we are," he replies, giving Nick one last hard look. Nick's fists are still clenched but I think he's reined his control in to one degree beneath murderous rage.

"Good. Now get out."

"What?" The look in Roger's eyes perfectly mirror Nick's. They are both confused.

My blood boils. "I am nobody's leftovers. If you had told me who you were in the first place, I would have helped you out and then taken you home. But I don't sleep with dirty, rotten liars."

"I didn't lie. I told you I'm in law enforcement."

"But you're no cop. You're a bloodsucker, waiting for someone to screw up so you can haul them back to prison and collect your cheque aren't you. Nick hasn't done anything wrong."

"How'd he get the black eye then?" Roger points to Nick's cheek and the slight bruising around his eye.

Shows how much attention I've paid tonight. Through narrowed eyes, I notice his face is still bruising. It's reasonably fresh.

"Maybe he ran into a door?" I say. If Nick hit someone, he wouldn't be standing here to defend his innocence. The cops would have been there so quick, he wouldn't have had time to think. Big guys like Nick look dangerous. With his shaggy brown hair, the almost menacing features when's pissed, and is that a tattoo sticking out from his shirt sleeve? I wouldn't pick a fight with him in a dark ally.

"I already told you. *He* hit me."

"You didn't hit him back?" Roger turns back to Nick.

Nick must be gritting his teeth hard. His answer comes out strained. "Why don't you go ask him?"

"Give me a name and I will."

Nick finally looks at me then. I don't know what he's trying to tell me when he raises his brows over you-know-what-I'm-hiding eyes.

I say the first thing that comes to mind, as stupid as it is. "I hit him."

Roger stares at me for a minute then swings back to Nick. "You can't be serious?"

I bristle. "Why not. You don't think I can kick his ass?"

"It's not that. Where is your bruise? If you hit him, your hand would be all swollen and it would hurt." Roger stalks toward me and grabs my right hand, his touch gentle as he turns my wrist over and examines my knuckles.

I snatch my hand away, guilt likely written all over my face. Another lie comes to cover up the first. "I didn't use my fist."

Roger smiles. He knows I'm bluffing and he's about to call me on it.

"I swung my handbag. Got him a beauty didn't I?"

Nick rolls his eyes.

"That handbag?" Roger asks.

"No, my other one. It's got buckles and stuff all over it."

"Do you want to press charges?" Roger asks Nick.

Damn. Hadn't thought of that.

"Of course not. I said something I shouldn't have, and she hit me. Fair's fair."

"Do *you* want to press charges?" Roger asks me.

Hmm. Now that would be interesting. Put Nick back in his box where my sex life is concerned. "No thanks. We're even now." I put as much emphasis on that statement as I can.

Nick nods.

The tense silence drags on and on as I take turns glaring at tweedle-dumb and tweedle-dick. I've had enough. My night is clearly over. There is no way I'm taking Roger home. My buzz is well and truly dead and I'm tired now. It's Friday. The end of a really long week. Suddenly I have the urge to curl up in a little ball and sleep all weekend.

Stuff sex. It's highly overrated anyway. I'd bet Roger isn't any different to any other guy I've been with.

"I'm outta here," I say and turn to leave. A hand on my arm stops me and I do some teeth-grinding of my own.

"No. Roger is leaving." Nick's voice, Nick's hand on my arm. He has something else to say to me.

"You can't kick me out," Roger says casually.

"The lady asked you to leave."

"Mel? Do you want me to go?" Roger asks softly, staring at me like he still has a chance.

Like hell. "Get out."

Standing with Nick, we watch Mr. Law Enforcement walk through the front doors and out on to the street.

"You won't get into trouble will you?" I question Nick once the door closes behind him.

"You're not going to ask me why I have a parole officer in the first place?"

"I overheard you talking about it the other day. Anger issues, right?"

"Yeah, right."

There is one thing I burn to know. "Who hit you?"

Nick laughs but it doesn't echo like Roger's. The sound is deep and rumbly and kind of odd. I don't think I've heard him laugh before. "You did."

"No. Who really hit you?"

"Matt."

"You mean, last night? Your brother-in-law Matt?"

"Yep. There's only one."

"But why?"

"You don't want to know. "

"I wouldn't have asked if I didn't want an answer."

"He wanted to follow you. After you stormed out, he wanted to know what we'd talked about and then he was determined to go after you and change your mind."

"He wouldn't have."

"He would have tried. You'd have walked home and then he'd know where you live."

I hadn't ever thought of that in this predicament. I've thought of the danger, yes, but not in real and practical terms. "Well, thanks for sticking up for me."

Nick's cheeks glow pink under the fluorescent light. "You too."

I supposed that's as close as he's going to come to thanking me for saving his bacon. It's good enough.

My mouth opens and a yawn escapes through my fingertips. I really am beat. All this to-ing and fro-ing is doing my head in. "Good night, Nick."

"Imelda?" His fingers touch my arm again, gentle but firm. "Can I walk you home? It's late and the bar's about closed anyway."

Immediately thoughts of Nick knowing where I live scare me but then when I think of who else could follow me home... I shiver. It's another stupid little detail that didn't previously cross my dense mind.

"I won't try anything on. I promise. It's too late for you to be out walking the city streets on your own," he clarifies.

"Ah. Sure, why not." Why not? He is so adamant about not hitting on me though. I'm a bit insulted. Maybe I'm not his type? He sure as hell isn't mine. Maybe from of this ridiculous nightmare, I can make a friend out of Nick. Instead of the boring nights at home with the cats, I can walk to the bar and hang out. An intriguing prospect. I don't really have male friends. Maybe that's a part of my problem? With a father who rarely makes an appearance, I haven't really had that whole male influence everyone raves about.

While Nick throws out the drunks, I sit on a bar stool and swivel, swinging my feet while he counts the cash register, my stilettos on the floor. With each minute that ticks by I become apprehensive again. Maybe the time has come for me to give up and admit defeat. I'm not the kind of woman men want for a one-night stand.

I'm barely a woman at all in their eyes.

I drop my gaze to my white office shirt and black slacks. There is nothing alluring about me. Sure I have a red bra under my shirt and a hint of cleavage peeking through the fabric where I'd undone the buttons, but that's it. My black pants are the bottoms of a suit but they don't do much for me. My clothes are still just clothes and I'm still wearing them...as armor.

There's my light bulb, I think as I smack myself in the forehead. Where's the skin? Like the bar chick from earlier? Even transformed slightly, I look the same as every other boring office worker in the city. I can be noticed now but not salivated over. That sounds gross but I want guys to want to fuck me.

At twenty seven years old, supposedly ready to conquer the world, I cower in the corner and wait for my interfering body guard to walk me home. I straighten my shoulders and sit up on the stool. I'm becoming a statistic. How many nearly thirty year old women are single and desperate and do all the wrong things in their pursuit of happiness? There has to be a number somewhere. There are numbers for everything these days.

Letting my head fall on the bar, I close my eyes and concentrate on blocking out everything around me. I have to find what it is that makes all those women fail so I can do the opposite. The voice of negativity in my alcohol fogged brain attempts to tell me I've already failed, and I know I should give up now, but I can't do that. If I'm to be a statistic, I want it to be the one with 2.5 kids, white picket fence, overly large SUV in the drive and a dog bounding around licking the faces of my family.

Will I still be sitting here, on this stool, in another ten years? Will Nick still pour the drinks or will he have moved on and found his own family? Will the drunk pool players still hit on every piece of fresh meat who thinks to enter *Johnnie's* doors? Will I be watching women my age now, doing the same things I am?

Dammit! Too many questions and not enough doing!

Nick's voice booms like a foghorn in the dark. "Are you ready?"

Was I? Was I ready to do anything it would take to embrace my womanhood and grab a hold of whatever fate offered me? Was I ready to look for more than just sex and a hot body and go beyond that? Here I am with real time to find a boyfriend, a soul mate, but what happens if I take Mr. Right Now home with me and Mr. Right walks by us on the street and assumes the worst of me?

"You alright?" Nick asks hesitantly.

I groan. "Don't ask."

"Look, I can call you a cab if you don't want to walk."

"No. No I need some air." Isn't that the truth? The humid abyss mingled with the alcohol makes it hard for my brain to grasp something that should be easy to understand. I'm a smart woman. Why can't I work this out?

"Can I ask you a question?"

If I say no, he'll ask anyway. "Sure."

"What are you really doing in my bar?"

"I already told you. I want to find a man."

"But in the last three days, you haven't had any bites."

"Thanks for rubbing that in."

"You just don't seem like the type to do what you're doing."

I bristle at that. "What do you mean the type?" I stand with my hands on my hips as Nick sets the alarm, closes the doors behind us and locks three solid steel deadbolts.

"I've seen 'em all, Imelda. Desperate, on a dare, lonely, naïve. You fit in to most of those categories but there's something different about you. I can't place it."

Is that a compliment? "I'm not doing any of this on a dare and I am not naïve."

"So are you desperate or lonely?"

Which one am I? Yes, I'm desperate but am I lonely? Until now, this week, I hadn't thought I was. Every morning I go to work and at the end of every day I come home. My friends and I talk on the phone all the time and my mum, sister and I have lunch together every few weeks when mum demands it. There are nights when I wish for company but for the most part, I don't have time to dwell on it. I was relatively happy until Monday night when my girlfriends triggered my headlong fall into this stupidity. At least I thought I was happy.

I stop walking. It's all their fault. I'm both desperate and lonely now and they had done that to me. They're supposed to my friends.

"I'm sorry, I shouldn't have asked," Nick said, his hands in the air. "It's none of my business."

"It's not that. When I hear you say it, I realize that I've fallen into a box."

"A box?"

"You just categorized my entire existence in a few hours over three nights. I'd say I'm in a box."

"That's a bold statement," Nick says quietly as we start walking again. "You're saying that you've been desperate and lonely your whole life and I know that can't be true."

"How do you know? What makes you so wise and all knowing?"

"If you've had such a hard life, you wouldn't be here looking for love. You'd be looking for a trick or a target to mug for your next hit."

"Drugs or prostitution? Are those the only two options for people who've missed out on the good things in life?"

"No." Nick says. "There are other options."

The night is suddenly cold. Is the sadness I see in his eyes under the street light real or is he ashamed of the labels he throws at people? "What's your story, Nick?"

7

"You don't want to hear my life story," Nick chuckles and shakes his head, keeps walking.

"You aren't going to tell me?"

"No."

"I answered your question-"

He cuts me off. "No you didn't."

I jog a little to catch up. "Fine. I'm a little desperate, but mostly I'm lonely. I'm not getting any younger and I don't want to be a forty-year-old career driven woman full of regrets."

"Can't you have the career and the man?"

"That's two questions and if you want an answer, you'll have to give me one."

He nods. If I wasn't staring at him, I would have missed the gesture. "What's with the anger issues? You must have done something pretty messed up to be sentenced for it."

"I did. And my anger isn't and was never the issue."

"Will you tell me what happened?" I shiver despite the warmish night. We are totally alone on the footpath, the road deserted as well, as if all the cars in the city avoid the street where we walk. It's eerie but at the same time nice to have some peace from the hustle and bustle. I feel safer since I'm not alone.

"It's really not all that exciting," Nick tells me. "A guy tried to hold up the bar one night, I got angry and laid into him a little. Judge said I didn't have the right."

"That's not all though is it?" He glossed over the important bits. I can tell.

"Okay, so I may have hit him a few too many times and then resisted arrest."

"Ah. That explains the sentence."

"Actually, that's the first charge I got stuck with. The cop I punched said I did it on purpose and of course everyone believed him."

"Did you?"

"Did I what?"

"Did you hit him on purpose?"

"Not the first time. That time was an accident but then he was swinging at me and I was swinging back."

The man is smiling. I can hear it in his voice. He enjoyed the fight. Idiot. No wonder the judge gave him the diary. She'd probably laughed when her gavel banged. Serve him right. Sort of.

"You said that's the first charge? Is there more?"

"Matt. Matt is the real reason this all happened."

"I don't understand. What has got to do with it?"

"Can we not do this?" he says, rubbing a hand over his face. "I get wound up when I talk about it and I'd just rather not."

"Okay, but at least tell me how the diary is going?" I ask instead, smiling.

Nick stops walking, his mouth drops open and he stares at me. "How much did you hear?"

Enough. I hadn't been eavesdropping. Not really. If he didn't want anyone to overhear, he wouldn't have talked about it at the bar. "That's it."

Silence descends so the only sound is the tapping of my heels and the thump of his sandshoes as we walk side by side. To the outside world, we must look relatively comfortable with each stride but a tension is brewing.

Then this one from Nick, "What kind of man are you looking for?"

"Interested are you?" I'm joking but he takes two big steps away from me so we are separated by about a meter and a half of footpath.

"I don't date patrons."

It isn't *what* he says, it's the way he says it. "What the hell is so wrong with me?"

"Nothing is wrong with you."

"Then what am I doing wrong?"

"What makes you think it's you?"

I stop again, forcing Nick to turn and look at me when I place a hand on his arm. "I'm not an idiot," I say with a shake of my head. "Guys just aren't this picky. I've been putting it out there and it's like I'm invisible or something."

"Maybe you're trying too hard," he suggests.

A laugh slips out but there's no humor in it. "Would that matter?"

"You're right. Probably not."

"So it is me?"

"Did you ever think that maybe you have that look that warns a guy away?"

"What look?"

"Yours alternate. Sometimes you smile like you're saying yes now but it's going to get really difficult come morning. Other times you wear your heart on your sleeve and that scares most guys. No one wants a one night stand, or a girlfriend, who's going to be hard work."

I bite my lip and ponder his statement. It's really hard to stem the tears that threaten with each shocked breath I take into my body but I refuse to cry over the fact that I don't know any of this stuff. Why isn't there a manual or something to save millions of women all this grief?

I'm so lost in thought I nearly walk right past my own building. "This is me," I tell him.

"Look, I'm sorry. I don't want to upset you."

"It's all right. I guess I wasn't prepared for any of this."

"Why are you doing it like this, Imelda?"

"Like what?" I'm tired, exhausted, and the tears are closer than I'd like them to be with a relative stranger who already thinks I'm bad news, a loser, a liability.

"Why can't you wait until you bump into the man of your dreams at work or at the store? Sign up for some online dating? Why did you pick my bar to start your little adventure?"

"Is that what you think this is? An adventure?" Is his opinion of me so low? And why does he have to say it like that? Like I'm the only pathetic person in a twenty block radius in need of a pity party. "This is my life and I happen to take it quite seriously." I poke him in the chest with every hurt word. Now I'm getting angry and it isn't fair but he deserves it for making me feel so cheap and nasty. "Maybe I want to find an everyday man who does everyday things like have a drink at a bar after a hard day at work. Maybe I want to feel loved or even sexy? Huh? Did you ever think that maybe I just want to be kissed so I can act for just one day like I'm an attractive, desirable woman who deserves to feel human for five fucking minutes?"

Nick's face shifts from angry to ashamed to incredulous during my very loud diatribe. At the end of it all, after I say things I'm not even sure I mean, he steps forward, cups my face in his warm hands and touches his lips to mine. For a second I stand, totally stunned. But only for a second.

His hands apply firm pressure and his face tilts and before I know it, I'm kissing him back. His hot tongue runs along the length of my lower lip so I open my mouth and let him in. Angling his head, he delves deeper, his taste on my tongue pure unadulterated male and I like it.

Nick's hair is soft as I run my hands over his head and down the back of his neck to rest on his broad shoulders. His shirt radiates heat and when my breasts press into his chest, a tingle shivers from my nipples right to my midsection where it turns to a low ache. This is what I'm searching for. Butterflies. I want to have a connection to another person and go wild.

As soon as I let that thought run through my mind, Nick pulls away, his hands shifting to my arms to steady me. I wasn't even sure I'd swayed.

"I thought you said I wasn't your type," I say, licking my lips, tasting his flavor on my tongue again. There is something peanut-ty about it, like he'd eaten a handful before we left the bar.

"You're not."

The flash in his eyes tells me all I need to know. "You kissed me out of pity?"

"No. I kissed you to show you that you're not revolting like you seem to think you are."

"I never said I was revolting." Oh my God, this skyrockets from dream to nightmare and still I stand there like a dazed teenager, reeling from a fake kiss. Damn this man's acting skills.

"You wanted to be kissed. Now maybe you'll believe you're not the hideous monster someone made you think you are and get back to living your normal life."

"You kissed me so I won't come back to your bar? You don't think I can pick up?"

"I know you can pick up but do you really want to? The guys who come to my place aren't coming in for a beer after work. They come to drown their sorrows or to get away from their wives and families and problems. They aren't the kind of men you want to take home with you."

As our argument grows louder, I get angrier. He says so many things and with each syllable dropping from the mouth that was just pressed against mine, I realize he just plain doesn't want me at the bar. All the rest is bullshit. "If you don't want me to come back to your precious bar, why don't you just say it?"

It's too dark for me to register what his eyes say as he steps away, deeper into the shadows but I hear his tone, loud and clear. "Fine. I don't want you to come back to the bar. Spend the weekend with your girlfriends. Get them to introduce you to a nice single guy with a good job and a mother who loves him. That's what you should be looking for, Imelda. My bar is full of losers and always will be."

I want to slap him. I want to tell him he got it wrong but my stupid brain chose that moment to actually listen to what he'd just said. Why hadn't Jess or Candice or Amy introduced me to any eligible single guys? Am I abhorrent even to my own friends or just too pathetic? While they're busy giving me shit and making me feel like a loser with a capital L, why hadn't they thrown any names into the ring. Surely they know guys they haven't already slept with?

"Have a nice life, Imelda."

I don't say anything, I can't. Humiliation isn't an emotion I'm used to dealing with but in the last few days, it's starting to feel like my second skin.

Punching the electronic keypad, I put my security number in and push through the glass door, sending it crashing into the wall. I walk past the elevators and take the half-flight of stairs two at a time, wincing from the pinch on my toes but it isn't bad enough to make me stop. I make it to the first floor and when I burst through the doors into my corridor, the tears start, one after the other until they trail down my cheeks, wetting my boring office shirt.

I can't see the lock my vision is so blurred. It takes a few attempts to get the key in and turn it to open the heavy double layered pine. I don't even have the energy to slam it shut the way I want too. Why did that bloody man have to make me think so much? And why am I crying my heart out just because a few of his words hit home?

This is what he wants.

To make me feel so humiliated that it will be too awkward to walk back through his door.

I wipe away tears and open my freezer. Taking out the tub of ice cream I keep there for emergencies, I grab a spoon and curl up on the couch. What I want to do is ring my so-called friends and ask them all why they'd never set me up on a blind date or taken me with them to a gallery launch or a premiere party. Maybe they'd tried and I'd been too busy? No. I can't remember ever getting that memo. I cry even harder, my tears dropping into the ice cream tub.

I need something to take my mind off it all. Flicking on the television I find a channel where the two British women tell other women what they're doing wrong with their hair and clothing.

After about fifteen minutes, I'm sitting forward, perching on the edge of the sofa cushion, my ice cream all but forgotten, the wet ring around the bottom of it staining my coffee table while tears dry on my cheeks.

I need an actual makeover. I'll show Nick he's wrong.

I'll show them all I'm not a loser.

Dear Freddy...

?

?

#

!

Fuck!

I got nothing. Bloody woman scrambled my thoughts and made me feel like a lech. I kissed her because she complained about being repulsive and then she gave me that look again. The one that says 'when are you going to propose?'.

Then she accused me of kissing her out of pity! I've never given anyone a pity pash in my life and I wouldn't start now. Why is it that women don't understand how much power they hold? She's a stunner but she thinks no one wants her. I just wanted to show her she's wrong and she throws it all out of context. Again.

She looks reasonably intelligent and can hold a conversation, but damn, I don't think all of her lights are on upstairs. Hopefully I set her straight and she won't come back.

I don't think I can kiss her again and keep up the pretext. She is hot! I haven't held a woman like her in my arms for a long, long time and it was good. But I don't need the temptation especially while I have a criminal conviction hanging over my head.

Freddy, I hope she gets the message. I don't think I can stand by and watch her flirt with the tossers drinking at my bar. Bloody hell, Roger almost had her tonight. Roger! That bastard doesn't deserve to breathe the same air, let alone score with a chick like Imelda.

But we won't go there. I wouldn't want you to think I'm going to kill him or something... My anger is not that out of control.

8

Saturdays are my day for sleeping in. I like to pull the quilt up to my chin and sleep until ten. Then I get up and make bacon and eggs for breakfast, read the paper and stay in my flannel jammies for most of the day. If there isn't anything I need to do or anywhere to go, I stay in the soft cow spotted fabric. Saturdays are mine for relaxing.

But not today.

I yawn and groan (I've been doing a lot of that lately) and stare at the LED clock next to my bed for the tenth time hoping the little numbers will come alive and suffocate me. Six am. On the one day I don't have to get up and fix yet another of Denni's night-time nightmares, here I am staring at the shadows on the ceiling, thinking about my own nightmares.

There is a particularly vivid one I can remember of my girlfriends. Candice, Jess and Amy all come to my sixtieth birthday party, all three hadn't aged a day but I had. My heritage had firmly taken a hold of my skin and it now looks more like stressed leather, complete with pigment blotches and wrinkles. In the background is my apartment but in the dream, trinkets cover every surface and granny rugs line every couch.

My nose twitches. I can practically smell the camphor and moth balls.

As my friends sing happy birthday to me with their perfect voices and perfect bodies and, well, perfection all around, I notice the front door standing open. When I shuffle to close it with legs that are slower and older, Candice bars my way.

"I'll get the door," she purrs.

Behind her shoulders, I can see hot men. In every shape and size and skin color, they're lined up from my hallway to the stairwell. As fast as my decrepit legs can carry me, I go to the window and see the hotties lining the street.

My mouth curves in a droopy smile. "Are they my birthday presents?"

"Hell, no," Jess laughs. "They're our friends and our lovers."

"What did you get me for my birthday then?" I don't want to be nasty about it but if it's better than all the hunks in the hall and on the street, then I want to see it. Now.

Then the sound fades and I hear the mewling. Amy holds a cane basket with the lid shut tight. "We saw these in the pet shop and they were so cute, we couldn't resist."

With shaking hands, I unlatch the top, open the cane and look in. There sits three of the most adorable little kittens I've ever seen. One is black and white with splotches of brown. One is white and fluffy and the other is grey with black socks.

One by one the kittens look up at me. Then they smile. Razor sharp teeth catch the light, evil eyes staring back at me.

That's when I wake up, screaming. Fluffy cries her outrage when I swat her off the bed. She must have been the one mewling.

My friends hadn't mentioned on Monday night, that the cats intent on eating my corpse when I die of loneliness are gifts from them for my birthday. Why hadn't they given me a hotty? They have so many. The bitches could have shared just one!

I have to calm down.

It really isn't Candice's fault or Amy's or Jess's. I'm not some kind of charity case who needs to be set up with leftovers or the ones who didn't make the repeat list.

Giving up on sleep altogether, I head for the shower. As the hot water runs over my body, loosening my tight muscles, I ponder what the day might hold for me. Wednesday through Friday I'd gone to work and then straight to the bar. Today the hours stretched out like a black hole of boredom.

I could catch a movie but I don't want to do it on my own. I can't call my mum. She'll know something's up the minute she answers the phone. And that's mostly because I don't call my mother out of the blue. Not anymore. My brothers are out of the question. We don't get along very well especially with all the taunting about me being adopted.

Two words spring to mind. Retail therapy. I rarely go shopping. I work too hard for my money to throw it away on clothes, shoes and handbags that may never see the light of day.

Hmm...

I have to get out the mindset that I'm not like other women living in this city. Why don't I own a pair of Manolo Blahniks? The most expensive shoes I own are the ones I picked up on Monday after work. It's not like my bank account will crumble after a day of shopping and luxury.

While I towel dry my hair, I take a look at it in the mirror. I want to style it differently today. Flashes of the TV show I watched last night sail through my mind. I definitely need a makeover. A haircut and a brand new outfit that isn't a little black cocktail dress could do wonders. Nick won't believe his eyes when I walk in to *Johnnie's* tonight. And I *am* going back. When he'd told me not to, I got angry. He has no right to tell me what I can and can't do. All he did was make me more determined. Childish, yes, absolutely. I never claimed to be all adult sophistication.

I don't bother straightening my hair or putting on make up. If I'm going to do it, I'll do it right. My first stop is a beauty parlor. My second will be some of the exclusive smaller boutiques in the city. If I can't find something awesome there, I'm in real trouble and should give it all up and wait on my couch to wither and die.

Six hours later my short jagged nails are replaced by acrylics, frenched with three pretty little pink flowers painted on each one. I sport a fancy new look, my dark brown dead hair cut to my shoulders in a choppy style that frames my face. It's much lighter and will be a cinch to do in the mornings. The hairdresser is an absolute miracle worker. Not only does she work wonders with my hair, she shows me how to apply makeup so my eyes appear darker and wider. Darker isn't something I've ever wanted my eyes to be, but the look is fantastic. Pink gloss sparkles from my lips and with the help of a little blusher, I have healthy color in my cheeks that isn't due to blushing.

I tip the woman almost as much as she charges me, I'm so happy with the result.

Next comes the hard part.

While I walk around in my plain old runners and comfy jeans, I pass a little non-descript boutique with a stunning dress in the window. Stepping into the cool interior, racks and racks of colorful clothes fill every available space. I don't stop at the dress in the window. I buy designer jeans and tops to coordinate. Two winter jackets, one a dark red for work that falls to my knees and is cinched in at the waist giving me a nice hourglass look. The other is a bomber style to go with the jeans. Dark purple with a matt appearance, rose gold buckles around the cuffs. Even the chunky zip is rose gold. I feel sophisticated.

A pair of black leather knee high boots compliment a gorgeous plaid skirt with a flirty ruffle around the bottom and a black knit sweater to finish the look. It's an outfit for winter but it will suit autumn as well. About three thousand dollars later I have another four pairs of shoes and nine complete outfits along with the two jackets. Don't ask where I planned to put it all in my tiny closet at home. Maybe it's the opportunity I need to throw some of the older stuff out. To get rid of some of my armor.

Wait till Denni sees me on Monday morning in my new suit. The darkest of browns, it's similar to the cut of the plaid skirt but without the ruffle. The pencil thin design fit like a glove and the matching jacket can be worn with the buttons done up or relaxed. I can either wear a bra and have awesome cleavage or put a camisole under it and have a hint of lace peeking from between the slim lapels.

This outfit leads me to a lingerie store where the fifty something year old lady fits me for bras that give me so much more than I have. The effect makes me lightheaded. I do have killer boobs! Along with my firm butt and reasonably flat tummy, I fit into just about anything I try on. Another five hundred goes in that shop. I've spent too many years thinking of my body as average when really, it's the clothes I wear that make me feel more like Mellow and less like a desirable woman. A few fitted blouses and push up bras and I'm a different person.

By the time the sun drops behind the horizon I'm exhausted. Not just physically but mentally as well. I feel like I've been on one of those makeover shows. My arms hurt from the array of multicolored bags clutched in my hands and hanging from the crook of my elbows. I've made the promise not to spend any more of my savings and head home but one more shiny expanse of glass catches my attention. Handbags and accessories. I really only have two handbags. One for work and one for going out. When I'd lied to Roger about hitting Nick, I'd fabricated a bag I don't own right along with the whole hitting him thing. Not that I don't want to hit him. I do. I really do!

Now I have the irresistible urge to own a bag just like the one I pictured in my head. I might just hit Nick with it tonight. God knows the man will say at least one thing to upset me.

Pride drives me through the evening and the wait for a suitable time to walk through the doors of *Johnnie's*. A late coffee perks me up and anticipation makes my blood thrum in my veins (or it's the caffeine). I wear the dress from the shop window. It's one of those ones that looks a bit like a sack on the hanger but with a belt around my waist, it gives me hips to sashay. The black material has big pink hibiscus flowers on it. Sounds garish, but it's a really hot dress and it's short. If I bend over too far, the world will see my new undies and beyond.

I just won't bend. Easy.

What I will do is the knock the socks off a certain naysayer and finally snag that elusive one-night stand.

·♥·♥·♥·♥·♥·

Dear Freddy,

I'm not in the habit of cranking out the diary in the middle of the afternoon before work but I feel kind of bad about kissing Imelda and some of the things I said were a bit harsh. She won't be back so I won't be able to say sorry. I don't know what the hell turned me into such a grade A jerk last night. Maybe it was the fact Roger was trying it on hard with one of my patrons when he was supposed to be keeping me in his sights. The man was working for God's sake. I tried to behave because he was watching my every move but when he kissed Imelda... Let's just say I wasn't happy about it.

Thank god she won't be back. Warm and fuzzy emotions had never got him anywhere in life and Nick doubted now would be any different.

He pushes away the feeling that makes his stomach hollow at the thought of never seeing her again. Never was a long time. She was pretty great.

And a pretty pain in the bum!

He had to snap out of it and get to work. There were other people to pour drinks for and be annoyed by.

9

Why is it that every time I stand before the big sleek doors of *Johnnie's*, I have an attack of the nerves that stops me in my tracks? Why couldn't the bravado from my insane day of shopping carry over and through into the pub itself rather than perching me on the stoop?

I know, for once in my life, I look totally amazing but here I stand. Unsure, hesitant, like a teenage girl again rather than the woman I want to be. It isn't about getting laid anymore for me. Don't get me wrong, I want sex, my body needs it, but now it's about pride. Ego isn't something I've been filled with but as rejection after humiliating rejection finds me alone in my bed, my pride smarts and I don't like it.

"Waiting for someone?" a deep voice asks from behind me. It's déjà vu from last night. My imagination playing tricks on me as I block patrons from entering.

"Nope," I answer as I turn. Craning my neck, I have to tilt my whole head back to meet a pair of twinkling eyes set on either side of a perfect nose placed on an even better-looking face. Now this guy is straight off the pages of a magazine. Shaking my head, I wonder if I'm still standing outside *Johnnie's* or if my wishful thinking has landed me somewhere a little more upmarket.

"Let me get the door for you then." He has a smile to light up the city and when the stranger brushes past me to press a hand to the door, his delicious scent does something to my insides.

I answer his million-watt smile with one of my own and walk ahead, slowly and with a slight swish to my hips. I don't do it entirely on purpose, the shoes make my gait more of a runway stride. I like it.

The crowning glory of the entire day, hell the entire week, goes to Nick and the look on his face when he sees me. I can't be sure which part of me walking in surprises him the most. Hopefully it's the fact I've come back even though he'd more than expressed his wishes in that department. The man had to know his pity pash was going to challenge me in ways nothing else could have. Or maybe he just doesn't know much about women?

A soft touch at my elbow brings my attention back to the tall stranger and his twinkly smile.

"Can I buy you a drink?" he asks. There's just enough shy hesitation that it's adorable.

As I nod, I can't help but feel like my day is looking up. Is it working already? Surely it can't be as easy as buying a new outfit? Denni had been right on so many other scores why not this one too? Looks really did count for everything and now that I'm hot, well, hotter, things are finally going to happen. "Vodka and lime. Thanks." Taking the bull by the horns, I hold my hand out and introduce myself while waiting for a scowling Nick to pour our drinks. "I'm Mel."

"Theodore. Well, Ted mostly."

"Well, Ted mostly, it's nice to meet you."

We are both chuckling awkwardly as our glasses are thunked on the bar. I want to tell Nick to settle down but instead, I turned my entire body to give Ted my full and complete attention. And perhaps a glimpse of my now killer cleavage.

"Do you play pool?" he asks.

I look over at the free table with only a slight stab of apprehension. "Not really."

"I can teach you?" Ted offers. Is he flirting or is he just as weird at this whole meeting other people thing as me?

I did pick up one valuable lesson after hours of random Google searches. Guys like to be smarter and better than the woman they are trying to impress. I'm not going to tell him I can shoot pool with my eyes closed and one hand tied behind my back. One good memory of my childhood is the pool table in the back room growing up. Rainy days were filled with ridiculous attempts at trick shots since my siblings and I had beat each other time and again. When there's no competition in the Mahari household, everyone gets really bored really quickly.

Taking the familiar weight of the cue in my hand, I relax my fingers and watch intently, making the appropriate noises as Ted racks up the balls. Wrong. He has two bigs where the smalls are supposed to be and the black is nowhere near to being at home but I bite my tongue.

"Now the purpose is to sink all of your balls first and then the black ball last to win."

I nod. Like an idiot. Or like a clueless female. I don't know which I'm more frustrated with. "Which ones are mine?"

Ted shakes his head and gives me the most patronizing look but, on his gorgeous face, well, I can handle it. My frustration eases and I relax as he says, "First you have to pot one. I'll break and then we take it in turns."

"Great."

I can't have played dumber but for once it's actually really nice to hand over control to someone else. I'm naturally competitive but guys don't like that. They're scared of confident women too. I know I'm stereotyping but when the shoe fits and all that. My own brothers hated it and me but that was one of the bonuses in my eyes. It was the only torture I could inflict to get back at them for all the adoption taunts.

The sharp crack of the balls hitting each other and the soft thuds as they bounce off the cushions puts me at ease. Not to mention the fact that Ted has a killer ass I can't stop staring at as he bends over the side of the table to take another shot. The dark denim jeans leave nothing to the imagination, outlining everything.

"You're bigs," he says. I only just wrench my gaze away in time before he can catch me perving. I'm sure my cheeks are an embarrassing shade of red but I don't care. I'm having fun.

When I lean over the table, I make sure I go for the hardest shot first, my hands in the wrong places so the pole bounces off the ball, the tip shooting up in the air and barely missing the overhead light. "Damn. I don't think I'm doing it right."

"Let me show you," Ted offers, standing behind me.

Long, strong arms reach around my middle, his hands over mine, the flutter in my stomach makes my fingers tremble. When his chest is flush against my back, he presses me forward a bit, positions my arms where they need to be, the rasp of his jeans against my bare thighs more erotic than I could have imagined. With a little pressure to my right hand, he pushes the pole.

The ball rolls into the corner pocket without a rebound.

Ted lets me go and steps back, clapping his hands. I squeal and do a little dance even though I could have sunk that ball had there been a brick wall in front of it.

"Great job but next time go for something a little easier."

"I like doing things the hard way," I tell him, my eyelids dropping a fraction. I want to ask Ted if he has a Mercedes parked outside. I don't think Nick will appreciate it if I ask Ted to bend me over the table right here.

But, once again I get ahead of myself. Right now, Ted and I are just two people playing a game of pool. I have to get closer. Maybe find out if he's a psychopath or a bail bondsman or a cheating husband. Maybe he's all three? He's too good looking to just be here on his own. Something has to be wrong with him.

I'm here on my own and there's nothing wrong with me. Or is there? How did I get here? I'd been so focused, so single-minded, exactly as I should have been according to my parents. But I'd missed out. On this. Drinks and pool on the weekend. How many times had I knocked my friends' invites back so I could stay at home and get a good night's sleep for the next day? I'm forever on call.

But I'm not a bloody doctor. No one's life hangs in the balance if I don't answer my phone. Denni might have to find solutions on his own and be a good employee for once. I make the resolution then and there to stop answering my phone after hours.

I take a big mouthful of my drink. I think it's lemonade instead of soda. Sweet and bubbly but with a citrus aftertaste. "So, Ted, what do you do?"

"I'm a business analyst."

"Awesome."

"You?" he asks before lining up a yellow ball and missing the shot by a mile. I nearly snigger.

I clear my throat instead and answer, "I'm a hotel events coordinator."

"Cool."

A thick silence descends as I fudge my shot and Ted misses the yellow again. He doesn't play the game well but he handles the pole like a pro. I almost laugh out loud. Inappropriate thoughts will only distract me from making flirty small talk. I want to turn my brain off.

"You have some great form but you need to grip the cue a little tighter with your right and lighter with your left."

Oh, so that's what I'm doing wrong? "Do you want another drink, Ted?"

"Sure, why not."

As I approach the bar, I realize I'm having a really good time. If I can get Ted beyond one liners and pool advice, maybe I can move onto questions like, 'Are you married? Girlfriend? Psycho?'

"Two more thanks, Nick. I'll take a couple of shots too." I'm not going to bring up the kiss and I'm definitely not going to think about the sudden dip in my stomach when he turns to glare at me over the bar. It was a non-event, a not going to happen again type of thing. Made very clear by none other than the caveman himself.

"He a mate of yours?" Nick asks rudely.

"Not yet," I purr, letting the intimation sink into his thick, caveman skull.

He eyes me warily and when I raise my brows, daring him to make another comment, he shuffles away to make the drinks. For a split second I wonder what he's thinking, his big blue eyes holding a hint of sadness but only for a breath, before it fades away. It doesn't matter what put the emotion in his eyes or what sordid shit went on his head. It doesn't concern me. I'm not his girlfriend. I might not even be his friend right now either. Strictly bar tender/patron relationship right here. I even flick the money to him like a shitty patron. "Keep the change," I tell him.

It pisses me off that Nick is so damned perfect, if you don't count his criminal status and the fact he thinks he's better than most of the people in here. Every move he makes is fluid and graceful. As he reaches for a bottle of vodka from the top shelf against the wall, his bicep flexes, the muscles shifting a tattoo that wraps around his upper arm. From here I can't tell what the picture is but the vibrancy of colors amazes me.

"What?" he asks, totally catching me staring at his arms.

My cheeks burn and I shake my head as I take the two glasses he offers. Only he doesn't let go straight away. "Be careful, Imelda."

"Haven't we already been over this?"

"I don't want to see you get hurt."

"No, you don't want to see me succeed. Then you can be right and I'll still be wrong."

"This isn't about wrong and right," Nick says with a roll of his eyes but that emotion is back, I can see it, but I think he's trying to keep it from me.

"What is it about then?" He's such a big shot know-it-all. Let him tell me my own motivations.

"It's about your pride and it's going to get you into trouble."

"So far most of trouble I've seen has come either *from* you or *because* of you."

He's wounded for a minute and then his grasp loosens on the glasses and he lets go. "Nobody invited you in here, Imelda. No one asked you to come back."

"And if I wanted your opinion, I'd ask for it, but you know what? I didn't ask for it and I don't want it or need it. I got the picture last night, loud and clear."

"I don't know what picture you think you got, but you're seeing it all wrong."

"I don't think I am. Why don't you stay out of my business from now on and I'll forget any of this ever happened?"

"I'm sorry. I really am. I'll stay out of it from now on if that's what you want." His hands rise in front of his chest in defeat. "After all I'm just the bar guy."

The smart-ass—and incredibly childish response—on the edge of my tongue wouldn't come out and I'm saved from any further argument when Nick fills two shot glasses and then turns and walks away.

Coward.

I'm more than a little preoccupied as I balance the drinks back to the pool table and Ted. He leans against the wall, swallows the last mouthful of his first drink and offers me the cue so he can take the fresh glass. "Everything okay?"

"Absolutely. Why wouldn't it be?"

"You were just arguing with the bar guy. He a friend of yours?"

Why does he suddenly seem so interested in my chat with Nick? I wonder if he's up for a little manly competition. I have never pegged one person against another but I wonder if the situation, and Nick's ego, warrants it. "He asked me out last week and is a little pissed that I said no."

Ted's look of friendly interest takes on another face when his eyebrows rise higher and his mouth turns into a little 'o'. "Why'd you say no?"

Oh, man. Another guy more interested in Nick than in me. I have to find another bar. But then Nick really would win. Damn, why he couldn't he act as though he doesn't know me? "Not my type."

"Oh?" Ted says pushing off from the wall and prowling toward me. "You have a type?"

I blush. I can't help it. I know my cheeks must be bright red and I don't care. No one has ever looked at me with quite that amount of sizzle in their eyes. "Not really," I gulp.

"Just not him?" Ted says, now standing only a foot away.

"That's right," I nod. "Exactly." I'm hypnotized by hazel eyes and a killer smile.

"Am I your type?"

All I can do is nod again. When his hand brushes mine to take my glass, fireworks explode somewhere in the vicinity of my long-neglected baby maker. Sure, it isn't the first time in the last three days a guy was able to turn me on but it's been so long and I've thought of pretty much nothing but sex for an entire week! No wonder my engine doesn't take much to rev.

Ted's smile melts into a grin and he steps back, sipping my drink from the exact place I had. "Your turn."

I feel like we're playing a game using words. I want to say something witty and sexy about when my turn would be but nothing comes to mind. For the third time in minutes, I nod again. My neck is going to break.

For the next hour we chat about inconsequential stuff and flirt. A lot. And drink. A lot. I let Ted beat me again on the felt but it's close. He's not a good player. I hold my breath as he hits the black into the pocket, the white only stopping about three millimeters from following.

"Great game," I laugh as I shake his outstretched hand. Before I know it, I'm hauled into his arms, his mouth descending on mine. Dazed confusion turns to savage lust when his tongue touches mine, his cologne an added spice to my vodka-soaked senses. The kiss is brief but fantastic. The only word in my vocabulary to describe our meeting of mouths is fantastic.

And I want to do it again.

"Dance?" he asks, his face as flushed as mine feels. *Fantastic.*

Ted is a really good dancer. The jukebox pumps out greatest hits from every decade except for this one but the beat is the same and it puts a rhythm in me that makes me want to move. Ted twirls me around a tight space between tables and I should feel self-conscious, silly even, but I don't. I feel like laughing and twirling and behaving recklessly.

This is what I want. Pure abandon. Spontaneity. Not planning something out for once in my boring adult life. I know I only have to whisper a few words of encouragement into Ted's ear and we'll be on our way back to my place but I'm enjoying myself too much to start thinking about the sex and whether Ted will deliver the goods.

"I bet they don't teach you how to dance like that at the Hilton," he says breathlessly.

I shake my head and laugh because it's less actual dancing and more just moving. "They don't teach those moves anywhere."

After dancing for an hour, I'm hot and well on my way to being drunk. Didn't I just want to be tipsy? Just enough to loosen the nerves I know are tightly coiled just under the surface of my liquored-up bravado. There's still crunch-time to consider and by the sultry looks Ted throws me again and again and the way he touches me on the dance floor, it isn't far away. One particular song I swear I even feel his erection grinding against me.

"I'm going to get us another drink," he says, and I know I should tell him I need to slow down but the words don't come out. Instead I give him a nod of encouragement.

Meanwhile, I hit the ladies to freshen up, flicking some water through my shortened hair to spike it out a bit. My neck is hot and I'm a little sweaty from all the fun. With all the excitement and dancing, I'd forgotten about the haircut, even the high heels hadn't bothered me while I'd moved and laughed. This is what I needed. A guy to take my mind off life and give me a night of rockin' sex. So far Ted is one for one. The room sways a little as I lose my balance. The shoes, I tell myself. Just a little stumble. I don't realize I've said the words out loud until another lady giggles from an occupied stall.

When I walk back into the bar, steady on my own two heel-clad feet, I notice Ted is back at the pool table, racking up for another game. All right, so I'll give him one more but then we are out of here. I need time to sober up a bit. Then we can head out of *Johnnie's* and back to my apartment. Maybe he's as nervous as me about the next move to make and needs another drink? I sure as hell don't know what to do. Am I supposed to ask him outright if he wants to come home with me? Maybe lick his ear and tell him I want to be fucked until I don't know my own name?

Butterflies take flight in my downstairs region and I smile. I'm going to do exactly that. Fuck it. Fuck the rules. Fuck Nick and fuck being a good girl.

Ted is so absorbed taking the first shot and I'm enjoying checking out his arse, he doesn't hear his phone ringing from the table between where the drinks drip condensation on the shiny surface. I pick it up with the intention of handing it to him but the face on the screen makes me stop dead in my tracks. Cold dread washes over me in icy waves.

There on the tiny display of Ted's phone (the same Ted who I, only a heartbeat earlier, considered taking back to my apartment) is Denni's annoying face, tongue poked out for the camera.

The dread turns to a burning hot rage as I continue to stare at it like I have no idea what it is, like the dots won't connect to make a full picture, just three-quarters of one, the phone still vibrating and humming a happy tune in my hand like it isn't about to spectacularly burst my bubble.

"Imelda?" Ted calls out to me, finally noticing something isn't right.

Everyone and everything in the bar disappears. The noise, Nick, the smells, the lights, nothing except for Ted registered in my sights. "You know Denni do you?"

"He's a good friend of mine. How do you know him?"

If Ted's voice hadn't squeaked on the second to last word, I could have met with denial, shook its hand and still got laid. Suddenly the ease of the last few hours, the companionship, the chemistry between us, takes on a whole new meaning. "This is so sick," I mutter to myself, the full picture finally becoming clear as day.

"Oh, come on. Denni thought we might be good together."

"So he gave you the direction of a pathetic desperado? God, it could have been that easy for you."

"What are you talking about?"

"Denni pimped you on to me. What else did he say?"

"Not much. Only that you were lonely after a bad break up and needed some cheering up."

"Bullshit." I didn't believe the lies for a second and Ted's too-quick answers seal his guilt.

"Look, Imelda, I like you. I've had heaps of fun tonight. Can't we forget all about this and behave like two consenting adults who are attracted to each other?"

Oh, now he was going to resort to condescension? Two consenting adults huh? "You think I'm going to sleep with you after...after all of this? You're dreaming."

Ted gets this look on his face like a boy whose candy was taken from him and stamped into the dirt. I watch apprehensively as he stalks toward me, his lips a thin angry line above his chin. "I didn't buy you drinks all night for you to back out now."

10

I stammer and stutter for a bit, my eyes wide with disbelief. I'm not prepared for this at all. It gets worse by the second. He really thought I was available for a few cocktails? But I was, wasn't I? That's exactly the message I was sending when a guy buys me drinks all night.

For sale: will perform sex acts for fifteen-dollar vodkas. It's like a sign is painted on my back.

I would like to pause my story right here to explain something about my character. I rarely swear more than the couple of now socially acceptable words. I hardly ever shout at anything or anyone and I never, never, ever resort to violence. And continue

"I want you to walk away right now, Ted."

He ignores my warning, advancing with that gleam in his eye that says he isn't going to back off, that he's not the kind of guy to take no for an answer.

"You are going to regret this." I give him his last warning. He doesn't know that my stomach is churning and my pulse is racing in my ears, the blood roaring in both fear and anticipation.

When Ted's hand reaches out to grab my hip, presumably to pull me closer, I really lose it. "Don't fucking touch me."

"I'm going to do more than that," he snarls and tightens his grip. "You owe me for a night of prick-teasing. You owe me."

I'm in my very own nightmare of hellish proportions with a guy who thinks he can take what he wants by force. All the warnings from my friends and from Nick run around like a broken carousel ride in my head. I should have listened.

I search the faces around me, silently begging for someone to step in, but they don't notice that I'm being assaulted right there, Ted's hands holding me still. I try to step back and signal for help. My tongue is heavy, sandpaper and wood in my mouth. Panic washes over me.

A woman near the bar looks in our direction but true to his word, Nick is staying out of it. Nowhere to be seen. Damn that man!

I find words and fling them at Ted. "Last warning, psycho. Leave me alone or I'm going to really hurt you."

His laughter I expect but it's his hesitation I need to take advantage of. After all, he can't carry me from the bar. Someone is very likely to notice that.

"What are you going to do, princess?"

The thought is tempting but I have something else in mind for Ted.

I lean into his embrace, put my hands on his shoulders as though I want to tell him something and balanced there on one spiky heel, I lift my knee with all the strength I have. The shriek that meets my ears is the best sound I'm going to hear all night. There is no way Ted can force anyone now. Just to bring it all home, I swing my fist in an uppercut meant for his nose but at the last moment, he moves his head back and my knuckle connects with the solid bone of his chin.

Something crunches in my hand but the adrenaline swamping me doesn't allow for anything else but the need to fight. Denni should have told Ted I have two brothers who made it their only pre-teen ambition to torment me. I'd kneed one brother so hard I'd been grounded for two weeks and he had to go to hospital for a quick bit of corrective surgery.

With my other hand, I thread my fingers through his hair, wrenching it from his scalp until my lips are in line with his ear. "I told you, you were going to regret that."

Suddenly the air swooshes out of my lungs as strong arms grab me from behind and swing me away from Ted like I'm the one who needs saving. Bit late for that now!

"I'm okay, I'm okay," I say to the brick wall at my back.

"It's not you I'm worried about," is growled into my ear.

Great, now Nick decides to intervene. Ted is making howling noises and as I peer under Nick's arm, I nearly laugh at the loser stretched out on the floor. Suddenly the pretty boy with the killer smile is just another dangerously temperamental guy who doesn't like to hear no.

Denni is so going to pay for this. He practically sent a predator to find me. What would have happened if we were back at my place and I changed my mind?

I curl my fists at the thought, crying out when the second finger of my left hand refuses to move. I bite down on a sob and shrug off Nick's tight grip to lift my arm to check the damage. Holy shit. My knuckle has moved and my finger is bent sideways and over at an odd angle. The sight makes me woozy.

"Are you okay?" Nick asks.

"I'm fine," is the mechanical reply I give. But I'm not fine. Not really. Have I ever been fine?

"You've broken your hand."

Deep breath. "No shit, Sherlock." When I think about it, it actually looks pretty cool. Could there be a more feminine injury to suffer than fighting off an attacker? I didn't think so.

"Where'd you learn to hit like that?" Nick asks as he gently rolls my wrist to survey the damage from different angles. God, it hurts so bad but his warm fingers on my wrist distracts me.

"I have two brothers. Older brothers."

"Thank god for that."

I continue to stare, dazed, at my hand in his and I shake my head when Nick asks if I want him to call the police. I hear him calling instructions for Ted to be thrown out on the street and to never show his face around these parts again and I smile a little.

"Imelda, you're not okay at all." Nick puts his hand on the small of my back and leads me to his office where he pushes me into a chair. "I'll get some ice."

"I shouldn't have done that," I whisper, still staring at the grotesque image that is my fingers, the skin already swelling over knuckles that don't look right.

"No, you shouldn't have. Another second and the guy was toast anyway. He's lucky you hit him and not me."

I tear my gaze away from my most feminist injury and stare into Nick's blue eyes as he places the icepack on my swollen hand. I flinch but hold in the scream that wants to undo me once and for all. "You can't hit anyone," I remind him. "You're already in trouble."

"I will not stand by and watch guys like that take advantage of helpless women."

I half chuckle, half sob. "I think we both know I'm not helpless."

"That's for sure."

We descend into awkward silence for a bit as he lifts the ice to examine my pink, raw flesh, his face close to mine as he leans in. I'd actually broken the skin when I'd thrown that punch. That had never happened with my brothers. They were always ready for my pathetic attempts at retribution. "I was aiming for his nose," I admit with a sniff.

"It wasn't where you hit him that's the problem, it's the way you held your hand. Classic rookie mistake."

"Oh?" He is so close now. I can smell his cologne over the stench of cigarettes and beer, feel his warm breath across my chest as he examines my hand.

Nick takes my other hand, turns my thumb inwards and curls the rest of my fingers over. His skin is so hot. "If you keep your hand like that, you won't hurt yourself as much."

I doubt that but tuck the information away for the next time someone tries to assault me. God, I'm the stupidest person in the history of stupid people. Ah, amend that. The stupidest woman. I hadn't fully considered the danger to myself. Amy tried to warn me to be careful but I'd laughed it off. Nick tried to tell me too. Why did invincibility have to be a disease you didn't know you were inflicted with until some asshole cured you of it? There really should be a checklist for dating and it should include, that men can and will follow you home. You might be assaulted. There's more but I'm having trouble forming sentences in my mind.

"Here," Nick interrupts my jumbled thoughts—he has a habit of doing that—and throws my handbag gently into my lap. My new handbag. The one I'd bought to complete my man-eater image. "Call someone," he says. "You need to get to the hospital for an x-ray."

"Aren't you going to say I told you so?"

"Will it help?"

"Not much."

"Then why say it?"

Just as he goes to walk away, I call out to him, "Thanks, Nick."

He turns back and shoots me an odd stare. "Any time."

Tears fill my eyes as I try to unzip my purse. In the end I have to put one end of the leather in my teeth and pull on the zip to get it open. Rummaging around, I finally find my phone and flip it open, searching for Amy's number.

I take a deep breath before pressing the call button. Maybe I can go to the hospital in a cab and save myself some trouble? I know I won't be able to hide this from my friends but I could use someone to hold my hand while a doctor pokes and prods me.

The button beeps as I press it, the sound like a signal for Satan to come and get me. It rings twice and then goes straight to *the person you have called is busy. If you'd like to leave a message...* I don't leave one. I don't want her to worry when she does eventually check her phone.

The next number is Jess. She answers on the fourth ring. "Hello?"

"Hi Jess."

"Oh, hey, Mellow. What's up?"

"Just wondering what you're up to?" There's a sob trying to get out and no matter how hard I try to hold it in, within two seconds of hearing Jess's voice, I'm a mess.

"What the matter, Mel?"

"I think I broke my hand. Can you come and get me?"

"What? How?"

"It's a long story. Can you come?"

"I'm so sorry, Mel. I'm working. Did you try Amy?"

"Yeah, no answer."

"Shoot. You're gonna have to call one of your brothers. Candice is in Canada for a commercial."

That'd be right. Just when I need one of them, they all have other things to do. "Can you bail early?" I ask.

Her sigh comes down the line. "I can't. I'm on my last chance with this new boss. If I try to leave before midnight, I'll be fired. I'm so sorry. If you can wait until then? I can come right after?"

"No worries. I'll call someone else." I don't wait for her to say sorry again. I can't bear it. Disconnecting the call, I let the phone drop into my lap. There is no way I can call anyone in my family. My brothers will demand to know everything and then they will want to hunt Ted down and kill him. I may be teased endlessly about being adopted but neither would back away from the chance to defend my honor or my person. There's my sister but she doesn't drive. By the time she gets a cab and comes from the other side of the city, I'll be finished at the hospital and tucked up in bed. I'm on own.

Nick pokes his head in. "Did you get onto someone?"

I shake my head and tears drip from my cheeks onto my new dress.

"Hang on a sec."

I barely notice when he leaves again. I feel like the biggest loser ever. Why can't things just work for me? Why can't I meet a guy who will like me for me? Why can't there be someone out there to make me happy, to drop everything and be there for me? I'd never need to come back to the bar ever again. I'd be safe. Happy.

"Okay, on your feet, let's go."

"What?"

"I can call you an ambulance if you don't want me to take you?"

I must have missed something huge. Nick stands there, car keys in hand, a jacket covering his tattooed arms, a hesitant look in his face. He hovers halfway between the doorway and where I still sit looking like he wants to be anywhere but here.

"You don't have to do this. I can get a cab."

"You can't see yourself right now, but no cabbie is going to take you anywhere. You're so pale you look about to faint. You're a little drunk and a lot hurt. I'm taking you to the hospital."

What started out as a great day full of possibility is going to end in a trip to the emergency room. "Thanks," I say with a sniffle. What else can I do?

Nick leads me out the back door to the ally where a sleek black car is parked half in, half out of a makeshift carport.

I look at the car and then at Nick. He waits for me to squeeze through the small gap between bricks and metal but I'm stuck.

"Don't worry. It's mine," he says. "I'm not stealing it."

I ignore that one. "What about the bar?"

"Suzie can look after things while we're gone. She knows what to do."

Suzie must be the woman I saw earlier watching Ted's attempted assault. The fresh memory makes me cringe. "The ice is dripping."

"Imelda, get in the car. The water will dry."

Just as I go to slide into the leather seat, my brain gets all funny. I pause halfway. It's one thing to let Nick walk me home, quite another to get in his car. No one knows where I am. I don't know where we're going. But Nick is not a serial killer and there are more than enough witnesses back there at *Johnnie's* to sink a ship, or find a missing woman.

The pain in my hand throbs mercilessly and so I sit and try to strap myself in. Every time I pull on the seatbelt, it locks up and won't stretch any further. "Damn it," I complain on a whisper. I finally get the seatbelt to stretch long enough but I can't get the clicker clicked in.

Nick reaches past me just as the belt slips from my hand. His fingers brush my hip as he pushes the metal parts together. "All set?" God, he's close. So close. The open part of his jacket brushes along my chest where the seatbelt is snug between my breasts and I lose my breath and my words. I nod.

I'm so embarrassed and so turned on. How can that be? The two emotions do not go together or sit well with me. If I was in the mood to be really honest, I'd tell him that the only reason I came back to the bar was to taunt him, to beat him, to prove him wrong. I lean my head back against cool leather. Now look at me. "I'm really sorry to be a pain in the butt, Nick."

I don't catch his response as the alcohol and the events of the day and night catch up to me. I close my eyes and shut it all out. He can take me anywhere as long as they have some painkillers and a soft pillow.

11

From his vantage point in the driver's seat, Nick kept glancing sideways to his passenger. With every corner he turns, Imelda gets paler and paler. He wants to floor it and speed all the way to the hospital before the shock of what she'd done really sets in.

His fingers tighten on the steering wheel. His heart still thunders in his ears and his hands itch to punch something. He'd seen Imelda's date getting pissed off, seen him approach her. That smug, predatory look on his pretty-boy face. Nick had witnessed that look plenty of times and it never failed to raise a protective instinct from deep inside. The little shit was very lucky that Imelda had struck out when she had.

Nick remembered the moment he knew he was going to hit the guy. He was about to swing but it was the same instant Imelda decided to rearrange his family jewels.

The guy was very lucky. Nick was very lucky. One more charge and he was looking at real time behind bars. No more slaps on the wrist for him. The diary was his very last chance.

"Are you alright?" he asks her for the hundredth time, making sure she hasn't passed out. Although it would give him the chance to carry her, hold her close. Ever since that damned kiss, she'd plagued his every thought. He'd only said what he had because he couldn't have a relationship. His life was too fucked up. Way too fucked up. Good girls like her didn't get in bed with guys like him. Guys who had violent tempers and jail time waiting.

"I think so," comes her very soft reply just as every muscle in his body tenses with the need to nudge her, make sure she's actually hanging in there.

"We're nearly there." He wants to lean over and comfort her and tell her it's all going to be okay but is it? He knows where an assault charge could go. Hell, the stupid diary is a direct result of losing his temper. That judge is going to have a field day when she finds out about all of this. Not that it was never going to happen again. He owns a bar. At the bottom of every bottle is a broken nose, a broken hand, a car wrapped around a power pole. It wasn't up to him what idiots did after over-indulging but he could stop defenseless women from being harassed. And he would. Every time. Even if it meant being locked up for it.

The bright lights of the hospital can be seen a mile away and when he pulls in, he has to tell the night guard why they're there and get directions to the ER. In total it's less than an hour since Imelda had needed to defend herself but it felt like years. He'd bet it felt like even longer for her.

When he'd seen her tears, felt the broken bone under already swelling skin, he'd wanted to go after the guy and smash him to a pulp. But then the pitiful frown when her so-called friends weren't available had pulled him back. She may not know it but she needs him.

Nick pulls the handbrake up and jumps out, opening the door for her, helping her out of the car. She's so fragile and small like this. Her pretty dress twisted around her hips and one of the pink hibiscus's had blood dripped on it. One minute she's inflicting harm and the next minute she's falling apart.

She'd been so self-assured when she walked in tonight. With her hair done up nicely and a different dress on. Her air of confidence was hard to miss. Nick had to admit he was surprised after what happened the previous night. He hadn't expected to see her ever again. He'd had to work so hard to hide his surprise so she wouldn't see how happy he was to see *her*. Just not there. In his bar.

Pulling on her arm, Nick makes her stop in the carpark, a meter from the metallic sliding doors. "Imelda, I'm so sorry."

"About what? This wasn't your fault." Her s's slur a little.

"Yeah, but if I hadn't said those things to you, if I hadn't kissed you... Damn, you could be wrapped up safe and warm at home instead of getting messed up like this."

"Nick, it's not your fault. If it wasn't *Johnnie's*, it would have been another bar. Turns out Ted had been sent by a guy I work with for...for...for pity sex."

Nick cringes at the emotionless explanation. "A friend of yours did this to you?"

"I want to hope he didn't do it on purpose but come Monday, I might need another trip to the hospital."

Her chuckle does nothing to ease his tension. What is the world coming to when women have to try this hard to pick up with no thought to the consequences from the dickheads out there? And since when does a guy send a psycho out to pick up his friend and take her home. Good thing Imelda found some common sense before they left the bar. She could have been in real trouble.

"Can we go in?" she says.

"Yeah, sure."

The sterile smell, the whitewashed walls, all bring back bad memories from his days as an amateur boxer. Like most teens, his father thought it would be a good way to release some pent-up anger and hormones, fighting in a ring with kids just like him. No one could have predicted how much he'd enjoy it. He would never have thought the sound of bones crunching and fists connecting with faces could make him feel so powerful.

He'd stopped when he'd found out how corrupt the sport was and just how dangerous it could be to the champ but not before he'd saved enough money to buy *Johnnie's*. He had a pretty cruisy life until the night he'd beat a guy unconscious. One minute he was talking and the next he was on top of him. It was the only time Nick had ever felt outside of his own body. He saw his fists fly, felt the blood spray, heard the sickening sounds but he couldn't stop. Even when the cop tried to take him down, Nick had still been unable to stop. Matt deserved every second of that beating. The things he'd said about Nick's own sister still haunted him.

As much as he'd enjoyed wiping the smug smile from his ex-brother-in-law's face, he never wanted to go there again. Not just because of the prison term hanging over his head but because it was a place he didn't like. He had no control when he was that angry. He couldn't stop. Sometimes he got to a point where he didn't want to stop. So he had to make sure it didn't start.

Nick banishes the morbid thoughts and sinks into a plastic chair while Imelda checks in. She comes back with a clipboard and a pen to fill out her personal details for the admissions nurse.

"Let me help you with that," Nick offers before he knows what he's doing. He should have dropped her off at the entry and run back to his bar, to the life that hung by an old plastic peg to a line about to snap under the pressure. He didn't need all this added hassle.

"Name?"

"Imelda."

"Your full name."

"Imelda Jane Mahari."

"Date of Birth?"

She leans her head against his arm and sighs. "January first, 1986."

"Address?"

And so it went on until he had her details sketched down on the thin white paper with all the boxes to tick. Medications, past history, etc. He did find out this was her first broken bone but not the first visit to the ER. Obviously her brothers were hard-asses, beating up on their little sister all the time.

Nick hands the clipboard to the nurse at the counter and then sits back next to Imelda. Her head droops and the melt from the ice leaves a wet patch on her skirt. She looks cold and lonely. Like a kitten dragged in from a storm.

God, now he felt sorry for her? Picking up a magazine, he flicks over which new celeb thinks Botox is the answer, another who thought adopting kids would save her marriage, an exposé showing before and after shots of models with and without makeup and airbrushing.

He doesn't read the articles, his mind is buzzing with unwanted visions of Imelda in her apartment all alone, crying, hurting. He can't stand it.

"Imelda Mahari?" a nurse calls from the doorway to the main hospital. The waiting room is almost empty but for them, an oddity in itself for a Saturday night.

Imelda stands but then sways on her heels which forces Nick to reach for her, hold her steady.

"Does she need a wheelchair?" the nurse asks, looking first at the semi-conscious woman in his arms and then back to him.

"I can carry her," Nick offers.

"I can walk," Imelda insists but then Nick scoops her up before she can utter a word in protest, her hand cradled against her chest, her cradled against his chest.

She doesn't have the energy to protest.

"This way."

Nick's shoes squeak out a rhythm as they walk down three corridors past rooms with crying, screaming, moaning patients already in beds. They must have been busy earlier in the night.

"I'm just going to give her a shot for the pain and then the doctor will come in and take a look at that hand."

The nurse speaks more to Nick but at the word 'shot', Imelda jumps up out of the bed and sways unsteadily next to it. "No needles," she says, her voice high, loud, frightened.

"Lie back down," Nick tells her. "It's just one needle and then you'll feel much better."

"Easy for you to say. It's not your arm she'll be poking the hell out of."

"It's one shot and you'll barely feel it," the nurse joins in the conversation, the needle in question in the air in front of her body.

Imelda takes one look at it and faints, falling on the bed, on top of her broken hand.

"Do it now," Nick tells the nurse before rolling Imelda onto her back and lifting her so she lies on the bed properly.

"She's not going to be impressed about that when she comes too," the nurse chuckles, dropping the needle into a bright yellow sharps container.

Nick doesn't care. He's not going to tell her anyway. She'd never have to know. What a baby, he thought. Of all the injuries he'd had in his younger years, needles didn't faze him. Never had. Having glass removed from a head wound without anesthetic was about the worst he'd sat through and survived. Every sliver of the wine bottle taken from his scalp he'd felt. Every stitch going through his skin, pulling at his hair had been like a knife over his head but he'd been drinking that night and the doctor hadn't wanted to administer anything. Stupid man thought Nick was off his face on drugs and not just blind drunk. By the time he'd finished, Nick was stone cold sober and regretting all the things he barely remembered.

After the nurse leaves, Nick sits and waits for Imelda to wake up. God, this woman is trouble with a capital T. In a few short days she'd made him hit one of his customers in direct violation of his sentencing conditions, caused a fight between himself and his parole officer, oh and then there was the fight they'd had in the lady's toilet. Then there was the kiss. He still hadn't really apologized properly for the things he'd said and done, mostly because the more he thought about it, the less he wanted to say sorry. He certainly wasn't sorry he'd kissed her. The circumstances could have been a little happier but if he had to be frank, he wanted to kiss her again. If only to shut her up sometimes.

Nick shakes his head and lets it fall into his hands, massaging his temples. How can one little tiny woman be so deaf, dumb and blind? Did she not hear what most of the guys in his bar thinks of her? He'd heard enough conversations tonight to know the majority of his patrons thought she was too high maintenance to bother with no matter how desperate she was. Which brought him to dumb. What she did was more than stupid. Gambling with her wellbeing for five or ten minutes of pleasure, in his book, it just wasn't worth it. What if the guy she took home turned out to be a murderer or, like the guy tonight, couldn't and wouldn't take no for an answer. Sure, she'd protected herself, quite admirably, but it didn't take into account a man's anger or determination. She'd got a lucky hit in but she had nothing to back it up with if the wuss came back for more. With a broken hand, she probably would have tried to kick him but he doubted her dainty little heels would have been up to the task.

Why couldn't she see what she did was ridiculous and futile? Even if she did find someone to take home, what did she think would happen then? They were going to wake up in the morning and say, thanks that was fun? Guys just didn't work like that. The only reason the guy wouldn't come back for more would be if she was lousy in bed. Nick snorted. He had a feeling she would be anything but lousy.

"You don't have to stay you know."

Imelda is staring at him, tears in her sleepy eyes, her voice so low and despondent it makes his heart hurt. "I'm not going to leave you here alone."

"I don't need your pity, Nick. I'm a big girl, I can handle this."

"And if they come at you with another needle?" He almost smiles when what little color she has in her cheeks drains away but he's sorry he had to say it like that to get his point across. "Thought so."

"You must have better things to do?"

Nick nods. "I do."

"Do you think I'm going to be in much trouble for this?" Imelda asks, looking down at her swollen red hand.

"If you do, better hope you don't get the battle axe I did for a judge."

He regrets those words when her eyes fill with fear. "Do you really think I could get arrested?"

"You assaulted a man." Nick holds his hand up to stop her from interrupting. Her mouth opens and her chest rises with an indignant breath but she does nothing more than huff. "But I wouldn't be too worried about him going to the cops. After all, he started it. You were defending yourself and a lot of people will back you up."

"Will you back me up?"

"Of course I will," he tells her and then gets to his feet and sits on the side of the bed next to her. "Why would you even have to ask that?"

"Well, for one thing, you didn't see what happened."

"I did so. That wanker deserved everything you gave him and more."

"I looked around for you and you weren't there."

"It's my bar. Where else would I have been?" He pushes aside his male pride to examine later. She'd looked for him? To help her? To save her? His chest swells and he wants to wrap his arms around her and squeeze her tight. But he doesn't.

Imelda doesn't seem to notice his reaction. In fact, she's deep in thought, her mouth closed, her lips pressed together in a tight, pale line. She gives him a little nod as though she's come to some conclusion inside of her own head. He wants to know what it is.

"Was there a second thing?" Nick asks. She'd said for one thing so there must be another.

"I...I..."

"Come on, say it."

"You told me never to come back. I thought you hated me."

"How can I hate you?" He's perched on the side of her bloody hospital bed after leaving his bar in the hands of someone else to be with her. He locks his gaze onto her and says, "I don't know you. I only told you not to come back so you wouldn't get hurt."

"I should have listened."

Nick chuckles. Her surly tone and the grimace on her face tells of her guilt and shame but she shouldn't have to feel any of it. Where the hell were her friends when she needed them? Why is he the one at her bedside when someone who loves her should be comforting her?

He's about to ask when the doctor walks in, picks up her chart and clucks his tongue. "Well, Imelda, looks like you broke your hand and dislocated a knuckle. We'll get an x-ray to make sure, then we'll relocate your wonky finger and fix you up with a plaster cast."

"Plaster?" she complains. "Are you sure? I couldn't wear a brace or something?"

The doctor shakes his head. "I'm sorry, no. That kind of break needs to be held as still and as straight as possible. It's plaster and a sling for you, young lady. We might be able to avoid surgery this way."

"Damn it," Imelda swears under her breath.

"What color would you like?" the doctor asks.

"Color?" She looks so tired and confused. How she isn't fast asleep yet, he didn't know.

"There are about ten different colors to choose from, from white all the way to black. I'll get the nurse to bring a color chart while we organize that x-ray."

A color chart? Were they picking fabrics for the carpet or the curtains? Imelda nods. What more can she do?

Nick swears. Karma better come for this guy. It better come in the form something really, really big too.

12

Why is it that every time life starts to go right, something has to blow up in my face to ruin it all? The last four days have been nothing but total humiliation, rejection after rejection, constant questions about my character and motivations, and now I sit in a hospital bed picking the shade of plaster I want to have on my poor broken hand for the next six to eight weeks.

To make matters worse, Nick sits through it all like he has a thumb tack on his chair and a permanent frown stuck to his face. He sits, then stands, then sits, then stands. When I told him to leave, I hadn't really meant it. Why would I want to go through all of this alone?

Alone...

The word reverberates around my head, thumping from one side to other missing every vital point of impact, avoiding crashing into the tiny, useless part of my brain still functioning. If the organ between my ears held any significance to me at all, I wouldn't have done the things I had since Monday. It was like my so-called friends dropped the bombshell of me dying alone with my cats and my brain had fled in fear of being tangled in the aftermath. As if the cats would eat that anyway. It wouldn't feed even one flea.

I watch helplessly as the radiographer positions my hand on what appears to be a lightbox, turning my wrist this way and that while I cry out in pain, biting my tongue so hard it bleeds. "Jesus, could you be any rougher?" I mutter under my breath while everything throbs in time to the rhythm of my heartbeat despite the pain killers.

It's not his fault I punched some guy in the head. It's not his fault my brothers had never taught me to throw a punch and not break something. It sure as hell isn't his fault I'm such a loser.

"I'm sorry, Miss Mahari. I'm not doing it on purpose."

"I know that but could you be a little gentler?" Maybe stop throwing my hand around like a batter's mitt and start remembering my broken bones?

"You make a bad patient," Nick comments from the open doorway.

"You would too if you hurt like you'd just stuck your fingers in a meat grinder. That guy's head must have concrete in it."

Nick gives her a weird look and says, "Are you serious?"

The radiographer looks from Nick to me, then back to Nick again and finally back to me. He's trying to work out the puzzle. Good luck, buddy.

"You hit someone?" he finally asks.

Nick is first to answer since the x-ray guy has chosen that moment to stretch my fingers out flat and I'm doing all I can not to scream. "She didn't just hit him. First she kneed him in the balls and then she punched him."

"Next time aim for a softer spot on his face," the radiographer suggests.

I groan. This isn't something they teach in high school. My lack of a masculine father figure left my two brothers to beat the shit out of me as a kid and then explain what they'd done in excruciating detail to my mother while I cried on the floor. Their lessons hadn't included punching. That would have left bruises and then my mum would have killed them both. My sister never copped any of the torment. She'd been sick as a child. With mum and dad at the hospital all the time, I was left on my own with the sadistic boys.

"It's a fact I will never forget," I promise both the men in the room. I'm definitely going to remember how to hit properly when I get to work on Monday and give Denni what for. If it wasn't for his meddling, I wouldn't have been attacked by Ted. I never asked him to set me up with his psycho friend. I never asked for help from him other than giving me advice. We're not friends. He only calls when shit hits the fan at work and I only see him in the mornings when our shifts overlap.

"You could press charges," Nick says into the quiet room.

I shake my head. Why would I want to go and stir the pot when I'm fine. Just fine. Apart from the hand, my body is intact. My dignity and pride have been pulverized but who needs those? Obviously not me. I hadn't been raped. I hadn't had my throat slit in my sleep or been abducted to parts unknown.

Tears gather again in my eyes.

Nothing had happened.

At least dead, I would have been released from the nightmare I instigated. Without pride it won't matter if I die alone anyway. I won't care. Seeing it coming did help, I thought. Maybe instead of cats I could buy a dog? At least then when I lie dead on the floor, he might howl my situation to my apartment block rather than eating me before I'm cold. In a building like mine, a howling dog would take less than twenty-four hours to investigate. An unseen resident wouldn't be noticed for months. Not until the smell annoys someone or my mail becomes a slipping or tripping hazard in the entry corridor.

"Hey, it's not as bad as it looks," the radiographer says, squeezing my arm softly.

I'm working on an answer but then he places a lead apron over my baby making bits (not that it matters since my bits won't be making babies any time soon) and he and Nick leave the room.

I sit perfectly still as the lights dim and a series of clicks and vibrations sound around me. In no time I'm back on the hospital bed in emergency waiting for the radiologist and the doctor to confirm what we all already know. I hope they aren't going to say they have to re-break the break. I've heard of that happening so many times to my brother's friends and I don't think I can handle any more excitement for the night.

My hand still throbs and the pain travels up my arm and into my shoulder. I wonder if I'm having a heart attack too. What a way to finish me off. No cats in the hospital and technically I'm not alone since Nick hasn't left my side. At least my friends won't be right if it ends here.

I have to think of something else. Find some focus. The alcohol buzz I'd had earlier has dwindled and gone and with that, every memory of the night flickers and flashes to the accompaniment of drums. Loud drums. I can only groan as each and every second of my humiliation is relived again and again. The only positive? Nick.

Nick doesn't hate me. He certainly doesn't like me but if he hated me, he would have pushed me into a taxi and left me on my own.

Sure, the frown hadn't left his lips and he hadn't relaxed for a second signaling that he'd rather be back at the bar than by my side. I don't care. Even when he chuckles or tries to crack a joke and his shoulders stay in the same tense position, I don't care. He's here. With me. He could have left. He didn't. Maybe I'm growing on him? I throw my head back against the plastic wrapped mattress. I'm hopeless. Growing on him? I'm a fool.

And Nick isn't my type.

I don't exactly know why. He's tall. Much taller than me, which isn't hard for most guys, really. I'm short. He's built. His biceps bulge and ripple when he works. That is super sexy even though gym junkies definitely aren't my style. A business owner with an awesome body. A girl couldn't and shouldn't ask for more. Throw in the hot tattoos and the couple of instances of chivalry he's already displayed—including a visit to the ER—and he's a pretty great package. For someone else. I have to tell myself that he's great for someone. But not me. I reckon he'd be great in bed but he isn't stable. Despite his hero routine, Nick has baggage. And a record. Imagine taking him home to meet the family.

Our eyes meet across the room and the clichéd sparks crackle. There *is* something between us. The kiss didn't come out of nowhere and I'd thought it was a pity pash but as his frown turns to a scowl, I wonder if it's something else entirely. Does he actually like me? Like, like me, like me? Why else would he stay all night like this?

The merry nurse comes back in the room, walking between us, forcing Nick's gaze from mine. We need the interruption. I need time to think. I have the feeling he'd been about to say something and I don't want the words.

"Are you feeling all right, sweetie?" the nurse asks.

"It still hurts," I say, another tear welling and then rolling over my lower lid and down my cheek.

"I can soon fix that."

This time when she waves the needle in the air, I don't faint. I just close my eyes so I don't have to watch. How can my night get any more unbearable? I'm sitting on a hospitable bed, my only company a guy who is harder to read than the financial review, a guy who'd first thought I was soliciting patrons and then pity pashed me to prove a point.

"There we are," the nurse says with a little pat to my aching arm. "Now, what color do you want for your cast?"

"I don't really care," I mumble.

"That's the spirit," she says as though she doesn't hear my words or the emotion behind them. "We have some green left over from a little boy we just patched up?"

"Whatever." God, they are some good drugs, whatever they're giving me. The pain floats away on a green cloud as I sink further back into the bed and close my eyes.

"I just have to make a call, Imelda. Are you going to be okay?"

"I won't come back to the bar again," I murmur with a nod, not really sure where the words come from or why my head bobs back and forth on my shoulders. I can't seem to open my eyes. I'm weightless and light and sleepy.

"Ever?" I hear.

"Not ever," I tell him.

"Is there something wrong with my bar, Imelda?" he asks.

Without the painkillers this conversation would be ridiculous but in my mind, it makes perfect sense and I smile. "It's dangerous."

"Only to guys like Ted."

I giggle. I want to see if Nick is smiling. I think I can hear it in his soft voice. He's never used that voice on me before and I like it. It's rough and soft at the same time. Like his hand as it curls around my not broken one.

"Aren't we friends now, Imelda?"

"My friends call me Mellow." I giggle again. Where does that keep coming from?

"What?"

"You know. Like a marshmallow. Squishy and round."

"I am not going to call you Mellow," Nick says. I feel pressure on my thigh. "And you're not squishy."

"Do you want to be my friend, Nick?"

"Sure I do. I haven't had a dull moment since I met you."

"So we're friends?" I ask. But all I want to do is sleep. I snuggle into the blanket. "Can you tuck me in?"

"Ah, okay."

He starts at my feet and legs, tucking the blanket in nice and tight. When he gets to my hips and ribs, I sigh and let go, giving in to the dark, giving in to dreams of Nick with a cape, saving the day.

~

Imelda sleeps for an hour before the doctor comes back to put the plaster on her hand. Nick checks in at the bar and tells Suzie she'll have to close. He hates asking for favors but there's no way he can walk away now. The high-as-a-kite Imelda can't get home on her own and he'd come this far.

No, what he's actually done is watch her sleep and hurt his brain coming up with reasons to push her away. But he's never met anyone like her before. The way she'd knee Ted right between his legs had been inspirational but then she'd even pulled his hair and said something in his ear. It was a scene straight out of a movie! Nick had only intervened because it looked like Imelda wasn't going to stop beating up on him. Suzie mentioned the cops had come by.

Ted was dumber than he looked to call them from where he sat in the gutter outside. They'd taken statements and everyone they spoke to backed Imelda's version. Thankfully no one wanted anything to do with a guy who could just take what he wanted. Suzie did mention they'd want to speak to Imelda once she was home from the hospital. She'd kept calling Imelda Nick's lady friend. "They're going to want to speak to your lady friend tomorrow, get her side."

As much he'd told her she wasn't his lady friend, she was. They were friends now. Imelda had said so. He wants to be her friend. Insane as that is when he's ridiculously attracted to the one thing he'd sworn off.

"This is really green," Imelda mumbles from the bed.

"You agreed to it," the doctor says. "If you want us to make up another color, you'll be here for at least another two hours."

She shakes her head. Nick almost laughs.

"Green will do. It will match...nothing. Not a damned thing."

13

Bang, bang, bang.

"C'mon, open the door. Mrs. Russel told me you're in there."

Bang, bang, bang.

"Go away." I want to yell but the sound doesn't travel. My head is heavy, as though it's stuffed with wet cotton wool. What the hell happened last night?

The banging stops, thank god, but I hear murmuring. Maybe one of my neighbors is telling whoever it is to piss off. I try to open my eyes but it's an effort. I have no energy. I'm a dead weight.

I lift my hand to wipe the sleep from eyes and instead pain erupts from my nose. I groan and complain but no one cares. No one cares that I'm hungover. That I want to die. Well, that's dramatic. I finally open my eyes and when all I see is blurry green, I squeak. Maybe I yell? I don't even know. Another groan is all I can muster.

A noise comes back to me but I'm too busy zeroing in on whatever is attached to my hand. Did I thump myself in the nose?

Memories start flashing through my muddled brain. Drinks. More drinks.

Flirting. Ted.

Scowling. Nick.

My hand! The blurriness from my vision clears and I'm staring at the plaster cast. This time I find my voice and I yell, "Fuck!" into the room.

"What the hell?" Comes from the hall outside my room.

"Imelda, are you alright?" Also from the hall.

Two voices. One male and one female. I grab the pillow and hold it against my face while I scream into it.

"Go away!" I tell them. Leave me to my abject humiliation alone. *Please*!

"Why is she naked?"

I'm what? I lift the pillow and look down my body. The blanket has shifted and I'm not naked but I might as well be. How did I get down to my bra and panties?

"She is not naked," the male voice insists.

My cheeks burn. My entire body burns. I probably look like a mottled, sunburnt, seal. With a green plaster cast on its hand. I peek from under the pillow over my left shoulder and sure enough the male voice belongs to Nick. A shirtless, covered in ink, Nick.

"How are you feeling?" he asks, concern in his eyes, no shirt on his torso. My entire vision is taken up by Nick. From his bare feet to his wide hips, jeans slung low, to his broad chest with a generous matting of golden brown hair, to his naked shoulders. The kind of shoulders that make my palms itch to find out if his skin is as smooth and satiny as it looks.

I congratulate myself for bringing my attention back to his face and not lingering longer on his pecs or other attributes. "What happened? Why are you still here? Did we?" Did I have sex and not even know it. I squeeze my thighs together and there's no discomfort. No twinge.

"No, we didn't. Of course we didn't. You fell asleep in the car so I carried you up but I couldn't just leave you alone."

"Imelda," the female voice chimes in. "Just what the fuck is going on?"

A second voice adds, "And who the fuck is this?"

I pull the pillow away fully and sit up in bed. They're not going to go away. "There's no need for so many fucks." Even though I'd dropped a few lately too. "This is Nick."

Jess eyes him, up and down and then back up again. "And who is Nick?"

"He's a bartender."

Amy sits on the side of my bed. She's my friend. She'll make it all go away.

But she doesn't.

"Imelda, what is going on with you?"

I raise my knees to my chest and rest my chin on them. "I don't know."

Jess isn't done. "I think it's time for Nick to leave. You've taken advantage of the situation, got our Mellow down to her underwear and then what? Did you touch her?"

"Oh my god," I cry as real tears fill my eyes.

Nick puffs his amazing chest out and looks like he's about to let loose so I jump up off the bed and clap a hand over his mouth. This brings with it a whole load of issues. I'm wearing nothing but my bra and panties. He's not wearing a shirt. I practically have to climb him to reach his mouth. My bare hand is pressed against his lips.

I really, really want to climb him. As I stare into eyes sparking with mischief, he looks like he wants me to climb him too.

No one says a word and it takes actual strength to look away. Have I shocked my friends? I have a half-dressed man in my apartment. I'm almost naked too.

Why am I almost naked?

When I meet Nick's eyes again with mine, the sparkle changes to a question. He's really enjoying this but he's also worried about me. It's sweet.

"Did you undress me?" I ask him.

He nods. He enjoyed that too!

"But we didn't...?"

He shakes his head.

I'm still pressed up against him and I really don't want to move away. He's warm. And sexy. And. Jesus! "We kissed again last night, didn't we?"

Jess and Amy snap out of their shock with a synchronized, "What?"

"Did I kiss you or did you kiss me?" I don't know why it's important but it is.

He gives me a pointed stare. I need to move my hand. I step back but now I'm more exposed. Nick isn't looking anywhere but my eyes. He didn't even raise his hand to move mine. He's being the perfect gentleman. Damn him.

"You kissed me," he reveals.

Shit. I probably did. When had I become this sex-crazed lunatic? I was the shy girl. The girl who didn't initiate conversation with strangers. The girl who shouldn't be standing in her undies in front of three other people. I reach for the robe hanging on the back of my bedroom door but I can't fit the stupid cast through the armhole.

"How bad is my hand?"

Nick sighs. "It's fractured. You'll be in the cast for six to eight weeks. The doctor says you can call in if you want to go over the break and the info again."

I hold the robe to my chest and sink down onto my bed, my chin flat against my collarbone. "I'm so embarrassed."

Nick chuckles and it's the last sound I really expect to hear. "I had fun," he says. "But let's not do it again."

He turns to leave and I call after him, "Thanks, Nick."

"Anytime, Imelda."

And then he's gone and I'm left with the accusing glares of my friends. My friends who hadn't been there for me last night. Who'd been too busy for me.

Jess has the good grace to wait until the front door closes before she rounds on me with a "What the actual fuck?"

· ♥ · ♥ · ♥ · ♥ · ♥ ·

Where to start?

Dear Freddy.

Last night was...hectic. Chaotic. Terrible. Kind of fun. In a messed-up way. Imelda got stuck with this guy who wouldn't take no for an answer ~~and she hit him! It was great!~~ And some stuff happened. I had to take her to the hospital because all of her so-called friends were too busy for her. She was crying and I couldn't stand it. I hate women's tears. Not because they shouldn't cry. I grew up in a houseful of women and there were always tears. I can't stand that she was crying over that wanker. She always seems so defeated. And desperate. But mostly defeated. Am I supposed to just stand by and watch her, night after night, day after day, get trampled on by assholes? I just don't get what her deal is. She's beautiful. She's smart. She's ambitious. How can someone like her not find someone to be with? I'd be with her in a heartbeat. If it wasn't for this stupid diary. If it wasn't for my 'issues'.

And for the briefest of moments, Nick wondered if he'd ever be in a situation where he felt like his life was under control, where his temper could be controlled, and he'd be lucky enough to be with someone like her.

14

What am I supposed to tell my friends about all of this? Amy knew I was going out and a guy was involved, possibly, but obviously no-one knew it had come to this.

Except for Denni. And I'm going to kill him.

Lucky it's Sunday and I don't have to face him yet. I'd probably break my other hand. I would ask myself why I'm being so uncharacteristically bloodthirsty, but this was the worst thing he could have done to me.

Or is this why I can't meet men or date? I'm just not cut out for it. Maybe I'm only good at my job. I'm organized and efficient. I'm just not really a people person. I can be friendly and put on a smile, shake hands, chuckle politely at bad jokes. But the rest? My broken hand speaks volumes about my inability to do the normal, everyday, people-y things. Like form new relationships. Get laid. Be an adult who can make it alone in the big wide world.

As I stand there and ponder my sad predicament, my hand begins to throb and the fuzz in my brain just gets thicker. Missy pushes the bedroom door open with her face and makes trilling noise as she jumps on the bed looking for a cuddle.

Maybe Jess and Amy will go home and I can just tuck myself back into bed and stay there forever? With my cats. They don't care that I'm awkward and not cut out for socializing. And they won't eat me while I'm alive and capable of dishing out the good, fishy food.

My eyes land on my dress where it hangs over the back of my antique velvet bedroom chair. I had been wearing that dress. Nick took it off me. Hung it so it wouldn't get trashed on the floor. My eyes burn and the last thing I want to do is cry but I'm so lost. It doesn't take a genius to work out I'm well and truly, totally, fucked-up.

I punched a guy in the face. Sure, I'd got into scraps with my brothers but adults didn't hit other adults. Except Nick had. That's why he was doing his anger management thing. He'd solved a problem with his fists and now, so had I. Not that Ted didn't deserve it. And more.

Did that make Nick and I kindred spirits? Sort of?

I open the door of my cupboard and pull out a black wrap-around dress. It's not the robe I want to wear but it is stretchy so I'm able to fit my ugly green cast down the sleeve hole. The dress is going to get wrecked if I keep doing it but I have to cover up.

I leave the underwear I wore on. I plan to have everyone out of my apartment within the hour so I can soak in the tub for the rest of the day. I take my time threading the ties through the hole at my hip but then I can't do the bow up. I only have the fingers of one hand and that won't be enough so I make sure the front closure is as solid as possible.

Inhale, one, two, three, four.

Exhale, four, three, two, one.

I repeat this exercise a few times until I'm ready to face my friends who are currently making tea in my kitchenette. Don't ask me why I'm so nervous. I should be mad at them. They weren't there for me. I would have dropped everything had one of them called me from the hospital. Good old dependable Mellow.

But, try as I might to muster the fury to turn the spotlight onto anyone but me, I can't. I'm not angry. They have their own lives. I'm frustrated. I'm upset with myself. I'm so fucking lost.

The murmur of their voices jolts me back to the fact that I can't hide in my room all day and they're here now. I need them now. I need to pour my heart out and see what advice they can give me because at this moment, I'm feeling pretty much like packing it all in.

"You can't hide in there forever," Amy calls in a sing-song voice. It's now or never.

"I'm coming," I call back and emerge from my hiding place, Missy on my heels thinking she's getting food rather than the pat she wanted.

"There you are." Amy smiles when I walk into the kitchen.

"Yep," I nod. "Here I am." My cheeks are on fire! I'm such an idiot!

Jess is holding a steaming mug, just staring at me with a weird expression. "So? Who was that?"

"That was Nick." I don't want to tell them anymore about Nick but he's now reluctantly part of the problem.

"And Nick is who? To you?" Jess asks.

"Nick owns the bar down the street, *Johnnie's*, you know the one with the big fancy doors on twenty-first?"

Jess and Amy both nod. Amy says, "What was Nick doing here and how did you break your hand again? I think we're missing a big chunk of action."

"It's such a long and humiliating story. I've been attempting to meet someone and *Johnnie's* is close by." I say all of the words, recount the entire night without dropping all the four-letter ones starting with F, while looking down at a stain on the countertop. I spilled beetroot juice there once and didn't clean it up right away.

Silence descends and then Jess speaks. "Why is this so important to you, Mellow? Are you so lonely?"

"Not really," I say back, but it's defensive. "Not in the way that I need to get a boyfriend or a roommate. I have the cats." It's dumb saying it out loud but they're great company. I don't even care about the cat lady element of rescuing the little fuzzballs. "You guys were teasing me and-"

Amy shakes her head. "We really weren't trying to have a go at you, Imelda. We were all just joking around. We're worried about you."

"Why do the jokes always have to come at my expense though?" I ask in a very small voice.

"That's not how they're intended," Amy says. "We're your friends. We want to see you happy."

"What if I don't know what happy is for me?"

"Do any of us really know that?" Jess offers. "You love your job. You're happy there. You love your crazy family."

I feel like I need to add, "Because I have to. I'm not sure I love my job anymore. Denni is the reason this happened." I lift my cast and stare at the green. It's even uglier under my four kitchen downlights, the rock-hard texture of the bandages crisscrossing this way and that.

My cup of tea doesn't feel right in my other hand but I know I'll have to get used to it with six to eight more weeks of it. The brew is hot and sweet on my dry tongue but I'm already tired and my hand is beginning to hurt again. I look around the room and wonder where Nick would have put the painkillers I must have been sent home with.

A mug is thunked down on the counter and Amy asks, "What has this got to with Denni? Denni from the hotel? Lazy Denni?"

Here goes. "He's been giving me advice on picking up."

Jess laughs. "Isn't he kind of a man-whore?"

I flinch and offer, "Yes, but who better to get sex advice from than a guy who has so much of it?"

Amy taps her chin. "Where do I start? Does the crude and politically out of favor phrase, man-whore, not tell you to be wary? You took advice from a guy who is probably sharing filthy diseases with women who must have such low self-esteem they don't care who they fuck or where."

I know some of these women and they have loads of self-esteem, confidence by the truck-load and an itch to scratch. "There's nothing wrong with random sex with random guys." I add the words to the conversation but I'm reciting someone else's bullshit. It's not mine.

"No, there isn't," Jess says, but with wariness and a pause so long it scares me. "For some people. Others need the connection. You're a connection person. You're emotional and caring and sweet. You need a boyfriend you can cuddle with after, not a number on your night stand for the next time you feel like a booty call."

The tears threaten again. I blame it on the pain. "What if I don't want to be that person anymore?" I raise my good hand when they both go to jump in. "I want to be sweet and caring too but I have this itch now. I don't think I'm going to be happy until it's been scratched properly." Why I'm speaking in metaphors I don't really know. They're my friends, I could just tell them I think about sex all the time now. That I have this knot low in my abdomen that won't go away. Like an actual itch deep inside and I want someone to scratch it so bad, to make it go away and leave only contentment behind.

"We all have the itch, Mellow. I have a great vibrator that does the trick."

"You have sex too though, Amy. You get out and meet people and have long nights of passion. I want *that*."

"So, meet a nice guy and let it happen gradually. You don't need to get it on today, this week, even this month. Let it happen organically."

I'm so frustrated I want to scream! "I was at *Johnnie's* to meet people. I would have been perfectly happy to have a one-night stand or meet someone nice, but all the guys were assholes. I thought Ted was going to be a good one. He started out so nice and flirty and sexy but then it turns out Denni sent him to find me. He practically served me up like a free ride."

Jess is trying not to laugh, I'm trying not to cry, and then Amy drops this, "What about Nick?"

"What about Nick? No one else could take me to the hospital so he offered. He didn't really have much choice. I might have been a bit drunk."

Amy says. "A *stranger* drops you off at the hospital. He doesn't stay. He doesn't bring you home. He especially doesn't sleep on your couch half-dressed."

"He was being nice. We're friends. I think."

"Why don't you seduce Nick?" Jess says it like it makes perfect sense. In a perfect world.

"I'm not Nick's type."

Jess chokes on her tea. "Who says?"

"Nick says! He told me after the first kiss."

In unison they ask. "How many times have you guys kissed?"

"Just twice."

Jess. "What was it like?"

Amy (with a sigh). "I bet he kisses like a caveman."

Me. "How would a caveman kiss?"

Amy. "Like he wants to eat you up in one bite."

Instead of a terrible picture of being devoured, I can see in my mind, Nick kissing me like he can't get enough. "I'd like a caveman kiss, I reckon. But I'm not his type. I kissed him the second time. He kissed me the first time but only because he felt sorry for me."

Amy. "Ouch. The pity pash?"

I nod. "Yep."

Amy again. "Damn."

"I'm hopeless," I wail.

Jess. "Not hopeless. No one is a lost cause, Imelda. You've just been acting off dodgy advice from a douche bag. You can't change overnight and you shouldn't have to. Your hair looks beautiful, I like it, but you've changed something about yourself to what...? Be more appealing to men? You shouldn't have to do that."

Amy. "I think you should talk to Nick."

Me. "About what? He must think I'm such a loser."

Amy. "He doesn't. I'd bet money he wanted us to leave so he could take the rest of your clothes off and make sweet, sweet love to you."

The spark was back to light to the dwindling hope and fired the burn in my cheeks. "You're just saying that because he was here with no shirt on."

Amy breathes once, twice, three times. Long, frustrated breaths. "I'm saying this as your very best friend, Imelda. You are as blind as the proverbial bat."

I bristle. Of course I do. "Am not!"

She keeps going. "That man is hot! He looked after you. He likes you."

I shake my head. "He was just being nice."

Jess mutters something under her breath and it sounds like, "He can be nice to me anytime he wants."

It's an off-the-cuff expression any one of us might utter but I don't like it coming out of her very pretty, very perfect mouth. I want to tell her to stay away from Nick. He's mine.

But he's not.

I'm not his type.

I'm not anyone's type.

·♥·♥·♥·♥·♥·

Dear Freddy,

Where do I start? This is probably not the best place to write down the events of the night but I have to tell someone and you're it. If I tell the guys, they'll think I've gone soft and gaga over a set of pretty chocolate eyes.

Yeah, yeah. Maybe I have. Those so-called friends of hers are so far up their own asses, they couldn't see how bad she hurts. Oh man, when I saw her knee a bloke in his jewels and then punch him in the face, I thought I was going to have to draw up a chalk ring right there in the bar. This chick would make me some money on the circuit. Except that the dickhead hurt her. A broken knuckle was not the ideal end to a good night. She should have been reveling in her femininity or whatever the hell it is she searches for because finding a guy is not her only agenda. She says she wants to have fun, find herself as a sexy woman but there's something else. I'm no shrink but I would say Imelda is lonely. I never wanted to get involved but it's too late for that now. The woman is a danger to herself but I think she finally realizes that.

The thing about loneliness is that it calls to other lonely people.

Damn! I am getting soft...

15

I spend the day sleeping, wallowing, eating chocolate curled up with three cats and I don't even care. Unless I die today, my hell-prophecy isn't going to come true. There's still time to save myself but what is my next course of action? I can't keep this up. The prowl just isn't for me. My friends are right about that.

I know I have to face Nick one more time. Just to say thanks for looking after me and for being a good guy. Because he is a good guy. It hurts me that I'm not his type but I haven't spiraled so low just yet that I'll scheme to change his mind. Seduce him. Hah!

What really sucks is that I want to kiss him again. I can't help it. I think I have a thing for strong guys. Guys who look like bad boys on the outside but have a heart of gold on the inside.

The issue is that he's exactly *my* type.

I wallow some more. Hit the pint of ice cream in the freezer for dinner, take some painkillers and go back to bed.

I call in sick on Monday with less than an hour's notice. Lucky Denni doesn't pick up the phone. Susan tsks down the line and tells me it's not like me, asks if I'm okay. She sounds like she cares but she's probably got a checklist of what to say when someone calls in sick. Another automated staff member ticking boxes to get through the day.

There's no major events this week or weekend so I don't feel bad. Actually, I don't feel bad at all. Denni tries to call twice during the day when he should be sleeping but I ignore his calls and hope he doesn't know where I live. I'm not ready to face him yet.

Jess checks in and I tell her I'm fine. I just need a day. She accepts that, offers to come around for an hour but I tell her I'm too tired. The painkillers, I say.

I search up broken hands on my laptop, which leads me down a dark path of randomly Googling stupid shit like 'depression in sexless women'. 'Why can't I achieve orgasms?' and also, 'Is there something wrong with me?' That one is no help at all. Every link is designed to make you feel better about yourself but it's on paper. It's not very helpful like that.

'How to pleasure yourself and not feel guilty' also appears in my searches. Also unhelpful.

I'm not on Facebook, Twitter or Instagram. I know. I'm not a real twenty-something if I don't have all the socials but I never wanted them. Now I feel left-out without at least one popular platform to connect and be connected with.

I make myself a Facebook account and stare at the screen for ten minutes waiting for the friend requests to roll in. I get one. From my mum. I ignore it.

I pay a ridiculous amount of money for the latest sex toy, a Satisfier Pro, from an online ad that has next day delivery. The reviews say will make you scream your own name in three seconds or less.

'*Unless there's something wrong with you...*'

Those words written in italics on my screen draw first blood. I cry into what's left of the ice cream. When it's time for bed, a gross heaviness weighs me down and I have to wonder if it's more than all the chocolate and crap I gorged on all day. I stumble across a site that is kind of anti-depression, the kind that says it's okay to lay on the couch for a bit but when you wake up the next day, seize it! Take your shitty situation and make something of it!

I am not cut out to walk around feeling sorry for myself. I'm no sex kitten, hook-up extraordinaire either. But I must be somewhere in the middle. I'm not a bloody alien. I don't think.

·♥·♥·♥·♥·♥·

Dear Freddy.

She didn't come back today. Part of me knew she wouldn't. All of me knew she shouldn't. Is it all right to confess that I kept looking up every time someone opened the door? Probably for the best, eh? No more trouble. No more temptation.

16

Monday night brings the crappiest sleep I've had in forever. I'm out of painkillers but I wasn't loving the way they made me feel anyway. So I spend the night alternating between throbbing pain and bad dreams. Each time I roll over to find a better position, I either squish my fingers or attempt to flex my wrist or even move it, only to be held back by the stiff, unrelenting plaster. It turns out green plaster actually glows in the dark too. So annoying.

I'm a person who generally sleeps with my arms above my head but have you ever tried to do that with a glow in the dark, two pound cast bumping against you, a jagged edge by my thumb catching in my hair after every bump and pulling at a single strand each time? No? Lucky you. I give up on sleep around four-thirty am. Needless to say, I'm in a foul mood and spend an hour thinking of all the things I want to say to Denni when I get to work.

I think about hitting him with my cast. It would hurt like hell for both of us. But I scrap that idea. No violence. No *more* violence. Sure, I'll defend myself if I'm ever in another Ted situation, or worse, but no random acts of revenge. Denni needs to be held accountable but I don't know how.

As the wee hours of the morning slip by I discover quite a few things I can't do by myself. I can't make an espresso without doing damage to either me or the machine so I switch to instant. I swear after every mouthful, trying not to cringe. I like coffee in the morning but I should have settled on tea.

I can't shower properly because I have to keep one arm in the air. I have pins and needles by the time I one-hand wash my hair. Which by the way, sucks too. In the end I settle for leave in conditioner and thank the universe for my straight hair that doesn't need chemicals or a flat-iron. I stand way too long and admire my haircut. I'm loving it more every time I see myself in the mirror. Something to smile about at least. Unlike the sling I have to keep my hand in all day. It's uncomfortable and will take a lot of getting used to too.

In the time it takes to digest the gross four-years out of date coffee and get the train to work, I've devised a plan to take care of Denni. It's underhanded. Definitely below the belt. But he deserves it.

I wonder how the conversation went. The one where Denni called his friend Ted and told him about this desperate chick he works with.

"Hey Ted, it's Denni. Wanna have sex with a desperate chick?"

"Is she hot?"

"Meh, she's doable."

"Sure, I don't have plans tonight."

"Awesome, fire away, man."

I was ripe for the picking which made my stomach hurt. All he had to do was buy me a few drinks and I would have been his. The sick feeling intensifies when it occurs to me that I could have slept with Ted and then found out later that it was all Denni's doing. Yuck. I feel violated despite barely being touched.

Sitting there on the train, pitifully feeling sorry for myself, and a lightning bolt of idiotic proportions slams into me.

"I am such an idiot!" I say. Out loud. *Crap.*

Here I am cursing Ted and Denni and vowing revenge, but I also thought it would that easy. Buy a guy a few drinks, share a laugh and a bowl of hot chips and then back to my place for a quickie. I'd flash a little leg, wink-wink nudge-nudge. Isn't that essentially what Ted had done to me? Bought me drinks, flattered and flirted. He'd definitely gone too far but I encouraged him. More! I practically asked for it. *Gag. Yuck.*

Okay, so my behavior hadn't been that bad but by the time I said no, and meant no, Ted had already got it into his head that we were a done deal. He was getting laid and I was meant to take it. No effort. No romance. Nothing special about it at all.

I think on it and I'd rather be romanced. I think I want to take it slow and fall for someone. For all of them, the entire person. Not just the orgasm they might offer. It would take more time but there it was. I am not a one-night stand. I want a boyfriend.

I'd listened to Denni as though he was not only the holder of the male bible, but the writer as well. I should have known better. With this revelation I'm feeling mildly sorry for what I'm about to do to him. But my revenge plans still stand. I could not go blaming myself for his stupidity any more than I could blame him for mine.

There's no doubt that the city is filled with guys with hard-ons to hang a wet towel from, but the body attached to the appendage has to be just as important to me. A body, I had hoped to ignore to get straight to the crutch of matters.

That one makes me giggle.

I'm losing my mind.

As the train pulls up to my stop, I decide I don't have to hurry today. Who cares if I'm a few minutes late? By the time my colleagues notice my hideous green cast, they'd miss the fact I might have grown a second head.

I take my time on the walk. It's not the day for it but my mind is all over the place. The autumn wind cuts through my knit top. I have no jacket because my hand won't go through and it's silly just having one arm in. Tomorrow I'll have to either cut an old jacket to wear or put on two knits. My clothes would be ruined by the time the silly thing came off.

With every shiver, my hand hurts even more.

When I finally walk through the staff entrance of the hotel, I'm like an icicle. I need to thaw out in my office before facing the day's work. And yesterday's.

I stop before the concierge desk, adopt an air of cruisy nonchalance and tell myself there's still time to cancel my revenge plans. There's still time to act like none of it ever happened and go back to normal. Pretend I never asked my man-whore co-worker for sex advice that nearly got me sexually assaulted.

But Denni doesn't come out of the backroom. It's Kyle. He gives me a smile and says, "Feeling better today, Imelda?"

I nod and hold up my cast. "I wasn't sick. Just broken."

"Ouch!" he says. "Do I want to know how that happened?"

"Probably not," I tell him. "Where's Denni?"

"He called in sick last night too. Something about a migraine, I think."

I nod. "Thanks Kyle."

The coward. That son of a bitch knew I'd tear him a new one.

I think about how revenge is a dish best served cold but I'm burning with fury and that's the best time to act. If I don't get this off my chest, I'm going to explode and take out everyone and everything within a four-block radius!

If I don't come face-to-face with Denni soon, I know how my day will go. I'll sit and stew about the many different paths available to an angry, hurt, betrayed woman. I'll think and then rethink and rephrase all the things I want to say in my mind until I forget which one will cut the deepest. I'll be so cranky and try to bottle everything up inside and then one very innocent, very well-meaning, bystander will say just one stupid word and that'll be it, I'll detonate.

At the wrong person.

I could call him? I ponder it as an option as I tuck my handbag into the bottom drawer of my desk, but only for a half a second. I need to do this in person. It won't be the same with the warm plastic and glass pressed to my cheek. Denni has to know he can't do this again to another woman and also, I want to watch him squirm.

He also has to know that treating women like living sex toys is unacceptable. He has to be trading on the boredom of the house-keeping staff and I don't like it. It pisses me off. He can't keep walking around like all women are ripe for a man's taking.

Ew. I pick up the phone and dial the number for housekeeping.

"Patricia speaking."

"Hi Patricia, It's Imelda."

"Oh, hi. How are you?"

"I'm okay, you?"

"Great. Twenty-three weeks and feeling like the back end of a whale but I'm doing better."

Patricia is a forty-year-old woman who'd left it late in life to have kids. She hadn't met her prince charming until her thirty-ninth birthday. Six months later they married and announced they were expecting their first baby. The first trimester had been hard on her but Patricia kept saying it was all worth it. It was all going to be worth it. I should take hope and heart from her situation, really. But I don't.

"Did you find out the sex?" I know she had a scan booked over the weekend.

"No. Bob decided he didn't want to know. This may be the only child we ever have so we'll make the experience as magical and surprising as we can."

"Fair enough. Well, I'll be buying pink so I hope you're having more girl thoughts than boy," I tell her with a laugh I feel is forced. I hope she doesn't notice.

"Buy blue. It's going to be a boy, I know it."

There's a pool going betting on the sex of the baby and the time Patricia will go into labor. I'd already thrown in my cash. Winner gets a dinner for two in the restaurant and all the money will go to the new mom, her husband and the bouncing bundle of joy.

"Hey can you do me a favor?" I have to get to the point of the call before I chicken out.

"Sure."

"I need someone with a bottle of bleach or industrial antiseptic to wash down the wall in the cloak room."

"You mean Denni's wall?"

I groan. This is bad. So bad. "Does it seriously have a name?"

"Yep. Pretty much everyone except for the higher powers know about Denni's wall."

It's a good thing the higher powers don't know. He'd be sacked on the spot. I consider spilling the beans but I want revenge. Living hell at work. No more Denni's wall. I really don't want him or anyone else fired.

"And then I want Ralph to install some coat hooks."

"How many?"

"Just make it so pointy Denni can't use it anymore."

"Is everything alright Imelda?"

I sigh. Dramatically. "Yeah. I just need a coffee."

"Are you sure?"

I pitch my voice higher than it needs be and reply, "Yep."

Then I hang up.

I give Patricia five minutes to make the calls and assign the tasks and then I stand and walk my way through the hotel to the staffroom. My green cast is heavy against my boob, the sling tight and unforgiving. I get so much attention from this one walk. I see the question in the eyes that follow my every stride. One waiter, Tom, looks like he's going to approach but then I dip my chin, let my shoulders sag, and push my way into the room we eat our lunch and drink our coffee in.

Just as I suspect, and knew would happen, Patricia comes storming through the door a heartbeat after I finish making my second cup of instant coffee for the morning and sit on a hard plastic chair at a sterile, white laminate table.

"Imelda what is going on?" she asks, sitting opposite, her eyes on my cast.

My bottom lip drops, my chin crinkles and tears well. It takes no effort at all to linger on the verge of crying my eyes out. I'm tired. I'm sore. I'm nervous. I'm angry. "It's a long story."

The door opens and three maids walk in, closely followed by Tom, the waiter.

After a chorus of 'what's wrong's' and 'please don't cry', I finally tell them my 'problem'.

"I have chlamydia."

The silence is one of shock. Of horror. Of disbelief. My co-workers are stunned and for a full minute I wonder if they don't believe a woman like me would appeal to someone like Denni. No one says a word. Until a sob catches in my throat, the sound audible in the small room.

Then the murmurs start. The exchanged looks, the uncomfortable squirm as the ladies present wonder if they might also have been exposed.

I continue. "I fell for his smooth words, the routine. I just wanted to see what all the fuss was about and now I have a disease."

"Is it treatable?" Patricia asks.

"It is for me, but apparently he's a carrier. He could give it to anyone at any time and you might not even know." I got this information from Google which I didn't fact check because it suits my purposes.

"Why didn't you use a condom?" This from Tom. A young guy. I want to smile at the way he says it, his tone. He isn't calling me an idiot, merely asking why I hadn't used my brains.

"It all happened so quickly. One minute I was minding my own business, the next he had me backed up against the wall and the moment kind of...took us away."

Five identical, outraged gasps met this revelation.

Patricia recovered first. "You didn't?"

Tom was next. "Yuck."

Delores, one of the maids who'd worked at the hotel for as long as I had cringed. "Are you sure it was from him?"

I stare her in the eye and nod. I carry off the indignant thinning of the lips well because I'm pissed off she thinks I'm having unprotected sex with all the men. I don't actually want to cause all of the women around me to worry but a simple STD screening isn't going to hurt anyone here. Someone should write a TV show series about the kind of sex hotel workers get up to when they think no one is watching, like that one on the boat. With three hundred beds in the place, there's plenty of opportunity and horizontal surface area, not even counting the cloakroom and all the vertical areas. "Denni is the only one I've been with in months."

"That bastard." Anya, another maid proclaims, slamming her hand down on the table.

"How do you feel?" Patricia wants to know.

"I'm okay. The round of antibiotics was administered on time so I won't have any lasting effects." God, shouldn't I hate myself right now? I don't.

"Do you want me to beat him up?" Tom offers.

I smile, through the haze of tears, through the pain of my hand and maybe a little bit of guilt at my own underhanded tactics. I lift the corners of my mouth and face the five of them, looking everyone in the eye before I shoot the last nail into the coffin that is now officially the end of Denni's sex-at-work life. "I just don't want this to happen to anyone else."

I listen to the plan they devise to quietly alert the other staff members amidst the pitying looks and pats on my back. I honestly don't care if they think I've caught something from Denni. I'm never going to sleep with a staff member. I'm a department manager. I could lose my job. Denni isn't in a position of power and since this is still the boy's club, he'd probably get a slap on the wrist in public and a high five behind closed doors. This kind of revenge is enough for me. I get up and leave the room.

Mission accomplished.

I don't know if I want to laugh or cry. I feel good that instead of taking it like a doormat, I've stood up for myself and ensured that Denni is going to be treated differently by our colleagues from now on. I've sliced up a little bit of hell to him that he didn't even know about yet. But this isn't me. I'm not the vengeful type. But then again, I've never been so angry in my life. Never felt so dirty and out of my depth.

When I get back to my office, I close the door and sink down into my chair behind the desk. What now? Do I just go about my daily work the best I can with only one hand? Do I wait for a hole in the floor to suck me down into hell for stooping so low?

Nothing happens. Not for a whole twenty-three minutes and fourteen seconds. I counted. Yes, I am just sitting there staring at the clock. My phone rings. I answer it and pray it isn't Susan.

"Imelda speaking."

"Mel, it's Kyle, I have a Nick on the phone from *Johnnie's*."

My heart skips a beat or two and my blood picks up a deafening roar in my ears.

"Are you there? Imelda?"

"Yeah, Kyle, I'm here. Did he say what he wants?"

"No. Only that he needs to speak to you."

Damn. I do wonder in that terrifying moment if he's going to ban me from the bar once and for all. I'm clearly a burden and also possibly bad for business. I'd been so busy rehearsing what I'd say to

Denni in my head, I hadn't given Nick much thought. Well, not this morning anyway.

"Put him through." The sooner it's over the better.

When the noise on the line changes to total silence, I'm not sure if Nick is there or not. I hope he's not there. I hope he's been disconnected. Lost in the nether that is telephone land. "Hello?"

"Imelda?"

No such luck. "Yeah."

"Hey, it's Nick."

"How are you?" *Polite. Nice.*

"I'm okay. How's the hand?"

"Well, my cast glows in the dark."

"Are you serious?" he laughs.

"Unfortunately." *Why is he calling*? And why doesn't he get to the point? Surely this isn't a welfare call? Or maybe he's worried about his business insurance? Maybe the cops want to press charges and he's calling to give me the head's up?

"So, you left your coat at the bar."

Damn. My new coat. "I guess I'll have to come by to pick it up, if that's okay?"

"Why wouldn't it be?" he asks, and I instantly feel dumb for putting it out there.

I mumble something that sounds like, "I don't know, don't worry," and follow it up with, "I have dinner at my mother's tonight but I can swing by after?"

"Sure. I'll keep it locked up in the office until then."

"Thanks." The word comes out heavier than I intend. Is this the right time to thank him for his help? For taking me to the hospital and making sure I was okay? For sleeping on my couch and possibly even feeding my cats? Because I hadn't topped up their bowl and yet it had been full of little crunchy biscuits. I decide it's not the right time. I'll do that in person. I might even apologize for all the trouble I've caused. Assure him that I won't be back. Was a thank you enough? Two words in exchange for the hero act?

For some reason my mouth engages without asking my brain's permission and I say, "Maybe we could have a drink?" Silence descends and I'm quick to jump back in with, "Just to say thanks, you know, it's probably the least I can do."

"I'm not allowed to drink on the premises. Sentencing conditions."

"Oh yeah." I'd forgotten about that. "Coffee?"

I can actually hear his intake of breath. "Look, come on over later and we'll see where we're at. Maybe one drink wouldn't hurt. You definitely owe me."

I force a chuckle, agree, say goodbye, hang up. *Shit*.

On a scale of one to ten on the my-life-has-gone-to-shit ruler, I'm already sitting at about seven.

I still have a family dinner to get through...

17

So. Family dinners. No one loves them do they? They bring with them the expectation of making nice. Of bullshit small talk. My mother will ask me how I'm doing, anything new, big promotion? She always asks this with hope in her big brown eyes.

She's an intelligent woman, my mother, but she doesn't understand that event manager in a hotel doesn't actually go anywhere. You can go to a bigger hotel with bigger events. You can move to an exhibition center or conference facilities. You can always move sideways and into more prestigious hotels but on the *what next* factor, there's no long list of roles to catapult myself into.

The planter boxes lining the paved path to the front door are barren again. My mother has the opposite of a green thumb. Every year she has a gardener plant a new array of flowers but she doesn't take care of them. They die. The planters are emptied and a new gardener is hired to 'do the job properly'. As I lift my hand to knock, I almost laugh out loud. I literally have a green hand and here I am thinking about people with green thumbs. I wipe my free hand on my skirt, run my fingers through my hair and plaster a smile onto my lips. I'm dressed appropriately according to my mother. I'm armed with a few made-up events from the past week which will show that I'm still being successful despite not having been 'promoted' in forever. There will be questions about my cast but I know well enough all I have to do is turn the conversation back to my sister and two brothers, and I'll be ignored. Like usual.

I knock and wait. It doesn't matter that I was raised here. We have to knock. We have to dress up for dinner. We have to come once a month and the only way to get out of it is to be out of town or in surgery. As in performing the surgery. I never go out of town and I'm (to my parent's disappointment) not a doctor. I'm also not a good enough liar to make good excuses. Imagine picking up the phone and telling my mother I'm off to Hawaii for a week. I'd have to tell her I got that promotion after all. It's the only way she'd believe me!

The door swings open and there she is. Impeccably dressed, made up and coiffed. On a Tuesday night. For a family dinner. It's ridiculous but we toe this line for her. We're too intimidated not to.

"Hi mom," I greet her and wait on the stoop. I have to be invited in. Like a vampire.

She looks me up and down as usual. Sometimes she tells me I look well fed (fat). Sometimes she comments on my clothing (terrible and tasteless). Sometimes she tells me my hair looks limp and I should see her person to get it sorted (I never will). I don't have to be the rocket scientist she'd prefer to know her gaze would be drawn to my hand.

"What. Is. That?"

"It's nothing really, I broke my hand."

"And green was the only color on offer?"

"It's a very long story."

"It always is," she returns with a delicate sniff. "You better come in before anyone sees you."

I always want to ask who will see me and why would they care if my clothes aren't designer enough or my hair is limp or my butt looks bigger because I've got the 'wrong cut of pants' on. Which one of her neighbors would walk over, knock on the door and say, "Jeez Sinta, what kind of product has your daughter been using sparingly on her hair? Why haven't you offered her the name of your salon so she can get it fixed?"

She didn't even notice the fact I'm wearing new make-up or that my hair is fresh. No one cares. Sometimes that's the best part of being invisible. Sometimes it's the worst. I probably shouldn't be upset that I don't get to pick between the two.

"Your siblings are already here. You're the last to arrive." The scolding doesn't pinch or bite. I'm too used to it.

"Mom, I told you, I don't get off work until six and then I still have to get here." Get on the first train, change to another, and then get a bus. This is another conversation we have all the time. All. The. Time.

"A taxi would get you here on time. Even one of those Uber cars would be better than the train."

And cost more than fifty dollars one-way if traffic is good. I need to change the subject. "How is everyone?"

"You can ask them yourself. In you go."

I'm ushered into the dining room. Alice is the first out of her seat but she stops and stares at my hand. I should have hid it behind my back. For three hours.

"What happened?" she cries.

My brothers stop talking and everyone stares at me. I squirm. I don't like this. The attention. I like to be the mouse in the corner when it comes to this family. "I fell over, broke my hand."

My mother enters the room making tsking noises with her mouth. "You were always a clumsy child."

I wasn't. I was bruised because my brothers were horrible. "It's nothing really. Six to eight weeks and I'll be back to new." I hug Alice, give Aadiv a squeeze to his shoulder and kiss Tanay on the cheek. They made my childhood hell but all grown up, they aren't so bad. If you take away their egos, bank accounts and incredible successes.

"What did you fall over?" Tanay asks.

"My heel caught on the edge of the elevator at work and I just kind of met the floor." I'd rehearsed this story all day until even I nearly believed it could happen.

Alice frowned. "Did you report it?"

I nod and take my regular seat at the dining table.

Aadive won't stop staring at the ugly green color so I drop my hand into my lap, out of sight.

Alice isn't going to let it go. "And what are they going to do about it? They need to fix the issue so it doesn't happen to someone else. Maybe a ninety-year-old grandmother or a child falls next."

This is what comes of having a career as a hospital administrator by the age of twenty-five. Everything is about the hospital visits and reducing ER waiting times, about health and safety and trip hazards, and not being sued.

"They'll fix it, Alice, don't sweat it."

Tanay asks. "Did you get a waterproof liner or regular?"

I sigh. "Can we please talk about something else? I'm fine. Really."

Our mother re-enters the room with a large earthy colored tagine held with immaculate designer oven gloves. She puts it on the table and then pauses, looks at me. "Something is different about you today, Imelda. I wonder what it is?"

"Could be the painkillers?" I offer with a choked laugh. Surely my abject humiliation and defeat isn't tattooed on my forehead just yet? When I looked in the mirror before leaving work, I thought I just looked tired. "I had my hair done too. That's probably it."

She shakes her head. "No. Definitely not that. Have you met someone?"

Change the record! I want to yell. Instead, I sigh. "I meet people all the time, mom. It's my job."

"Don't be crotchety," she tells me. "I think you've met a man."

I think about Ted and my broken hand, Nick and my broken love life. "It's the painkillers," I assure her.

"So, Alice, how's things down your end of town?" My sister inherited a penthouse apartment only steps away from the hospital she works at in one of the richest areas of the city. She asked me to move in with her once but the commute is too long for me.

"Ugh," she grunts and then looks up through her lashes. Our mother doesn't like grunts, groans or, you guessed it, sighs. Thankfully she doesn't notice and Alice continues. "The air-conditioning in our building needs an upgrade. Daniel is being his usual shade of shitty about it."

I choke on another laugh, a real one this time, as my mother shoots her a dirty look. Ladies don't use vulgar language. Apparently. "When isn't he?" I ask. She's had problems with her neighbor for so long, nothing surprises me when it comes to his behavior anymore.

"What makes things worse is that I'm looking after Jia for a week."

We all fall silent for a moment. I ask, "Jia? As in baby Jia? Lanfen's baby Jia?"

Alice is careful not to groan this time. "Don't look at me like that. It's only for a week."

Tanay says, "But you hate babies."

Alice bristles. "I do not."

Aadive throws in, "A week as in overnight as well or just watching her during the day?"

Before Alice can answer, our mother asks, "Why don't they have a nanny?"

"Because they don't need one," Alice says through gritted teeth. "It's going to be great. And besides, there's no one else. I can take Jia into the hospital in the day to visit and then bring her home with me for the nights."

My sister has always been very vocal about not having children. Ever. She loves her goddaughter, but does she know how hard this will be? I don't say anything because as long as we're talking about her, no one is focused on me.

More food is added to the table and finally it's time to eat. That means less than an hour until I can leave. Less than an hour to keep quiet about Nick and how I really broke my hand.

We talk about Alice's building works and her bad neighbor situation, Tanay's upcoming trip to Africa where he will operate as a doctor without borders for three months. Aadive answers questions about a modern design for a heritage building his architectural firm is about to begin work on. Conversation flows around the single glass of wine we're allowed to have. Anymore and we might get honest or, *gasp*, straightforward, and that wouldn't do.

Sometimes I wished these dinners were fun and full of laughter. Other families (television families) drink bottles of wine, tease each other, guffaw and poke fun. When we were all teens we had dinners like that. Then my mother fell in with the country club crowd, my father deserted us, and this is what came of it. Formal, stiff dinners, with impeccable manners, smart casual clothes and polite conversation.

If I was a horse, I'd be biting at the bit, tossing my head and raring to run. There is of course, no horsing around beneath this roof.

My brothers help my mother clear away the dishes and tidy the kitchen, we take turns and it's theirs tonight. That just leaves me and Alice at the table.

I speak first and I speak quickly before anyone else comes back. "How can you be this calm about taking care of a baby?"

"How can you sit there and lie about how you broke your hand?" she retorts without missing a beat.

I really shouldn't let her get in my head but as I take a breath, she's there, in my brain, poking around.

"Because the truth is ridiculous. I know you're not clumsy and you don't wear the type of heels to get caught in a narrow gap." She rubs her hands together and slides forward on her chair. In a very loud stage whisper, she says, "Ooh, tell me everything! How drunk were you?"

"There was alcohol involved, I won't lie. To your face," I add.

"Oh my god, please tell me everything!"

I watch as Alice jumps around in her chair, thinking she's going to get a hilarious and ridiculous story about how I did something dumb while drunk. And I guess it was dumb and I was on my way to drunk when it happened... Deep breaths. "I was attacked by an arsehole at a bar."

I don't get any more words out when Alice becomes dead still and sputters. "What?"

"It's really not that bad," I rush to assure her. I should have started with, *I'm okay, remember I'm okay*. "He didn't get much of a chance to touch me. I punched him in the face. That's how I broke my hand."

"I would have done more than that! I would have murdered the bastard."

"Believe me, Nick wanted to try, but don't worry, Ted won't be hurting any more women for a bit. At least until he pulls his balls out of his stomach."

"You kneed him too? Oh man, I'd love to have seen that."

I shake my head. "No, you wouldn't. It was terrible and embarrassing and I just feel so stupid."

"Uh, you defended yourself against a predator. There's nothing stupid about that! I am so proud of you!"

Why is she saying it like she'd never in a million years think I can take care of myself? "Thanks," I mutter.

"But wait." *Urgh, she's not done.* "Who's Nick? And what were you doing in a bar? Not exactly your scene."

"And what exactly is my scene?" I ask before I can think better of it.

"No, I don't mean it like that, Mels, it's just that you usually sit at home or go to restaurants with the girls. Bars have never been your thing."

Defeat fills all the hollow places in my belly. "They're not my thing at all, evidently." I raise the cast and cringe. Tears burn my eyes again.

I think maybe tonight after catching up with Nick, I might put on a good crying movie and allow myself a few more moments.

"You still didn't say who Nick is." Can't get a thing past my sister. Beautiful and with a head full of brains.

"Nick is the owner of the bar. He took me to the hospital to get patched up."

"What about the posse?"

My family have been calling Jess, Amy, Candice and me, the posse, ever since we became fast friends. "I was there on my own."

Now Alice is really confused. "Why?"

I make sure we're still alone in the room and that my mother isn't coming down the hall. I really don't want to tell her what's going on but it all kind of blurts out like a form of verbal diarrhea squishing past the fingers I'm holding over my mouth. "I was trying to find someone to have sex with."

"Okay, kinda gross. Why?"

"I really don't want to go into the why's. I'm embarrassed enough."

"Is someone pressuring you to do this? Is Nick pressuring you?"

"It's not pressure, okay, it's just that..."

"Just what?"

"I don't think I've ever had a real orgasm." I whisper it. So softly I hope she doesn't hear me right. "I haven't been in a relationship in forever and I really, really don't want to die an old cat lady." Big, fat, hot tears fall down my cheeks and there's nothing I can do to stop them.

Instead of laughing at me, Alice gets up from her seat and sits next to me, giving me the biggest hug she ever has in our entire lives.

"Please don't cry about this, Mels. For some people it's a medical condition in itself. Not everyone *feels* the same as the next person."

That's even more depressing.

"Why didn't you just take care of it yourself, find out if you can even achieve? Why leave it to a bloke?"

My sister had sworn off men a long time ago. She works even more than I do. She doesn't have any cats either. Just her, all alone in her big, penthouse apartment. At least she'd just die and then get discovered when the smell got too much for her crappy neighbor.

"It's not the same," I sniff and pull back, wipe my eyes on my sleeve.

"Of course it is. You might do it with a pig and still not get to the big O. What then? My advice would be to buy yourself a little gift online, buy a movie with it, turn the lights down and go crazy."

I know my eyes are open extra wide. My mouth is also open. "Is that what you do?"

A sparkle lights her eyes and she's mischief in a second. "Yep. It's not normal not to want. I just don't want the pubes on the shower soap and the wet towels on the floor to go with it."

What had happened to us? No one in my family wants a relationship. Probably because we barely know what a loving and warm one looks like. Our parents are so stiff and formal all the time, even to each other. We sometimes joked that we were all adopted. There's no way those two had sex, let alone four times to get each of us. Maybe I'd inherited this untouchable persona from my frigid, prudish mother? Along with my darker skin, big brown eyes and straight brown hair?

"I already bought one, but I don't know if I can." I admit it out loud because it's true. Of course the best thing to do would be to get myself off so I would know if I can or if I can't but I'm so nervous about that too. I don't know how to do it myself. I'm just not much of a masturbator. Never have been. Sure, I tried once or twice, but nothing came of it.

"You can," Alice says.

"I'll think about it."

"Now, more about Nick."

"There isn't much to tell. I'm not his type."

"Is he your type?"

"I didn't think so but what if my normal type is the reason I'm single and orgasm-less?"

"Do you like Nick?"

"Yeah, I think I do. He's a great guy and would make a great friend."

"But not boyfriend?" Alice wonders out loud.

"He's got too much baggage. He's cute and he's really nice. He has great arms, like really great, but he's not looking for anything."

Footsteps come down the hall and I swear her to secrecy as I wipe my eyes and pull myself together. "Not one word."

"My lips are sealed. Just no more bars alone? Deal?"

We lock pinkies and I consider my secret safe. I don't count going to the bar later as alone. Nick will be there.

18

If I say I'm nervous, it will be the biggest understatement of the year!

It's just one drink. Well, maybe not even one drink since Nick isn't allowed and I'd had enough to last me the rest of the year. I have learned, through this whole ordeal, that alcohol isn't good for me or my decision-making skills. Some people probably thrive off of liquid courage but clearly I'm a person who needs all of my thinking brain cells for actual thinking! I hate it when my mother is right about something. In this case, it's that one glass *is* enough.

I'm still asking myself if it was a good idea to tell my sister the truth. If she tells anyone in our family, I'll be the brunt of every single joke for the foreseeable future and beyond. I suppose I have dirt on her too though, if she did tell. Like the fact she lost her virginity at fifteen and not the eighteen she told our mother. I don't want to use it but in the family tactics warfare game, I have to play to win.

My steps are slow as I walk in the street-light along the footpath towards *Johnnie's*. There's a few people around but not many. It's late. Ten-thirty-ish. For about thirty seconds, I ponder walking right past and going straight home. My hand hurts and I'm feeling the lowest I ever have. My stomach is in knots and I could throw up on command. Do I really need that new jacket I'd left at the bar? Did I have to volunteer to come and grab it right away? Did I have to offer to stop for a drink? All regrettable choices to add to the lists I'm making in my head of all the things never to do again.

The doors to *Johnnie's* are closed and it's deadly quiet. Weird.

I push through and there's no one inside. As in the place is empty.

Until Nick pops his head up from behind the bar. He smiles. I smile back. This won't be awkward at all, I realize with an inward groan.

"Do you want to turn the lock behind you?" he asks. But it sounds more like a question than a command and I gulp.

"Closing up early?" I lock it anyway. He saved me when I needed saving. He's hardly going to do anything dangerous. In his bar. With a sober woman who isn't his type.

God, I'm paranoid! Where was this emotion when I should have felt it? Back before I was attacked by bloody Ted?

"It's so dead tonight. No one else is coming in. I don't get many early nights so I take them when I can."

And then it happens. I think of Nick in bed. You know when you can't unthink or unsee a thought or an image? Nick's chest is that thing for me and now Nick in bed is too. I bet he has satin sheets and some sort of dark, leopard-print bedspread. I want to hit myself in the head to dislodge the image. Naked chest. Bed. Slippery satin.

"Do you want a drink?" he asks, clearly unaware of my inner turmoil. "Coffee maybe?"

I'd be awake all night. Then again, who could sleep with this image in their brain and the slow burn in their belly anyway? Not me. "Sure. Thanks."

"Where did you go for dinner?"

Small talk then? Probably better that way. "Just to my mum's. We have a family dinner every month. They're torture but it's not worth missing."

"You're dressed nicer than dinner at mom's," he comments as he grinds beans and heats milk.

"Um, thanks. You don't know my mother. She's a perfectionist so jeans aren't suitable dinner wear."

"I bet she got a kick out of your cast. Can't exactly match that to anything fancy looking."

I'd said almost those exact same words at the hospital, hadn't I? I narrow my gaze and ask, "Are you making fun of me, Nick?"

He chuckles. "Not at all. What you wear to dinner with your folks is none of my business. You look nice is all."

I clear my throat. "Thanks."

We're both silent while he pours dark, steaming liquid into two mugs and then stirs in a little bit of warm milk.

I don't know how to break this ice. This is the exact reason alcohol helps.

"Are you done now?" he says into the awkwardness between us.

We're both sitting on stools now, facing the bottle shelf of the bar. It has a mirror backing and I can see my face in the reflection. I can see Nick's too. He's looking down into his coffee.

Can I pretend to misunderstand? Should I? "I honestly feel so embarrassed. I promise this will be the last time you see me. Unless we pass on the street or something... But I won't say hi. I'll just keep walking like we're total strangers."

More silence. Fun. Until he says, "Maybe that's a bit extreme."

The tension in my belly does some sort of cartwheel. I turn the cup so the handle is in my good hand and then sip the coffee to buy some time even though I did say no thanks to the brew. "I'm sure you could do without the hassle that is me."

He chuckles again and damn it, I like the sound. "It's been fun," he says. "Sort of."

"Oh sure, *you* get punched in the face. I punch someone *in* the face. We're a barrel of laughs, you and me."

"It's not the first time I've been punched in the face and it definitely won't be the last."

"How's your diary coming along?" I chance a sideways look and his cheeks are pink.

"It's the most ridiculous thing I've ever had to do."

"I kept a diary in high school," I confide.

This time he looks at me, turns on his stool and gives me his full attention. His knee brushes my knee but I try to ignore it as he continues. "What did you write in there?"

I attempt to laugh it off. "Stupid teenage girl stuff. You don't want to know."

"I really do. How do I know if I'm doing it right if I've never seen one before?"

"I am not showing you my high school diary."

He raises a hand to grip the bar and his blue eyes open so wide. "Wait a minute. You still have it? Why?"

I shrug. "Posterity? Stupidity? Those years were really hard for me. I had to write it all down or I'd go insane. I wasn't really a talker."

He laughs harder. Deeper. Courser. "I don't believe that."

I look at him, turn on my barstool. "I was really shy!" But my protests sound awfully defensive and he keeps laughing.

"So, what? Crushes? Bitches? Was it like a stabby book of girls you'd like to get revenge on for being mean?"

I put my head on the bar, my good hand blocking him from my peripheral. "I really don't want to tell you."

His warm fingers tease mine aside and he's so close I can smell the coffee on his breath as he says, "No, really, I want to know. Please?"

"Fine." I give in. I might as well. Also, I can't think straight. He's too close. "Mostly it was a period tracker." He grimaces and I smile at the direct hit. "But also, it is full of boys and bitches. It's all the things I wanted to say to all of the boys I both loved and hated. My parents took me to a psychologist as a child hoping to fix my shyness and he suggested the diary as a way to say all the things I couldn't articulate out loud."

"So, witty comebacks? Insults? That sort of thing?"

I roll my eyes. "There was nothing witty about thirteen year old me."

"How did you overcome it? The shyness?"

He's so serious now. As though he's genuinely interested. I shrug again. "I grew up. Finally realized that people can't hurt me in the way I probably thought they could. My dad used to shout a lot so I would make myself very small and very quiet." I see the look in Nick's eyes and I'm quick to add, "He was never violent. Just loud. We couldn't ever do anything right. He left after a while. I came out of my shell. Eventually."

Nick finishes the last of his coffee so I do the same. He says, "I'm kind of glad you came out of your shell, but also, kind of wish you didn't after the last week."

I know he's kidding. It's not funny. It isn't.

"I guess I better grab my jacket and get going. It's late and I have work tomorrow."

He gets off his stool and I follow him down the corridor to his office. "Oh, did you get to have it out with your co-worker? Danny? Was that his name?"

Nick unlocks the door and flicks the lights on. The space is small. Cozy.

"Denni, and no. He's playing chicken and stayed home."

"He's likely scared you'll be out for blood."

"Hmm." I make the non-committal sound but it doesn't come out the way I intend.

Nick turns to me. "What did you do?"

"I may have told a few select people that Denni gave me a sexually transmitted disease."

"Which one?"

"Chlamydia."

Nick shakes his head. But then he seems to think of something. His eyes are wide. "Have you slept with this Denni guy before?"

"Jesus, Nick. If I could get nailed at work, why would I be here?"

As soon as *nailed* crosses my lips, I want to pull it back.

"Imelda, this is dangerous, what you're doing."

I hold up my cast-wrapped hand. "I get that now."

"Why is sex so important to you anyway, why now?"

"I told you, I just don't want to be alone. It's perfectly normal for humans to crave contact with other humans." I can't tell him how bad I am at sex. How I think I'm broken or worse, missing something on the inside.

"You also said you wanted to do it the old fashioned way but now that you haven't, what next? What if you don't find someone? What then?"

Can a girl groan any more times in a day? Bad groan, not sex groan. Damn it! The heaviness in my belly turns to butterflies when Nick hands me my jacket and his fingers brush mine. He's too close. I can't breathe.

What did he ask? Oh, yeah, what next? "I don't know."

He looks puzzled for a moment. "Don't know what?"

Is the air getting thicker or is it just me? Is the room getting darker? What is wrong with me? I need oxygen. "I don't know."

He's standing so close. There's not a lot of space in here. My back is to the door and he can't leave if I don't leave. It's tight. I don't want to leave.

He steps closer and I'm frozen to the spot. His eyes are bottomless and his tongue flicks out and wets his lips. "Don't know what?" he says again.

I don't manage another word. He reaches out a hand, hooks it around my waist, pulls me close until I'm flush against his chest. My breasts squish and I drop my jacket and maybe my handbag. I don't know anymore.

When his mouth touches mine, I'm lost. It's like he's been waiting all day to do this. His lips are firm as he sucks my tongue into his mouth and explores with his own. His hands are on my back, my shoulders, my ass as I'm pulled in closer than I thought was humanly possible. When he nibbles on my lower lip I want to wrap my legs around him and ease the ache pounding in my lower extremities.

As Nick trails wet kisses down my jaw, my cheek, my collarbone, his hands gentle and I miss the pressure instantly.

"I'm sorry, I'm a little rough," he whispers against my overheated skin. "I'll be gentle."

It's in this one moment in time that I can call a stop to this. I wanted it so bad, but with Nick? Didn't it complicate things?

Complicate what? my subconscious roars in my head. Nick and I don't have a thing. I'm not even his type. I should be worried about that but I'm not. It's just sex. This is what I want. No strings. No second-guessing. Just mind-blowing sex.

His fingers trail against the hem of my skirt and I know what I want.

I step back in the small space and almost laugh at the look on his face. He's confused. Not angry. Not likely to push me. I like that even more. Despite what he thinks of himself, he's a gentleman at heart.

His arms fall to his sides and lifts one hand to rake it over his face. "I'm so sorry, Imelda. I shouldn't have done that."

"Oh no you don't," I tell him with what I hope is a warning in my tone.

His confusion triples but he's watching what I'm doing with my hands. He watches me lift my skirt, hook my thumbs in my thong and slip the scrap of fabric down to my knees where it falls to the floor around my heels. I've never done anything like this ever. My heart is beating so hard I think I might pass out before I can get Nick's hands back on my body.

"It's too late for apologies, Nick." I step back into his personal space and rise up on my tippy-toes so my face is almost level with his chin. "No going back now."

19

A different groan meets my ears and for once it's not a noise I've made. Why isn't he touching me? I've just left my panties in a puddle on his office floor and he's standing there like I'm riddled with the plague. Or chlamydia. I've done something wrong. My body is hot and then cold and then hot again and I wonder how I can run out of the building without having to reach down for my underwear, handbag, coat, dignity.

I'm sinking back onto my feet ready to actually die from humiliation when his strong arms lift me right off the floor. His mouth mashes harshly onto mine and I don't care. The kiss is dirty and hot and hungry and I match him in urgency. My legs wrap around his waist and he's holding me up while we kiss like two starving lunatics. In a move reserved only for porn and midday movies, he uses one arm to swipe the contents of his desk anywhere but the dark surface and then sits me on the edge, his thigh between my legs and my one good hand tangled in his hair.

"Last chance to say no, Imelda. Tell me I'm not the guy."

Fucking hell. He's kissing me everywhere. All of my exposed skin. A few buttons of my shirt have come undone and I don't know if it was him or me and then he's burying his face in my cleavage while he squeezes my breasts in his palms.

I feel like I have to do something so I undo a few more buttons and then reach around and unclasp my bra. I want his mouth on my nipples. I want his mouth everywhere. He doesn't need instruction and I clearly don't need air either. I try to inhale and shrug out of my shirt and bra at the same time and that only serves to push my chest right into his face. He doesn't seem to mind as he licks and laves and nibbles. The cool air hits my skin and I know I have goosebumps all over.

Nick has the look of a hungry wolf as he comes back to my mouth. More items fall from the desk onto the carpet. He grins and then pushes me so I'm lying back. I think there's a stapler under my left shoulder so I lift a hand to get rid of it and he takes advantage all over again. His calloused palms make their way from my shoulders, down over my breasts, my ribs, my stomach, my thighs. This time I groan. The need to pull my feet up to the edge of the desk and show him how wet I am overcomes me but that's too much for me. I know it would be. That is not the Imelda I know. But then again, neither is this vixen with her boobs out, lying on a desk half-naked while Nick is still in control and fully dressed. I'm losing my mind and he's staring at me like I'm his next meal.

He's thinking something. It's there in the gleam in his baby-blues as he surveys me. If we were roleplaying, I'd say he's the king and I'm the concubine.

"Nick?" I say hesitantly into the gap between us. I'm so unsure and I don't want to be but rejection right now is going to break me.

"Just give me a sec. I'm...taking a mental picture." His grin is beyond cheeky when he flashes it at me, his head tilting to the side. His lips are pink, and his hair is mussed.

My reflexes are shot and my brain is slow so when he flicks my skirt up and drops to his knees between mine, I've only got enough time to lift my head before he licks me. Right there. His hot palms press against my inner thighs and I obey by opening my legs a little wider. I'll do anything he wants me to if only he does that again.

"So wet," I hear, muffled, his voice vibrating through me.

My breath is coming in short pants and I stop fighting the urge to lift my ankles. I need more. I brace my feet against Nick's shoulders and his chuckle does even more exquisite things to my insides. One of his hands is on my butt and the other... "Oooh," now a moan turns into a little squeal when his finger slides in all the way to the knuckle.

There's pressure everywhere and my skin is heated and I'm not getting enough oxygen. I try to breathe deeper, longer, but he's pressing everywhere with teeth and tongue and mouth and fingers. I want to push him away but instead I thread my fingers into his hair and urge him on. I'm grinding against his face because I'm so close, so torturously close to... something. It?

And then he's gone and so is the sweet torture.

"No, don't stop," I plead, my thighs falling to the desk, my feet swinging. He laughs like I'm joking. I'm really not. I feel violent. Violently in need.

Nick stands up but doesn't move away. He pulls his wallet from his pocket and says, "You're going to give me a brain injury with that cast if I stay down there."

Jesus, I forgot about the cast. Did I thump him? "What if I promise to be more careful?"

Another chuckle. A zip releasing. His cock in his hand as he pushes his jeans down just far enough to be out of the way. "Next time. If I'm not inside of you soon, I'm going to lose my mind." He rolls a condom on and I'm suddenly, finally, scared. The oral was great and I think I was close to the big O but what if this doesn't work?

"Relax, Imelda."

I try to. I really do. Nick pulls on my thighs until I'm a little closer. He leans down and kisses me again. I can taste myself on his tongue and soon the kiss is hungry and dirty again. I like these ones. These kisses that feel like a drug. They're naughty but so incredibly hot.

He's nudging between my legs and I lift my thighs to his hips as he guides his cock into me, sliding home better than I thought he would fit. He lifts my arms, one hand to his shoulder and my cast over the other shoulder to rest against his back. "Try not to hit me with that," he says between nibbles on my bottom lip and jaw.

I'm sort of sitting up now and as Nick withdraws slowly, a hiss squeezes between his teeth. It's not the same feeling as when I was lying down with his mouth on me but I like it, this feeling of being filled. The desk is hard under my butt but Nick thinks of that and works me so he's taking the weight of me into his palms and protecting me from the biting surface. He's done this before, I think.

Or he's holding on so he can slam back into me, which he does, and moves the whole desk with a shuddering slide across the carpet. Each time he slides out and then back in, he hits this spot. It's on the inside and on the outside and it's nice. I didn't know I had this spot.

My hands explore beneath his t-shirt and I want to taste his skin but I have to settle for his neck, his stubbled jaw, his earlobe. That hits Nick's button. His movements become firmer and rougher and furious and those feelings build back inside of me until once again, I lose my breath, and collapse back onto my elbows on the desk.

"Stay with me," he urges, relentless in his rhythm.

There it is again, that anxious feeling like something is going to happen. I'm hot and hotter and burning, my muscles tense until I'm squeezing my knees hard enough to bruise his hips, surely. I'm making animal noises but so is he. I close my eyes and attempt to let go but I can't. I don't mean to hold back but there's something in me that just does. But then he does something different. Nick reaches between us and presses down on my clit with one single finger pad. I know there's lips and mouths and dicks and hands but it's that one single finger that is my undoing.

I come like a wild thing and my insides contract and pulse without direction as I hit the moon and stars like I'm being thrown around inside a pinball machine. Nick jerks once, twice, grunts and groans, jerks again, and then he collapses against me, peppering little kisses against the bare skin of my shoulder, his own breath hot and harsh as we drift down together.

There's only one thought left in my brain. My lips curve into a smile and I don't know if I want to sob or laugh.

I did it.

I'm not broken.

· ❤ · ❤ · ❤ · ❤ · ❤ ·

I've done something, Freddy, and it's not very smart. Hell, it's not smart at all. But it was totally worth it. ~~To see Imelda. I mean, to give Imelda.~~

Shit.

What did he mean? There's no way he could tell the judge about this. He couldn't write it down in this diary that would definitely be read by another person. Although... He scratched his chin with the end of the pen. Could he use this to show the judge that he wasn't the big, bad wolf others thought he was? He wasn't going to outright lie but if it looked as though a woman could be capable of being in a relationship with him, would that soften him in the eyes of old Judge Battle-axe?

Dear Freddy. I've been so worried about Imelda being hurt by someone or messing up my bar with her drama that I didn't really see her. She'd beautiful. She's smart and funny and so ~~innocently naïve~~.

That didn't actually sound good. He crossed out innocently and naïve.

She's smart and funny and so great.

And yet he was beyond lame. Nick scrubbed his face hard with the heels of his hand. He shouldn't have gone there with her. This was going to bite him in the butt in some way. He'd searched and searched but he couldn't find one ounce of regret. Imelda got her sex and he'd been able to give it to her. Safe. Scorching. Office sex. He'd never done that before. He'd had offers but that was his work place. He did not have sex with women in his office because they'd come back and they'd hang around and he didn't need or want that.

Except, he kind of hoped Imelda would be back. He'd helped her get dressed and then driven her the few blocks to her apartment where she'd just got out of the car, shut the door and disappeared into her building. She didn't invite him in. She didn't say 'thanks for the good time'. If she hadn't had that silly smile still on her kissable lips, he'd have thought she was having second thoughts about what they'd done. Maybe he should have followed her? But he was parked in a tow zone and it was late and he was exhausted. Weirdly exhausted. Like he'd been wound up and didn't even know it.

He signed off and tucked the diary back under the pillow on his bed. He might live alone but there was no way he wanted to leave this thing out in the open for anyone else to find. What he wrote in the diary was between him and the judge.

Now that he'd discovered someone like Imelda, he had to hope the diary would get him out of the hot water and into a normal life. If there was any such thing.

20

Four hours. Four pretty good hours spent with a smile on my dial. That's how long I'm at work for before Mr. Rodney, the hotel manager, stops by my office wearing a different kind of frown than usual. Midday was a crappy time of the day. Too late for a snack, too early for lunch but close enough that you had to keep an eye on the clock so as not to lose a minute of your upcoming, well-deserved hour of peace.

I had been happily daydreaming about orgasms and imagining what Nick would look like fully naked. Not that I was going there again. He's great, don't get me wrong, but we're so different. And anyway, I had to remember that I wasn't looking for Mr. Right. I was only looking for Mr. Right Now, for now. And I'd achieved my goal. I'd proven to myself that I wasn't broken. I was done.

"Denni called me yesterday," George says, as he settles his considerable bulk onto the inconsiderable chair opposite my desk.

"Oh?" A cold sweat settles between my shoulder blades. "Is he feeling better?"

"Did you know he is my nephew?"

I shake my head and mentally let out a string of classic, crude curse words. "No I did not." It did speak billions though. No wonder he's never been fired for his cloakroom antics.

"He told me about what happened."

"Did he?" I'm careful with my response. I'd seen this happen before. My father had been the best at the *is-there-something-you-want-to-tell-me* game. He'd sit me down and softly say, "is there something you want to tell me, Imelda?" He never had to follow it up with, "because I already know something and you're going to pay worse if you lie". We'd always spill our guts. Every. Single. Time. But George wasn't my father and he wasn't my mother and I was good at this game too.

"He confessed everything."

"Did he?" I don't break eye contact. If it's George's intent to make me sweat, he's doing a shit job.

"What he did was inexcusable."

"What he did was probably against the law." I expect my heart to start up its death march against my ribs, which is my body's natural response to anxiety and being put on the spot by my supervisor, but I'm calm. Why am I calm?

"Are you thinking about going to the police with Denni's role in this?" George asks. I watch a bead of moisture slide down his ruddy complexion to drip off his chin and onto his navy sweater.

I don't need to take any more action than I already have with the chlamydia claim so I shake my head. "No, George, I'm not going to tell anyone about this and Denni shouldn't either."

George nods. "So it's forgotten then?"

I narrow my eyes and hold up my bright green cast. "Could you forget about it if you looked like this? Denni did this to me and he should at least come here and see it. Apologize for it."

"Will that help?"

I want to utter the famous *for fuck's sake* but I don't. I don't say anything.

"He is really sorry."

I inhale. Then I exhale. "So he should be," I say, fidgeting with the stapler on my desk.

"He had no idea Ted could be like that. They've been friends since primary school."

"Well, maybe Denni needs to rethink the company he keeps."

"Ted made a mistake. He got a little drunk and acted out. What guy hasn't?"

"Sir, do you have any daughters?"

"Three," he replies warily. He has to know where I'm going to go with this.

"Would you want one of your daughters to come home from a night out with this," I clunk my arm on the desk between us, "on their hand? Would you then like to hear the tale of how she broke her hand on some guy's face because he wouldn't take no for an answer?"

George's face goes this shade of red we're all very familiar with here at the hotel. His eyes bug and his fingers twist together nervously. I don't know how he got his job here but he isn't very good at it. He lacks the confidence and the sternness to lead.

"I didn't think so," I mutter.

George doesn't get up and leave like I'm willing him to with my Jedi mind tricks. He obviously still has a point to make but he's taking his bloody time getting to it.

So, I wait.

And wait.

And wait.

Until finally he speaks. "I don't know where to go from here, Imelda."

That snags my attention. "What do you mean where to go?"

"You may very well be brought up on assault charges-"

"I beg your pardon?"

"The police have been in contact with Ted and when he told them you hit him, well, they weren't happy about a citizen taking the law into her own hands."

"A citizen who was defending herself. Do you know if he'd waited to attack me until after we left the bar, maybe we get all the way to my apartment, I could have shot him and been in less trouble, so don't give me any of that assault crap. Ted was totally at fault and I have dozens of witnesses."

"That may be," George nods. "But the fact of the matter remains that there will be an investigation and you are obviously still very upset about it."

"George." My tone is one of danger and warning. I am not getting fired for this. If I leave this office, it's of my own accord. Because I've made the decision that I'm bored out of my mind and want to find something new to do. New people to be annoyed by. None of this was my fault. *Except...* It was my idea to hang out at the bar. It was my idea to take advice from Denni. If I'd stayed in my lane, in my pathetically sane and stable life, none of this would be happening right now.

"The board have decided to give you the week off. Maybe two depending on how long this all takes."

"You can't be serious!" Mortification washes over me. "And what did you tell the board?"

"I told them you and Denni are having a personality clash and that you both need to take some time out. He had the best of intentions, Imelda."

"My ass he did!" I shoot to my feet and plant both hands on my desk with a thump and thud. "This is completely unfair. How do I appeal?" *Time out*? Like a fucking recalcitrant child? I'm so angry.

"It isn't a tribunal,' George says. "There is no appeal. You will tell your co-workers that you have decided to take some vacation time. It isn't as if you don't have any."

"Do I have a say in this at all?" I have loads of vacation hours owing but that's not the point.

"Only if you go quietly and then come back when the dust settles. Make a fuss and maybe you don't come back at all."

I turn my back on the man condemning me for something I hadn't planned or provoked and swear under my breath. "Unfuck-ingbelievable." I don't usually swear a lot out loud but I'm furious. Denni had started a chain reaction of unwanted events that might ruin my life. I should have done more than spread a rumor. I should have punched him too.

"Imelda?" George's voice comes from somewhere behind me, hesitant, unsure, unsteady.

"What if I tell everyone what Denni did? Make it public?" We both know I won't. Doormats don't bite back. They just sit there being functional and quiet and low maintenance while stronger people walk all over them.

"That's your choice but it's a slippery slope. Denni knows things about you now that he could tell too. Don't make this into anything more than it already is."

I sigh. Pick up my handbag. "I'll go quietly."

I pack up my things, my coffee cup, my favorite pen I bought with my own money, the scarf I keep over the back of my chair for cold days when the air-conditioning is turned too low. It's not like I'm packing to leave for good but if this gets worse than it already is, I want to be able to tell George to stick his job and not have to come back for anything.

I'd always loved this job. I worked so hard to be the best I can be, to show the men in the hotel industry that I'm just as good, if not better, than they are, and this is how it turns out?

If I'd stayed in my lane, this wouldn't be happening.

If my friends had kept their opinions to themselves, this wouldn't be happening.

As I emerge into the sunshine of another cool but clear day, I can't even be all that sorry. I'm getting a week or two off, fully paid, and I had sex. AND I had an orgasm! I'm not even worried about what the future holds since I've proven something to myself.

I stand a little taller.

I'm different today.

I've been feeling it since I woke up with a huge, stupid smile on my face.

The huge, stupid smile is still there as I make my way home in the middle of a workday. If I can do this, I can do anything I set my mind to.

I stop for a newspaper and more ice cream on my way back to my apartment. My usual route would take me right past *Johnnie's* but just the thought makes my tummy somersault so I take the long way. The coward's way. My hands are full with my office stuff and two shopping bags but I drop everything when I check my mail and notice a small box wrapped in brown paper with my name on it. If I was waiting on a check for a million dollars it would take two weeks but order a sex toy online and it only takes forty-eight hours. My hands are sweaty as I put the box and a few letters into the bag with the ice cream and then let myself into my apartment. I put away the perishables and leave my new purchase on the bench. I make myself a cup of tea but my thoughts keep coming back to my impulse buy. Really, I didn't even need it now. I'd achieved the big O. There was the tiniest part of me that wondered if it was a fluke? Maybe Nick was just a little bit magic and it was all down to him? Maybe I'd never have another orgasm with another man ever again and he'd ruined me and I'd only ever think of him even if I was in bed with the love of my life? *Fuck.*

As I drink my tea, I stare at the little package. I try to distract myself with stuff to do over the next week or two. I could shop. Go away for a few days? See the countryside? Go to Hawaii? A massage and spa day sound amazing. My last mouthful of cold tea is unpleasant. As is the heavy feeling low in my belly. It's back. How can I be turned on? I'm only trying not to think about orgasms. But not thinking about sex is exactly like thinking about sex. Once the thought gets in, there must be only one way to get it out. Previously I'd just starved the feelings of any love and poof, gone. Then I'd purposely made myself too busy to think about sex. No sexy books, no risqué movies and no questionable Google searches. It's like my inner libido had just dried up like those vampires on the television who didn't get any blood to drink.

Terrible analogy, but apt in this case, although it did tell me I've watched too much Netflix lately.

The little package isn't going away and neither is my curiosity over it. How does it work? Does it work at all? And because it's not creepy enough having cats who aren't even technically mine, Harry jumps on the kitchen counter and bumps the package with his head. He's purring and pushing the box closer and closer to me. It'll fall off if I don't do something with it. The laws of cats and gravity and cats pushing things off benches captures my attention for all of thirty seconds.

I snatch it from the cat and make a decision. I'll run a bath and see what happens. I bust the box open on the dining room table and then take the little gadget into the bathroom. If I feel like giving it a whirl, I will. If I don't, I won't. I'll just tuck it into the back of my underwear drawer and forget all about it...

21

I have quite a clinical brain. I'm a realist and if I can't touch it, taste it, smell it or see it, I'm not likely to believe it. A few times over my teen years and my early twenties, I tried my hand at masturbating (pun intended). *God, I hate that word.* I hated trying to pleasure myself even more. It never worked. I'd never get the right angle or be in the right mood. I even tried it drunk once and just wound up hurting myself when my finger slipped and I gave myself a fingernail slice to my own clit.

So, I gave up.

It's one of those things I put in the box labeled, 'can't and don't want to do it', in big red letters.

Seems the sex toy might go in the same box type of box. It said waterproof so I tried it under the water. I can't find the right spot with my non-dominant hand, and the water is too hot. I get out of the bath all sweaty and feeling less clean than when I got it. And it's hard to dry yourself with only one good hand. The only place to sit or get comfortable is the toilet seat and that's kind of yuck. I feel so stupid even trying it on my own. Masturbating just isn't something that particularly appeals to me, and my history with it isn't great. That kind of trauma lingers a long time and I can't shake it off. I also can't handle looking down at myself like that in a sitting position.

I'm in the kitchen making yet another cup of tea (can you tell I have a tea-when-I'm-bored problem?) and I'm wrapped in my fluffiest dressing gown, with kittens on it if you can believe that, when there's a knock at my door.

I'm naked under the fleece but it's probably just one of my neighbors come to complain about one of the cats who isn't even mine. I think Harry likes to pee in the corridor but no one can prove it. I'll apologize, tell them I'm sick, cough a little and send them away.

I swing the door wide to launch into another "I'm sorry, Mrs. Russel but there's nothing I can do. Harry is kind of-"

It's not one of my neighbors. The word, *asshat*, dies on my lips.

It's Nick. And he looks great. Worn jeans, t-shirt. The kind that hugs in all the right places. He's not smiling. He looks concerned. This cannot be about Harry the cat.

I open my mouth and then close it again. What do I say? Thanks for the orgasm? "If you've come to apologize or use any words that sound like mistake, I'm going to slam the door in your face."

Now he grins. "I came to check on you. I called you at work but they said you'd gone home sick and wouldn't be in again this week." His grin disappears as does the dimple on his chin. "I was worried I'd hurt you."

"What do you mean by hurt?"

He looks up and down the hall. "Can I come in?"

I'm naked. "Sure."

"Are you sure you're okay?" he asks.

I'm naked. "Of course I am. Why wouldn't I be?"

His cheeks get really pink and I'm stuck just staring at him, waiting for whatever it is he's about to admit to. I don't have to wait long.

He breaks eye contact and scuffs the toe of his shoe against the floor. "I can get kind of rough. Not on purpose. Just that I don't know my own strength sometimes and then I get carried away..."

Intriguing. "Do you?" I clear my throat with an *ahem* sound to try to disguise the fact that my lady bits wake up at the carried away part and my mouth dries in an instant. "Well, I'm fine. You don't have to worry about me."

It's disconcerting when his gaze comes back to mine and then he looks me up and down. "Why are you home sick then?"

I attempt to summon fury. It doesn't work. I'm just hot and bothered now. The robe. It must be. I just need to put some cooler clothes on. I need to put clothes on. "My boss sent me home. He found out about Denni and Ted and decided it would be best if we both took some time off."

"What a dickhead," Nick mutters.

"You're telling me," I say back. "Nick, why were you calling me at work?" *Again.* I know I didn't leave anything behind this time. I'd even made sure to collect my panties from the carpet.

"I just wanted to make sure you were okay today. Things happened kind of fast and then you didn't really say anything. You just ran off."

"I didn't run!"

"You didn't say goodbye either."

"I was processing." *I still am.*

"Did I overstep? Go too far? I've never had sex in my office before."

The admission was strange. The thrill that stole through me was weird. "Oh?" It's all I can manage. My cheeks must be fire-engine red by now. If I'm going to examine what happened last night, I'll do it alone. Not standing here like this with Nick.

"Imelda?"

"Yeah?"

"Can you say something? Anything. If I don't know how you feel about what happened, how am I supposed to know what to say?"

I know he's not looking for an ego stroke. He actually looks uncomfortable. Unsure. I smile to try to let him know I'm fine. Really, really fine. But I'm not fine. I'm so hot and bothered and hot. I try clenching my thighs together but that does nothing. I need to be sitting.

"Why don't you sit down and I'll make you a cup of tea?" Bad idea but I have nothing else to offer except for gross instant coffee. We probably do need to talk about it. Even if just to say thanks for the big 'O', see ya round!

Nicks nods and I run the three steps to the kitchen. I make the tea but what I really want is to put clothes on, only if I tell him I need to put clothes on, he'll know I've got none on. I nearly give into the urge to slap myself. I should have said thanks for coming, now get out.

His voice floats to me from the next room. "I deleted the tape too, just in case you were worried about it."

My hands stop mid-tea and I think my heart stops too. My chest feels like an elephant has stepped on it. "What?"

"The surveillance camera in my office. I wiped the tape first thing this morning."

Why am I so bad at this? Nick is showing genuine concern and taking care of the business I haven't even considered and I'm being an idiot, worrying about everything and anything and everything but apparently not the stuff I should be worrying about.

I force a laugh and say, "I bet you watched it first," as I round the partition from the Kitchen but he's not on the couch. He's at the dining table. With a box in his hands. He's staring down at it, ignoring the cat twining around his ankles.

"Ummm." I nearly drop the tea. I set it down on the table instead. My hands shake and I think my insides are going to explode and leave a hell of a mess. "I can explain."

Nick stammers a little but then he looks up at me. "New purchase?"

He's angry? I don't get it. I've missed something vital. "It was an impulse purchase a few days ago. It just got here." By way of explanation, it's pretty crappy.

"Did you fake it last night?"

"Fake what?"

His eyes are cloudy and grey and he's so pissed off. "Did you or did you not fake an orgasm last night? Because if you faked it to make me feel good about myself, you could have just said you weren't there yet."

"I didn't fake anything. I orgasmed." I'm so quick to rush in with details that I add, "It was my first one and it definitely happened. I think." His eyes flash murder and I add more. I can't seem to shut up and even raise my hands in a defensive gesture. "Only because I've not really got anything to compare it to but something different than the normal stuff very definitely happened. I think."

"What the fuck are you talking about? First orgasm? That's not possible." Something dawns on him and he does a complete one-eighty from furious. "Oh, my God, tell me I'm not your first, ever?"

"I wasn't a virgin! I just had never...got...there. You know..."

"Never?"

I shake my head and feel like sinking right through the floor. "Never ever."

"Is this why you were so set on finding a guy? So you could have an orgasm?"

"Sort of. I honestly thought I was maybe broken."

Nick snorts. "The men you dated were the broken ones if they never satisfied you."

I try to reach for the box still in his hands at the word, *satisfied*. The Pro after it written in big, gold letters brings me back to the fact that Nick is holding the box that my sex toy arrived in.

He snatches his hand back and now the box is over his shoulder and I'm losing my balance, teetering in front of him. "Not so fast. Where's the vibrator? If you orgasmed last night, why are you playing with this today?"

I plant my feet and cross my arms over my chest. "That is none of your business."

"It is my business. I'm making it my business, Imelda." His other hand reaches out and snags the belt of my fluffy robe. He pulls gently and I step forward.

"What are you doing?"

"Well, now I'm wondering what you were doing before I came in. Were you using this?" He puts the box on the table next to the cup of tea he's probably not going to drink. He unties my robe and I just let him. I have no mind of my own when there's the potential for Nick's hands, or mouth, to be on my body.

Fresh air brushes my skin and the intake of his breath takes it away again. "Did you come before I got here or were you waiting?"

"Waiting for what?" My voice is so breathless and I'm a little lightheaded with the anticipation that this could be round two. I'm only slightly distracted with the fact I'll find out if last night was a fluke.

"Waiting for an extra set of hands maybe?" His fingers are cool as he spans my waist and then my hips and then my bare backside. He then drifts up to my ribs where he skirts the edges of my breasts with his thumbs. When he blows gently on each nipple, I want to take his head in my grip and keep him right there, encourage him to take it further. To take me further.

"So," he continues, "is this what you've been about all along?"

I can't think and I don't want to talk. I just want to *do*.

He keeps talking. "You said 'sort of' when I asked you. Is there more? Another reason you were so keen on a one night stand?"

I manage one pesky little word. "Why?"

My left nipple disappears into Nick's mouth and my hips buck of their own accord as electricity sets my blood on fire. He transfers his attention to the right and then bloody talks again. I want to tell him to shut up. "If we do this," he punctuates his words with a single, delicious finger sliding between my legs. "It's not just one night and it's not just one orgasm."

"Mmhmm," I mumble incoherently as my head falls back and my heels slide apart on the carpet.

He gets the hint and adds a second finger. I could get addicted to the feeling of being stretched from the inside out by him. A light

nip to the skin over my ribs makes me all at once ticklish and even
more turned on. If that's possible. I'm holding onto his shoulders
and resting my shin against his thigh as he works me into a frenzy of
need. I'm careful of my cast this time but I'm nearly at the stage of
begging and I want him inside me so bad I think about asking but
the words don't want to come so I tilt his chin up andd kiss him. I'm
fully naked and doing unmentionable things in the middle of the
day with a bad boy and yet I can't ask what I want. Can't demand
what I need.

My shyness is something that will never truly go away and it holds
me back in so many avenues of my life already. What's the worst that
can happen if I ask for what I want? Nick says no, he leaves and I'm
left in this state but at least I won't have to see him again if I don't
want to. If I die from mortification, it won't matter anyway. I'll be
dead.

"You're thinking," he comments, slowing his movements and
looking up at me. "Either I'm not trying hard enough or you're
having second thoughts? We don't have to do anything you don't
want to do."

"That's the problem," I huff with frustration. "I do want to do it,
I just don't know what *it* is."

"Just say the words. Do you want to me to keep doing this?" he
bites down on my nipple and I cry out in pleasure and just a little bit
of exquisite pain. "Or this?" he's rough as he fingers me quick and
hard.

The room is spinning and I'm desperate to hold on. To hold on
to my sanity and Nick and my dignity.

"Maybe you just want to be fucked again? Like last night?"

I whimper and I don't even care anymore. I like the dirty talk. I like everything about this exact moment in time. I don't feel shame or embarrassment, just pleasure and need and a fierce longing to sit straight down on his cock and ride it until oblivion takes over.

I reach down while kissing him hard on his stubbled mouth and unbutton and then unzip those well-worn jeans of his. When I fold down his jocks and take him in my hand, he wraps a fist in my hair and deepens the kiss, his fingers inside me never skip their rhythmic beat.

He's harder than I thought possible and the tip of his dick is already wet. I want to taste him but I'm too far gone to cool it down, to drop to my knees and give him the satisfaction I right now need more than my next ragged breath. I push his hand away and sink onto his lap, my wet heat gliding easily over his.

"Condom," he rasps, his mouth so close to my ear, one fist still in my hair.

"Pill," I say back, sliding up and down his length, enjoying the moment to just feel, enjoying the moment to be in control even though I know it won't last. I don't actually know what to do next, only that I really like this position.

As I find a speed my body likes, he yanks on my hair even harder and sucks my exposed neck, my earlobe, my shoulder. He loosens his grip and pushes the robe off my shoulders until it's in a heap on the floor. I'm completely, totally exposed now. My front door is unlocked. My cats are somewhere in the apartment and my retired neighbor is probably adjusting the volume on her TV set to drown out the noises I'm making.

"Where's your sex toy?" Nicks asks.

"Bathroom," I reply.

"We need it," he says.

"No, we don't. I need you to sit still and be quiet," I tell him.

Nick chuckles but then I'm lifted, his hands on my backside, his cock still inside me. I squeal and my insides clench around him. He swears and tips his head forward against mine. "If you do that again, this will be over too soon."

I test him. My pelvic floor is better than I knew. He swears again. Then he's shuffling into the bathroom. He spots the satisfier pro. "Pick it up," he tells me.

He bends at the waist, still holding me like I weigh nothing at all. I grab the toy.

When Nick reaches my bed, we go down on the comforter together but he doesn't come all the way down like I expect him to. I'm lying on my back and he's over me but not crushing me like I want him to. He's staring at me though and I don't want to slow down. I want to speed up. I clench again and he slides out only to come back harder, with a slap of pelvis against pelvis. "Don't start something you can't finish," he tells me.

A smile stretches my lips. "Why can't I finish it?"

"You didn't come before I got here, did you? With this?" He takes the toy from me and presses the button until the sound of the buzzing is loud between us. He lays the rubber head of the toy against the back of his other hand and mutters something I don't hear.

I shake my head back and forth across the mattress.

"Why not?"

"It wouldn't work."

"Did you turn it up?"

"I was too scared."

"Of what?"

"Stop asking questions and get on with it!"

Nick grins and rocks a steady pace almost instantly. "Are you still scared?"

"No, God, please stop talking."

"And we're doing this? As in more than once or twice?"

"Yes, yes, I don't care, whatever you want. Just keep going. God, harder, harder."

The unmistakable crinkle of plastic and foil meets my ears and he pulls out long enough to roll a condom on but then he's back and he's relentless and my breath is long gone and stars and spots are swimming in my vision.

"Let go, Imelda," he grunts between grunts.

"I'm trying," I wail and the buildup is there, it's in me as surely as he is, but I can't seem to tip over the edge. I screw my eyes shut and grab handfuls of the blanket so I don't hurt Nick with my cast if I throw my arms up.

A strange object is placed against me, down there, and I can feel the buzz against my pubic hair but it does exactly nothing like it did before. Until it gets a suction. And I'm off like a rocket.

I think I scream. It happens so suddenly and I'm not ready. I thrash and my hands go to his chest, his arms, his shoulders. I'm pushing and pulling and my body is literally pulsing and jerking and I'm making feral animal noises but I'm not the only one. Nick's thrusts are wild too and he's making the bed slam up against the wall. His roar bounces off the walls and can probably be heard on the street as we both come and come and come.

When he collapses on top of me, I realize he still has all of his clothes on, his jeans around his knees.

I don't care about that either.

All of my thoughts and doubts and confusions float away and it's just him and me.

I like it. I like this.

· ♥ · ♥ · ♥ · ♥ · ♥ ·

Dear Freddy,

I like her. I really, really like her. She's funny and smart and adorable and sex on a stick. I like that she's not scared of me and I don't have to be scared of physically hurting her. I like the way her hair smells like coconut and her skin is smooth and she has real curves and a real laugh and she's amazing.

I thought I had to protect Imelda but she's strong. She might not know what she wants but she sure knows what she doesn't want.

I thought I was in trouble but this could be fun. A lot of fun.

22

"Do you have to get to the bar?" I ask Nick, my legs folded over his as we lie on the bed and get our breaths back. It must be about four in the afternoon and *Johnnie's* opens at five. I'm still naked as the day I was born and his junk is out of his jeans, his t-shirt pushed up his stomach a little. I should cover up but he's seen it all now. No sense in playing the prude when I'm numb and tingly and boneless.

"Yeah but give me a minute. I don't think I can move."

I roll onto my side and take the hem of his shirt in my fingers, lifting the fabric as high as it will go and kissing his chest, his ribs, his abdomen. "How many tattoos do you have?"

"That depends."

"On what?"

"On if you count them as individual pieces of art, I have a few, but they're all connected now so it makes just the one."

"Did it hurt?"

"A little."

"Does it have significance?"

"A little."

I want to ask another question, get to know him, lick his abs, but a knock on the door brings me back to the fact I've just had day sex. Broad daylight, no holds barred, sex in the day-time.

Nick begins to chuckle. "It's probably one of your neighbors making sure you weren't just murdered."

"Surely we weren't that loud?" I ask, heat flooding not only my cheeks but every part of me. The rumble of Nick's voice and laugh against my bare skin makes me want to roll right on to him and go again.

"*We* weren't, *you* were." From somewhere, I find the will to get to my feet, I leave the bedroom, scoop up my robe from the dining room floor and am just shrugging it on when the knocking comes again.

"I'm coming, keep your shirt on!" I almost giggle at the words I say every time one of my delightful neighbors knocks incessantly. Today, it takes on a new meaning!

"I told you Mrs.-" I really have to stop assuming every knock is Mrs. Russel from down the hall.

"Jess? What are you doing here?"

She looks me up and down and instead of blushing, I'm about to freak out. Really freak out. This thing between me and Nick is my secret. Sex in the day-time is my secret. I need a secret. I need Nick.

"You texted, I came right over as soon as I could."

"You didn't have to do that."

"I can't believe those idiots have fired you." She pushes past me. "Get dressed and we'll go and get ice cream."

"I didn't get fired," I rush to assure her. "I'm on sabbatical."

"Sure, that's what they say today, but what if it doesn't get resolved? What then?" Jess shoots me a stare over her shoulder that implies I haven't considered that already. Then she makes a beeline for my bedroom.

"Where are you going?" I call after her but I'm too far away to physically stop her. So I call, "Jess, stop!"

It's sharper than I intend. I just don't want her barging around my apartment like she owns it. I don't want her to find Nick either.

Too late. He steps out of my room and leans against the doorframe, hands in his front pockets, shirt snug, hair mussed. At least his jeans are zipped.

Jess is quiet for a second. Only one. "What. The. Fuck."

Another knock sounds at the door and it suddenly feels like a circus. I leave Jess and Nick to give each other the stink-eye and find Amy and Candice in the hall.

Amy says, "What's the 911? What happened?"

"Jess called a 911?" Of course she did. If we message 911 and the person's name, we're all supposed to drop everything and turn up.

Candice. "Yep, are you okay? What's going on?"

Jess doesn't just walk out into the living room, she stomps. "False alarm, girls. Mellow doesn't need us, seems she has him." A wild gesture including a thumb goes behind her.

Nick says, "No one has anyone. I just stopped by to make sure the patient is doing better."

"From her bedroom?" Jess shoots back.

Everyone is looking at me and I'm naked under my robe and there's too much happening in the small space. What should I say?

Nick saves me. Again. "I have to get to the bar. I'll see you later?"

His question throws me. Does he want me to meet him at the bar or is he coming over after? It doesn't matter, heat is already pooling in my middle and I wish my friends hadn't popped in to support me. I'm the worst.

He comes to stand in front of me and in my head I'm chanting, *don't kiss me, don't kiss me, don't kiss me*. But then he does. Gentle at first, and then I'm breathless and his tongue is in my mouth, his hands on my hips to keep me steady. Those hands! That kiss!

A throat clears. A cough. An *ahem*. He finally pulls away and I think of the spectacle I'm providing my well-meaning besties. They've never seen me like this.

Because you've never been like this.

My fingers rise to my tingling mouth. "Bye, Nick," I manage to utter.

He smiles. Like a wolf. "Bye," he says back. Then he saunters out of my apartment without a parting shot to anyone else. He bounces along like a man who just got laid during the day.

The explosion of voices is expected. But unwelcome. I'm a little pissy that they couldn't rock up when I needed them but now, here they stand, ruining a perfectly lazy afternoon.

I hold both hands in the air. "Before the Spanish inquisition gets started, I'm going to put some clothes on."

Candice laughs and adds, "You go girl!" and taps me on the butt like a football player when I pass her.

I hear Jess scold her with, "Don't encourage her."

To which Candice says, "Someone has to!"

Amy's voice filters out with, "Nick is kinda hot."

I close my bedroom door on them and sink down onto my just-used mattress with a silly smile playing on my well-kissed lips.

I'm not broken. Not broken at all. Not only can I get off, I've done it with a man who knows how to play. And I played back!

As I emerge from my sex-scented bedroom wearing comfortable leggings and an old, soft t-shirt, the mood is weird. My friends are acting weird. Candice is tapping the empty sex-toy box against the surface of the coffee table and Jess and Amy are sitting in hostile positions, arms crossed over chests and frowns almost identical. I need to start throwing out my rubbish and not answering my door.

"Ok," I start with a sigh, coming to a stop in front of them, my hand on my hips and an exaggerated eye roll for good measure. "Let me have it."

Jess begins. "Are you being pressured in any way? By Nick, or anyone else?"

Amy follows very quickly with, "We know you're a smart girl, Mellow, but love can make you so blind. It makes smart people do dumb things."

Candice doesn't seem to care what the others are saying. She holds up the box and says, "Does this work? I've read some pretty spectacular stories about it but is the hype worth the price tag?"

I snort a laugh and nod in her direction. "Totally worth every cent."

Jess. "Can we please be serious for one second?"

Me. "I am not being pressured into anything and Nick is not one of those dumb things dumb people do. I'm having fun! You guys told me to get out more. I did. I am."

Candice. "We didn't mean for you to jump into a relationship with the first guy to pour you drinks."

"Nick and I are not in a relationship." I want to add that he's more than the guy who pours my drinks but he isn't. Not really. I know next to nothing about him other than he owns *Johnnie's* and his sister has a sleazy ex. But if we're just sleeping together, I don't need to know more than that, do I?

Candice rolls her eyes. "He may as well have peed on your leg just now. That was an ownership kiss."

My voice is higher than I want it to be when I say, "It was not! He may have been a little territorial sure, but you all kind of came in on the end of something here. You caught us off guard."

"Us?" Amy says. "You're referring to you and Nick as us. That sounds like a relationship. And we didn't just catch you off guard, we nearly caught you having sex."

I know I don't have to explain myself to my friends but this behavior is out of character for me and I'm having trouble processing in my mind. Maybe if we bounce a few things around, it might help me? "Nick and I are starting to become friends. Sort of. Anyway, we're not in a relationship. The *us* is only that we were the only two here. I'm pretty sure we're just fucking." I say that last word with a really big smile on my face. Is it for shock value? Absolutely! Are they shocked? They sure are!

Candice rallies first but it's not the high-five I imagine. "Make sure that's what it is, Mellow. Just because he's a bad boy doesn't mean he won't want a commitment if you fuck more than a few times. If you're really clear from the get-go that it's just sex, no one gets hurt."

"So I should put a number on it? Or a time frame?" I sit and lean towards her, elbows on my knees and eager for the advice. "Is that how it works?"

"Jesus!" This blaspheme from Amy. "If you have to ask, you're going to get hurt. You're just not this kind of woman."

The silence descends and through teeth clenched against hurt I ask, "Just what kind of woman am I then? I think we've already established that I'm an all-around doormat who never has any fun, no meaningful connections, no god-damned orgasms or good times for the good little doormat. Am I just supposed to sit around waiting for something to happen to me?"

Jess. "Wait. What do you mean no god-damned orgasms?"

Oh dear. My cheeks are so hot. I feel about two feet tall. I'd left that part out hadn't I? "As in, if I don't have sex, there'll be no orgasms."

Candice reaches over and taps me in the head with the empty satisfier box. "That's what this is for!"

Amy is staring at me with one of those penetrating stares that you feel all the way deep down inside until it finds the truth. "Spill," she demands.

"Fine. Fine. I had never had an orgasm."

Three mouths fall open at this revelation.

Candice. "Never? As in never ever?"

Jess. "What?"

Amy. "That's impossible."

I throw myself back into the sofa. "Believe me when I say it is possible. You guys sat here and told me I was going to be eaten by my cats, alone, dead and alone. You talk about all the sex and all the orgasms and all the ways you do it. Nothing makes a girl realize what's lacking when everyone else is doing the doing."

"We honestly didn't mean to make you feel like shit, Mellow." Jess says it and the other faces echo the sentiment.

"I should probably thank you. All of you. I've been so stupid and should have told you what I was doing. I could have avoided *this*, I'm sure." I hold my cast in the air and there's a chuckle or two.

We talk for a little while, hostilities cease, we're back to four women sitting around talking about sex and stupid boys like Denni. They can't believe I'm paying a career price for his betrayal, they can't believe what I did to get back at him. I don't tell my friends about my relief of having the week off. I don't tell them how bored I am with my job, with the hotel, with my life. They'll think I'm having an early mid-life crisis. Maybe I am?

Candice and Amy offer to stay for dinner, Jess has a 'thing' she won't talk about. "Nothing important," she tells us all. We don't buy it but also don't push. There's enough tension here without another drama to add.

I hadn't realized how far we were all drifting apart until my life blew up. Sure, we have our cards nights but there's barely a phone call between us anymore. It's all Facebook status comments and messenger groups. We haven't watched a movie or gone out to lunch in forever. Or maybe they had and I was too busy at work?

Why did my life suddenly become kind of blurry? Like the last ten years or so were hazy and possibly misspent? Ugh, where did my post-sex bliss bubble go? I want it back.

After assuring my friends that I'm perfectly fine and don't need a babysitter, I'm once again alone in my apartment. Except for the cats. Maybe I'm not perfectly fine and maybe they should have stayed.

The silence suddenly feels different. Oppressive. Unfamiliar when it should be familiar. Uncomfortable when it's always been comfortable.

This is my apartment.

This is my life.

Only, now everything has changed and it's meant to be better, not...alien.

Harry curls himself around my ankles with a loud purr and Missy climbs onto my lap and starts kneading my thighs, her claws sharp. They're waiting for me to turn on the TV and get comfortable. To settle in for the night with a few movies and lots of cups of tea.

And I can't do it.

I have so much energy buzzing through my veins and I don't know what to do with it.

Shower first. Then something new. It's the week for it and I think embracing it might be the only answer.

23

Lucky I have flat shoes on because I've been walking aimlessly for two hours. I visit a park. Sit by a water fountain. Watch some birds as they fly from one group of tourists to another, crumbs being thrown like a cue to take flight.

Sure, it's relaxing, but I'm bored. I like having something to do. I enjoy being busy.

The other problem with boredom is it gives your brain time to really think and what the girls said earlier keeps circling in my brain. Make sure Nick knows this thing is temporary. Make sure we're both on the same page about it being a little bit of fun but no more.

Yes, Nick will make some girl happy one day but not me. He has too much baggage. He has a temper. He has muscles and strength and he's big and can get out of control. *Lose control*, he'd said. I liked it when he got a little rough. The memory of his fingers in my hair is an instant turn on, the strands all pulling at once while my body straddled the pleasure and pain lines.

I have to find something to do.

I notice a new movie premiering at the cinema, a chick-flick, so I buy a ticket and some popcorn and go in. It's okay but not the best. At least it's dark when I walk out which means I've successfully wasted an afternoon. Just one afternoon, out of fourteen.

I turn my phone back on and there's a message from Nick.

-Pop by for a visit if you're bored

Pop by? The distraction techniques aren't going to work while I'm thinking about Nick constantly and clearly he's thinking of me too. I think what the hell, one drink can't hurt.

When I get to *Johnnies*, it's in full swing. There's an extra TV and it seems everyone is wearing yellow and black. Sports game? I wouldn't know since I don't follow any teams. Or any sports for that matter.

Nick sees me before I see him and I'm still turning in circles taking in the atmosphere when I bump right into his chest.

"This place is nuts!" I yell over the crowd.

"Semi-finals kicked off today. Every mad sports fan and his dog is out."

So different from the day before when you could swing a cat and not hit anyone. I cringe. I hate that saying.

"I guess you'll be getting off late then?" That was not disappointment souring in my stomach. I ate too much buttery popcorn.

Nick cups his palm to his ear to say he can't hear me and then threads his fingers through mine and pulls me down the corridor and into his office.

"Who's watching the bar?" I ask, a little breathless, a little anxious, a little nervous.

"I put extra staff on for game nights. I can sneak away for a minute."

All the things we could do in one minute...

Nick is more grounded and can't be thinking of what happened when we were here last. "What did you say out there? I couldn't hear you?"

I struggle to calm my breathing and not flick glances at the desk behind Nick. "I was just saying I guess you'll be here most of the night?"

"Probably. Something wrong?"

"I just think we just need to talk about some stuff."

Instead of being worried, he looks intrigued, even though usually when a girl says we need to talk, it's code for bad. "Talk about what?"

I swallow past the lump in my throat and beyond the door I hear a cheer nearly raise the roof. "I, uh, just want to set some ground rules...for this." I wave vaguely in the space between our two bodies.

Nick catches my hand and gently pulls until I'm flush with his body. He leans back on the edge of the desk and then I'm in the space between his legs, my chest against his chest. "Ground rules, you reckon? Can't we just do what we do and see what happens?"

Do what we do sounds like fun but the girls were right. "I don't want you to get the wrong idea."

Nick just smiles and it's a bit patronizing. "And what idea would that be?"

A collective groan comes from the bar and I feel like the people out there are narrating the story in here. "What we're doing, what we've done, it's just sex, right?"

"I'm not thinking marriage if that's where you're going. Do you want a relationship, Imelda? Or do you want a good time? Or maybe you want both?"

I shake my head. I'm adamant about this. *I just don't really know why.* "Just a good time. Just sex."

"So let's set some ground rules then. Midnight booty calls?"

I nod. "Sure." I'm on vacation time, I can pull a few all-nighters. My inner tingles get heavier and burn a little. I have to concentrate on breathing in, breathing out, don't let him see how turned on I am, just being here, with him.

His hands drop low on my waist and then lower still to my butt, a cheek in each large, calloused hand. "Can I take advantage of the situation when we're alone?"

His erection pushes against me and I wriggle my hips against him. I'm actually going to combust. "Absolutely."

"Naked pics?" he asks.

"Never," I laugh.

"Are you going to sleep with other people, Imelda?" Teeth nip at my neck before my skin is sucked into his hot mouth and now I'm melting.

"No, no I don't think so. You?"

"I'll barely have time to keep up with you, I reckon."

Compliment or insult? I don't know. Once again, he's stealing reason. And my clothes. The button on my skinny jeans is released and my fly lowers painfully slow. Eight fingers dip into opposing sides of my waistband and push down, taking my panties all in one swipe.

"There's people out there, Nick."

"But they're not in here," he murmurs.

Before my jeans hit my knees, he turns us so my butt is against the edge of the desk and then turns me again so I'm facing away. My back is cold for a moment and then the lock on the door clicks into place.

"Is this a good idea?" I ask, all anxiety and anticipation rolled into one stomach flipping emotion. I loosen the grip I have on the desk with my good hand before I do damage to that one too.

"What is it you want from me, Imelda? Orgasms you like, I know that. Do you want danger? Games? Straight up sex?"

"I don't know." His hands are scraping up from my exposed hips, under my blousy shirt to cup my breasts through sheer lace. My nipples are pebbled and when he rolls them between forefinger and thumb, my head tilts forward and I bite my bottom lip to keep from making noise.

"They won't hear you," Nick tells me over my shoulder. He pushes my hair out of the way and kisses my collarbone. Then he pushes my jeans down a little further. "So what's it to be? Danger? Games? Sex?"

"I don't know," I repeat. Being in a semi-public place with my pants around my knees isn't normal and I can't think.

"I want you to tell me what you want. Find the words. Do you want to me to do this?"

A single finger slides along my butt until he reaches right down south but instead of penetrating me like I need, he slides back up, between my cheeks. I'm mortified. "Not that. Never that."

"Good, not much fun that way. Tell me."

"I want you to touch me."

"How. Be specific. We don't have time for coy."

I'm far from coy but is that how he sees me? Playing games? Playing hard to get? Is that how I come across? I don't mind really, because that means he hasn't figured out who the real me is. Once he does, he might run.

I decide to see where coy takes me. I reach behind and take his fingers in mine and guide him back south. I want him to play with me but the only way to do that is to bend over. So I do. Nick's sharp intake of breath makes me smile. I lift one leg the best I can with my jeans around my shins and rest the edge of my knee against the hard surface of the table. "Would this work?" I ask, poking my butt out a little as I put my casted arm down to steady myself on my elbow. I'm going to have a bruise there but it will be totally worth it.

Nick clears his throat. The muffled zipper sound reaches my ears followed by a crinkle of foil. He's well prepared with an endless supply of condoms. He tests me first with one finger, then with two. I must be wet because there's nothing stopping him.

He positions me and then slides all the way in. The desk doesn't move but I push back. Hard.

"Tell me exactly what you want."

"I want you to fuck me. Now, Nick. Hard."

"How hard?"

Is that excitement in his voice or is he as on-edge as me? I wish I could see him but it doesn't matter. "Just don't hurt me."

My jeans leg is turned inside out and snags on my ankle and shoe as he pulls it so I can lift my leg a little higher. He braces under the back of my knee, his palm flat on the desk, deepening the position, and then he's relentless. I can't move. I can't push back. I can only hold on as he fucks me from behind, never slipping, never losing pace, going harder than I thought was physically possible.

I muffle a scream into the corner of my elbow as the room loses focus and my world shatters into a million tiny pieces.

As I perch there, collapsed on the desk, my cheek flush to the timber, I think in fragmented, fleeting notions.

Everything I've ever known about sex is turned on its head. I know it doesn't always have to be in the dark with the lights off. I know there are lots of different positions, different ways to do it. In bed, out of bed, in a chair, bent over. I just never knew how *good* this could be. How sensitivity could be increased like this.

I just never knew.

I'm slumped on the pesky stapler and a stack of invoices with a ridiculous smile on my face, my jeans half on, half off, a kiss to the side of my neck. I'm boneless and satiated and I suddenly know the only way I want to spend the next two weeks is naked, with Nick.

I wonder how terrified he would be if he knew that?

Dear Freddy,

I don't know what I'm doing anymore. I whistled in the shower last night. Whistled! I feel a thousand pounds lighter and haven't had a violent thought in days. Even the most annoying customers just make me smile, or worse, laugh. Even if my brother-in-law came to the bar right now, I'd pour him a drink and then forget about him like I've been trying to for the better part of a year. I'm not going to say my temper is cured or in a box or anything like that but I'm in control. I know I am.

And it's all her. Imelda. I know it's probably just that great sex with a willing partner is a relief in itself but she really listens to me and wants to know about my day. It's been a while since I've been with someone who isn't completely self-absorbed or shallow AF.

Too much information? Probably but he thinks too much might be better than not enough. It's not like he's sharing intimate details to brag. He just wants the judge to see that he can be a functioning, not-angry member of society.

He wants to write more and is a little pissy that this stupid diary thing is working for him. He didn't want the judge to be right. He wants this to get him off the hook, but how can these pages do that? He's still not sure so all he can do was write stuff down every day.

Not the really personal stuff. Like how touching Imelda is like setting his brain on fire and then still trying to string two thoughts together while watching the flames. He secretly likes the potential conflict with her friends obviously thinking he's not good enough for her, or that she's too delicate for the likes of him, he'd yet to work that out too.

To Imelda's face, he was really blazè about having fun and taking it easy but imagining being with her was taking its toll. He was having trouble concentrating and had to count last night's till four times before it balanced. After-sex is supposed to be about bliss and satisfaction, but he just wants to do it again. And again. And again and again and again.

Nick eyes the pen in his hand and shakes his head. If he doesn't get his shit together and stop acting like a sixteen-year-old boy, he'll never get any work done. He has books to update and invoices to pay.

His phone vibrates on the desk. The same desk he'd had her on. Twice now. He hardens in an instant.

Is it her? Booty call? At ten in the morning?

We need to talk. Now. (phone message)

So much for no violent thoughts in a few days. His sister's idea of talking is always her yelling at him for something. Their last 'talk' was predictably over her sometimes ex Matt. She still thinks he's a good man somewhere inside despite their pending divorce. Nick was bloody sick of trying to convince her otherwise.

Just as he's about to message her back, his phone vibrates again. His pulse leaps into an instant gallop.

Come over if you're free. Read the first message.

I'm naked and can't get this toy to work. Came soon after.

Nick had always prided himself on being a family man. The matriarch of their family was as fragile as a broken butterfly so it often falls to Nick to sort out the messes his siblings get themselves into.

Can it wait? I'm kind of busy. He hits send, picks up his keys and wallet and heads out to the street.

The next message comes as he's about three meters from Imelda's building door. He practically ran straight there. Which is difficult when a man is hard.

His phone screen lights up and he slaps his forehead hard.

Sure. No worries. See you later maybe?

He'd sent the message to Imelda instead of his sister. She must be really confused and probably a bit embarrassed. For all her words and actions, Imelda is really a lot more innocent than she wants to let on.

He pauses on the sidewalk and ponders his two options. Three if he counts going back to the office and finishing up the work he's meant to be doing.

He should know life wouldn't let him get too comfortable for too long...

24

The hardest thing about stepping out of your comfort zone and daring to be someone or something...more, was the backfire. No matter what I do in relation to becoming someone different, I'm destined to do it badly.

It took me two hours to get up the nerve to send a dirty message to Nick. I kept typing words and then deleting them. Put my phone down only to pick it up again and then put it down. It doesn't help that I'm bored out of my mind! Work is a great distraction and now that I'm distraction free, there's nothing to occupy my stress or anxiety. I'm second-guessing everything, overthinking the rest, generally being restless and at a loose-end. I don't like it all.

Three cups of tea and my morning coffee means I'm riding a caffeine high and my heart is racing from the stupidity of my actions.

Can it wait? I'm kind of busy.

Only seven words and they're seared into my retina. Of course Nick is busy. He's running a successful business. He has a family. Probably loads of friends too.

I pull up the message group I have with my friends and start typing.

I: Anyone around to save me from myself?

Candice sees the message first and the three little dots undulate on my screen like a very small Mexican wave.

C: What did you do?

I: Sent Nick a dirty message.

C: With pics?

I: No, thank God!

C: Nothing bad then? Where's the fire?

I screenshot the very short exchange and post my abject humilia-tion to the group for everyone to laugh at, at their own leisure.

C: Ouch. He better not have tapped and run.

The thought had crossed my mind but then I'd sent that needy one liner, *see you later maybe?* I should have ignored it all. Or just answered with a 'K. Maybe a 'your loss' GIF to top it off. I wondered if there was a masturbating GIF? Truth be told, I wasn't naked and hadn't taken the toy out of the drawer where I'd chucked it. I burned the box too. With matches. In a little ceremony only my cats and one neighbor could have possible seen in the alley behind our apartment block. Not one other person would know I'd made the purchase, just the bank. And the online store.

I'm bored and thinking about Nick. There. I'll admit it. In my mind. Not out loud.

C: Do you need me to come over? I'm not doing much.

I: Let's meet somewhere? Have some lunch? A boozy lunch!

Candice names a place and time and I post a thumbs up. The others are obviously busy. They'd not even read the messages but if they got them, they could meet us there.

This I can do. A long, boozy lunch for the virtually unemployed.

I race into my bedroom and throw my t-shirt off, sending it flying somewhere in the vicinity of the hamper. I feel like someone who has been denied the outside world for months and now I finally get an outing even though I was out in the alley early this morning breaking up a catfight. I can't afford vet bills right now.

I'll drink a few and hope for five minutes of sunshine and forget my humiliation.

I've just slipped my shorts off when the doorbell buzzes.

"Timing," I mutter under my breath. I know it's not Mr. Patterson upstairs. He's already pushed his window high to yell at me about starting fires that could burn down a whole city.

There's no way it's Nick either. I push my plastered hand through the sleeve of my robe and try to pull the other side up my good arm with my bad hand. The door buzzes again.

"Keep your shirt on!" My favorite line by far for those who push my button too many times.

I've complained exactly 2072 times to the building super about the lack of security in this complex. One buzz from the outside and everyone opens the front doors. If you're leaving, you hold the door wide for any stranger to come on in. I've given up.

"Who is it?" I call through the door when there's no one's image reflected in the peep hole.

I think I swear a little when Nick steps into view.

"I can explain," he starts with. "That message was not intended for you."

And now I'm standing in my panties and not much else after telling him I'm naked. What to do, what to do? All the experts say you can't die from embarrassment but I'm probably about to prove them wrong.

"Was that for your other girlfriend?" I call with a healthy dose of pettiness.

"Let me in, Imelda."

I have never liked being told what to do. By anyone. Least of all the men in my life. My brothers, my dad, my teachers, my boss. Nick is different. I unlock the door but make sure my body language tells him he can't come in.

His gaze takes me in like a starving caveman. "Am I too late?"

I'm confused. "Too late for what?"

He takes one step into my apartment and sweeps me into his arms with a kiss I'm not expecting. I hear the door shut. He must have kicked it with his foot. I should complain at being manhandled. I don't. I kiss him back. Like a starving cavewoman.

When he lets me draw breath again, he pulls back and says, "My sister wants to talk. You want to play. I was meant to tell her I was busy, not you. Never you."

I'd never considered myself to have ice around my heart like a bad cliché but I must because some of it falls away letting Nick nestle inside like a stray cat with one paw over the window sill and those big, pleading eyes saying, *take me in*.

"Ugh." The throaty noise I make isn't pretty. "And now I'm busy. I just told Candice I'd meet her for lunch."

"What time?" Nick asks, settling me on the kitchen counter as he undoes my robe.

"I wasn't naked when I texted you," I rush to clear up. It's as close to, *I'm not that desperate*, as I would admit out loud.

"Why not?"

"I was bored," I clarify.

"So I'm literally the toy in this situation? You can't just take me out when you want to play, Imelda."

This tart inside me is banging on the walls to get out and show him what she can do. The daring vixen would lean down, undo his pants, take him in hand-

I can do that.

I do that.

He's hard and hot in my palm and I'm beyond thinking about playing it safe or being a prude or conservative or whatever I might be.

I use more force than is probably necessary when I push on his shoulders. He is puzzled when I slip off the counter and drop to my knees. I don't give him time to react.

I don't give myself time to overthink. I just do.

"You're supposed to be wallowing in misery but you're actually glowing. What gives?"

I laugh at Candice's wide-eyed, suspicious reaction. Meanwhile I assumed playing it cool was the way to go by the time I got to lunch a few minutes late. I'm also a hopeless actress.

I had to get a cab instead of the bus or train or I wouldn't have made it at all. "I swear it all happened so fast!" I offer by way of vague explanation.

"What happened?"

I fall into the seat opposite and Candice pours still water into a glass for me. "Nick came by."

She stops pouring. "I thought he was too busy? Aren't we commiserating a tap and run?"

"Please stop calling it a 'tap'," I beg her.

She puts the carafe of sparkling water down on the table and stares at me. She's wearing aviators at an outside table but the position of her eyebrows says she's about to grill me. "What do you call it? And if you say making love, I'm going to throw your drink on you."

I roll my eyes and since my sunglasses are just the el-cheapo brand from a dollar store, she can see the action. "It's not making love." My insides heat up and I have to squirm into a position that doesn't remind me I was having sex not long ago. Hard, fast, furious sex. Just the way I like it apparently. "It's not tapping either."

"Fucking?" Candice asks, just as the waiter comes by to take our drinks order.

"I can come back?" he says, looking from me to her and back to me again.

"I'll take a glass of rosé, thank you."

"Vodka, soda and lime."

"The hard stuff already?" I say.

Candice just shrugs but there's something off. I hadn't noticed it because I'm the most self-absorbed person in the world right now. "How are things going with you?" I ask.

"We're talking about you," she says back.

"I think I want to talk about you. Spill." I hold my good hand out to her like she always does to us. Candice loves other people's issues. She always has. Then she doesn't have to dwell on her own. Which are usually that she has too many guys on the line, or she gained a pound, or she has too many job opportunities but 'they're, like, so far away'. Like France, or the Swiss Alps. Poor thing.

First there's that shrug again and if it wasn't quickly followed by a forehead-line-inducing frown, I'd blow it off as easy as she was about to. "Candice, what is it?"

"I think I did something silly."

"Something or someone?"

"All right, someone."

"Is he married?"

Candice shakes her head but her bottom lip trembles. "She isn't married."

"She? As in you did a girl? What's the problem?" Candice and Jess weren't all that worried about man or woman, penis or vagina. They'd never hidden the fact and Amy and I don't judge.

A long, deep inhalation from Candice and I'm thinking I might have to shake the information from her, but then she speaks. "You know the advice I gave you, to make sure you both know what you're getting into? If it's just sex, make it clear."

"Yeah, I remember. What did you do? Don't tell me she's pressuring you for more?"

Candice shakes her head and an actual tear rolls from behind the aviators, down her cheeks to soak into the crease of her mouth.

"Oh my God, Candice, what is it? Do we need to go to the police?"

A broken laugh that's more of a sob is muffled in a napkin and she keeps shaking her head. "It's not her. It's me. I think I fell for her."

"And she doesn't want you back? I'm missing something."

"That's the problem, she does want me. We've been seeing each other for a few months and now she wants to do a meet the parents thing."

"A few months? And you didn't say anything?" But then it hits me. "Oh dear," I mutter. Now I understand. "Your dad is not going to like that, is he?"

Her back straightens. "You know what? I'm an adult and I can make my own damned decisions. I don't need anyone's approval to live my life the way I want."

"Um." I don't know quite what to say. I should echo the cry with her but it's not that simple is it? "Take it from someone who is a continuous disappointment to her parents, it's not that easy." It's not actually approval you seek from your family. No one needs another person's okay to do or be what or who you want. I wonder what would happen if I arrived at family dinner with Nick at my back?

Acceptance would be nice. If only they'd first accept that not everyone wants to be a doctor, or wildly, certifiably successful or even some award winning something.

I sigh. "Why couldn't we just have the type of folks who are happy if we're happy?"

"I think my father lives to tear me down. He saw the last shoot I did for FHM and nearly shit a kitten."

I grin and point out, "That suit was almost transparent. I'm not surprised he didn't like it. What did he say about your nipple piercing?"

"He didn't even notice until some new recruit was pointing it out to his buddies in the dorm. I had to hear about it for over an hour."

"Why didn't you do that thing where your phone 'cuts out'." I make air quotes.

"He doesn't fall for that anymore."

Being an army brat had to be so much harder than being the failure of the Mahari family. Candice's dad gets reposted every four or five years. Her mother is happy enough to pick up and move each time but the real fight started when Candice told them she was staying put. At that stage her modeling had been for Target catalogues and fashion designers. Fast forward ten years and she was the feature of every man's spank bank. She'd done calendars, magazine spreads (and I do mean spreads) and appeared on the front pages of many men's mags. She was beautiful, skinny, tall and perfect.

Her father was career military and strictly religious.

"What are you going to do?" I ask.

"I don't know, but I have some time. Dad's overseas for a few more months anyway."

"Are you going to meet her parents?"

"Next week."

"Are you nervous?"

"Not at all, actually. She's been queer and proud since she was eight. Apparently her parents are likely to hug me and welcome me to the family."

A make a sheesh sound through my teeth. "So you're swearing off the almighty penis?"

"I'll have to live vicariously through you for a bit," she laughs. "Tell me what happened with Nick that made you late?"

"That message was him blowing off his sister. He'd meant to tell her he was busy so he could come around and..." Could my cheeks get any hotter? I doubted it.

"And?"

"Get blown by me?" I offer. I'm burning up and using dirty language in a public place. I'm not even sure the context is right.

Candice laughs harder than I expect her to just as the waiter comes back with our drinks. Lucky, or I'd be wearing hers. It takes her a while to calm down and then she does that thing where she gets serious in a heartbeat. "And he's not pressuring you is he?"

I think of the shock on his expression when I fell to my knees. The pressure of his hands in my hair as he pulled the strands. He even gave me the half-hearted 'you don't have to do that'. After that, the rest is a bit of a blur. I do have a bruise on my butt from the kitchen bench. Turns out it's not quite the right height for sex.

I smile. "I am fully consenting, don't you worry about that."

Candice returns my smile with one of her own, and a nod. "Good. It'd be hard to kick his ass! He's big!" And then she leans forward and asks, "He is big, but is he *big*?"

And just like that, I find out what I've been missing out on with my friends. This easy camaraderie and the kiss and tell. Only, it feels...weird, too. I know Candice won't tell the whole world what I tell her, but it's disrespectful to Nick, isn't it? I want to be that person who giggles and holds her hands apart to give away just how satisfying he is, but I can't.

So instead I say, "Tell me more about your lady! Does she have a name?"

And I'm relieved to turn the conversation around. I don't really want to kiss and tell after all...

25

As I spend more time with Nick, I come to understand that despite wanting to fit in better with my girlfriends and talk smack with them about boys, it's not what I wanted at all. I felt left out for so long because I wasn't able to participate in the conversations but now I find myself sitting back and just listening.

My one week of purgatory from the hotel predictably turns into two. I spend the mornings with Nick, in bed, on the lounge, on the carpet, in the shower. Wherever and however we want. I've barely done anything but sleep and have sex.

And there's still something missing. I love the thrill of waiting for the knock at the door. The text, sometimes illicit, sometimes not. It's Nick's day off and we're planning to not have sex. He's bringing takeaway and I get the first pick of what movie to watch.

It's weird. We're just going to be hanging out. My idea, which seemed good at the time but I'm now questioning it. I'm even wearing the least sexy clothes for hanging out. I've never kidded myself of where I think I sit on the scale of fugly to scorching. It's a massive boost to my ego when Nick can't seem to keep his hands to himself. So I have on sweats and bed socks up to my knees and a top that says 'Cats, Books, Coffee'.

He eventually knocks and for the briefest moment, I consider not answering. What am I doing? I wouldn't even wear this outfit for my friends let alone for my... I was thinking boyfriend but he isn't. We're just sleeping together. Only, today there's no 'sleeping'. When I told my girlfriends Nick is just a friend, I was close to the truth. Friends with benefits? Isn't that the term?

When I do open the door, he leans in and kisses me straight away. Not even a hello. It's that drugging, goes on forever, type of kiss that sets off the fireworks in my body. "If you keep that up, we're definitely having sex."

He laughs and walks straight to the kitchen with a familiarity that makes my weirdness feelings intensify. "Is that a promise?" he asks.

I smile but I don't know what to say.

He stops getting plates out for the Chinese food that smells divine, by the way, and looks at me. Really looks. "I didn't want to ask over text but why the sex ban? That time of the month?"

I roll my eyes.

"I have sisters, I'm not completely insensitive."

I'm not really sure what to tell him. Not that time of month. I had sent the text in a moment of pure exhaustion. My body is feeling very well loved and to be perfectly honest, with myself, I need a break. A sex break. I nearly laugh. I went from the longest drought to having too much of a good thing. But I don't feel like being on my own and Nick asked what I was doing.

When I don't answer, he comes around the breakfast bench and looks me in the eye. "Are you breaking up with me? I brought you Chinese food."

Now it's my turn to laugh. "No, no, nothing like that. I just..." God, why am I drawing blanks right now?

Nick beats me to the punch again and I wonder if he's a mind reader as well as sensitive and caring and gentle and great in bed. "It's okay if you're a little confused. This thing has happened kind of quickly."

"This thing?" I repeat. "I thought we weren't going to label it. Just have fun."

He frowns. "I've been having fun. I thought you had been too? Was I wrong? Is that what this is about? You can be honest with me, I can handle it."

I shake my head. "I don't know."

"Don't know?"

"I don't know anything anymore. Not really. I think I'm enjoying myself a little too much and now I'm worried about getting hurt, or hurting you."

His expression relaxes and he leans back against my counter, his t-shirt fabric pulling across his chest the way the muscles in my abdomen do when I see his arms and ink. It turns me on in an instant.

"Ah," he says, as though all the puzzle pieces just dropped into place. "You want to change the terms of our liaison."

I chuckle. "Liaison? That's a label."

"I don't care what we call it. Fun, relationship, liaison. As long as you're not putting an end to it today."

"We're getting a little caught up," I point out.

"So what? We keep having fun until it's not fun anymore."

And then I fit two pieces of this puzzle together in my mind. It's fun but I'm stressing about where it's going to go. I'm stressing about where I'm going to go. It's why my teeth and jaw hurt when I woke up this morning. My job will never be the same and I have to accept that painful truth. I don't want to go back to the hotel where there's zero respect for women, for co-workers, for management. Everyone does their own thing with no regard to anyone or anything else, especially Denni.

I'm sick of it. Done.

As much as I like hanging out with Nick, he isn't really boyfriend material, is he? He has a busy job working nights and a criminal record for beating someone up. He's right now caught up in a court case. I once asked Denni if I could potentially miss out on Mr. Right while I was having fun with Mr. Right Now. I needed to get back in the saddle and work out if I was broken and I'm not. I should call an end to things with Nick before it gets any more complicated. But I don't want to.

My insides warm and I go to him, put my arms around his neck and kiss him. I rarely instigate touching and usually wait for him to make the first move but I'm ready to admit that I really like being around him and I don't want it to stop.

"Let's not change a thing," I murmur into his ear. I know he likes this. I know it turns him on.

He groans and squeezes my butt, but then he lets go and sidesteps me, back into the kitchen where he shoos Harry away from the food, gently lifting the cat back to the floor. "If you're serious about the no sex thing, you can't do that again."

I have power here. The power to choose my workplace. The power to say yes or no to whoever and whatever I want. I am not the doormat my high school yearbook said I was most likely to be.

Candice had put it perfectly. *"I'm an adult and I make my owned damned decisions."*

I was so distracted by my own thoughts of a brighter future that I didn't follow along with the movie. I suddenly wanted Nick to leave so I could start my job hunt. We barely said much while the movie was on and I yawned so much towards the end, he kissed me goodnight and then left.

I couldn't think fast enough and it was all about me.

First things first. Put in my resignation letter.

Dear Freddy,

Today I hung out with Imelda at her apartment. Again. Nothing different lately. Except that she was different. I thought she was calling things off but that didn't happen either. Maybe she didn't want to end things to my face in case I got angry?

Which I wouldn't have done.

I'll give her some space to sort out whatever it is that's got her so distracted and see what happens.

Nick really did feel as though his diary has gone the way of a teenage girl again. He wanted to put something else in the entry but there was nothing else. The bar was doing great. Holding steady both financially and also patronage wise.

His regulars kept spending money. His events were well attended if not particularly well planned on his behalf. Mostly he spread the word on the socials and relied on people to share the events. Sports and bars went hand-in-hand and there was always a game of some sort happening somewhere in the world. Australian Rugby came to end around the same time the NFL kicked off so it was currently high season for the flat screen.

He probably needed to start thinking about a Halloween party. The demographic of neighborhood was always changing and to change with it, he had to attract more of the Imeldas of this city and slightly less of the footy crowd.

That would occupy some of his time while he gives her space. He wouldn't message her until she got in contact with him.

There was no way he wanted her to fully know just how much he liked being in her company.

26

I've had a busy week. For an unemployed person. Hitting send on my resignation literally takes my breath away. I'd go so far as to say I had a minor panic attack and nearly clicked 'undo' to recall the email. And then something really, completely bizarre happened. A weight lifted from my shoulders, I took a deep breath, deeper than I had in years (as wanky as that sounds) and it felt good. I'm lighter despite the financial doom coming my way in around nine weeks. I have some vacation pay and may have sort of blackmailed one more paid week out of George. I shouldn't go so quietly but I'll make it easy for the hotel, for Denni. For me.

The response I receive within ten minutes wishes me well. It's at this point that I nearly cry, nearly become hysterical, actually. I pace until the feeling of peace comes back. I'm doing the right thing. That job is going nowhere. I'm going nowhere. The last thing I want to do is face Denni over the lunchroom table, or see him every morning. I am so replaceable that no notice was needed for me to do a handover.

I'm sorry for my brides for all of thirty seconds but they're not my brides, are they? They'll cope.

Really I'm just talking myself into my decision all the while trying not to completely freak out. As much as I was getting bored, I was comfortable there. No new experiences, only one or two new staff members at a time. Almost no situations where I was surprised or put on the spot. Great for a person who had spent half her life being terrified of everything.

I pause, mid-pace, foot three inches from the carpet of my living room. What am I going to tell my mother? We've already established I am not a good liar, nor do I want to be one. Her reaction will be epic, I'm sure.

As I sink onto the sofa, my head in my hands, heart racing, the logical side of me knows she can't do anything more than frown and express her disappointment. It's what I've been avoiding my whole life. Each time I shied away from one of my mother's friends or refused to hug, air kiss or talk to a veritable stranger, she would make this tsk sound. *The sound of her embarrassment*, my siblings and I named it. Each time she had to pull me away from her skirt or stop me from hiding behind her, she would thin her lips and tell me I had to snap out of it, that I was making her look like a terrible mother.

My only reprieve was school. The teachers didn't make me hug strangers. They rarely pushed me to openly contribute since my grades were perfect. Then again, I probably just lucked out with my early teachers. By the seventh grade, I could whisper a short oral speech without holding a bucket to vomit in. By the ninth grade I'd made a few friends and could lift my voice loud enough to be heard.

By university I'd pulled my shit together, 'snapped' out of it for the most part, or so my mother believed.

Really, I had just learned to perform on command. I learned to not cringe or pull away when someone leaned in for a hug. Candice, Amy and Jess knew how real my struggle was to take part in conversations and get close to people so they'd often run interference. It wasn't so much by choice that I didn't make many personal connections. I was born that way, shy, withdrawn, the outsider. My family laughed about it. My friends accepted it, accepted me.

Would Nick? If he knew the real me? The one who sometimes uses lame excuses to avoid parties and dinners so as not to make small talk. While I don't love isolation and had thought my life was becoming lonely, I do love the silence. No one to impress with my inane crappy nuggets of supposed wisdom. No awkwardness to cover with babble.

I don't even know why I'm worrying about whether or not Nick will accept the real me. He's not boyfriend material. I have to stop dwelling on the what ifs because we are just having fun. No labels. No strings. No messy complications.

My phone pings with a message and I open an invitation sent via email from *Johnnie's*.

It's a Malice in Wonderland themed Halloween party but the invite is flat and doesn't have much information on it. I notice it says (TEST) at the top line.

I send a text to Nick.

I: Um, got your invite. It needs some work.

It's been five days since we saw each other and this is the first communication we've had since our non-sex day of movies and a quick, awkward goodbye. I've been busy and the radio silence was weird at first but then I didn't want to push anything since I'm the one who keeps reinforcing the *just fun* boundary lines. It scares me a little bit how much I only want to put my very best foot forward with Nick. How I don't want to do anything to stuff this 'thing' up and yet not push it too far or hold it back either.

Is this what people in relationships do? Second-guess every word, written or said? Confuse and twist every scenario into something it's probably not until you want to scream? I seem to spend a lot of my free time thinking about what Nick is thinking about. I'm exhausted. And yet, it's all I really want to do. Ask Nick what he's thinking. How he's feeling. What's he doing.

I lost count of the times I picked up my phone this week to message him or call him, only to put the phone down and leave him be. I keep telling myself he'll call when he's free. Our week of non-stop sex had to slow down eventually. Or had I killed it? By suggesting the movie day?

N: I'd take suggestions. Gladly! What are you doing right now?

My stomach flutters.

I: Not much. Are you at the bar?

N: Come on over. I'll make coffee. Or cosmos ;)

The winking emoji turns up the flutter.

I: On my way.

I'm at his beck and call. I don't even care!

There's a fully formed hurricane in my tummy when I strip right down to nothing at all before slipping on a pair of delicate lace panties. Nothing goes with my cast and I'm still not completely happy about it so I push the offending green through the arm of a black jersey dress (courtesy of the sister box). I wonder about the need for a bra but ultimately decide not to wear one. It's only been six days since Nick's hands were last on my bare skin and that's five days too many. I'm hoping he'll let loose in his office like the last two times I've been there.

This new part of me, I'm learning to love. I've been frightened or dubious about sex for too long and now that I've discovered how amazing and freeing it can be, I'm converted. Nick doesn't judge me or try to correct me either. A part of me knows that since he's a man, he's going to prefer me to be as free as I feel I can be. He is getting a lot of sex as a result. But he also didn't mind the movie day. Or the thought of it, anyway. He could have made an excuse about being too busy but instead, assumed I was on my period and brought food.

Maybe he is boyfriend material? The hurricane kicks up a notch and I'm dizzy for a moment. I have to steady myself.

Don't do this.

Don't do this to yourself.

It's just fun.

I slip on a pair of open toe wedges and a light coat and head out. The nights are cool but *Johnnie's* will be warm. By the time I get to the bar, I have stopped thinking about Nick as my boyfriend. My mother would probably have a stroke if I bring him for a family dinner. Which leads me to think about my family. No one has ever brought a significant other to a family dinner. We're all married to our careers. My parents definitely should have thought of that before pushing us so hard down the path of academia and serious jobs.

I wonder if I arrive at dinner jobless and hand-in-hand with a tattooed hunk, if it will get me out dinners for a little while? I might ask Nick if he's up for the challenge.

I'm chuckling to myself when I walk through the doors at *Johnnie's*. I don't even care that I don't work here or that I'm not Nick's girlfriend, I make my way straight to the office when I don't see him behind the bar. Suzie is there and waves me through.

I knock softly and go right in when I hear him call out. He smiles when he sees me and pushes his chair back from his desk but he doesn't get up. I have no idea how much I've missed him this week until I see him. I've been busy, he's been busy. We're not a couple. No strings and no obligations.

And yet I'm so happy to see him, I shed my jacket while I'm taking steps and climb right onto his lap. Our lips meet and something shifts inside of me.

"Hello," Nick murmurs when we break apart for much-needed air.

"Hi," I say back, sheepish that I've not even stopped for pleasantries. I didn't even close the door. Anyone could wander the wrong way from the toilets and see us like this. My dress probably isn't even covering my butt right now.

I make to stand and bring some semblance of normal back to this moment but he stops me. Both hands on my hips. He kisses me again and again.

"It's been a long few days," he says when he's finally ready to let me go.

I step back, wipe my mouth, smooth down my hair and my dress, shrug and say, "I figured you were busy when you didn't text or call."

"I wanted to give you some space. The other day you seemed to have a lot on your mind."

I did. "I quit my job."

His eyes grow wide and he stares at me like he's never seen me before. "What? Why? Because of that asshat? Did they force you into this, because that's illegal!"

I close the door of his office before someone actually does come along and overhear us. I then come back and perch on the edge of his desk next to him. "No one forced me into anything. I just didn't realize how much I was beginning to hate it. The job. The people. The politics. I need something new."

"But to go from employed to unemployed? Aren't you worried about paying the rent?"

I should be. "I'll find something."

"Can you pour a beer?" he asks.

I shake my head. "I don't think so. I've never tried."

"Well, let's start with this party invitation. I'm not very creative, as you can tell."

Nick goes to stand up and let me sit on his chair but I stop him and sit on his lap, my back to his font. The invite is on the screen and I can see right away that he's using the wrong software. Part of my job is—was—designing menus and programs. Playing with graphics and social media teasers. I love—loved—that part of the job.

"Have you got any great images you can use?" I ask.

His hands slide down the outside of my thighs until he reaches my hem. "Mmhmm, I sure do have a great image but it's in my head."

I ignore him and go to bring up his computer's menu to see what other software he has. "This is going to be difficult with this dumb cast," I say, more to myself than him.

Another mmhmm is murmured against my shoulder as his hands wander aimlessly beneath my dress. Okay, maybe not aimlessly. I relax my thighs a little and let him do his thing. I have no intention of stopping him. I have six days of pent up energy to unleash and if he wants to start now, I'm on board. Literally, since I'm not shifting from his lap.

"You can keep working," he says over my shoulder.

"What's the pay like?" I ask, as he hits a sweet spot between my legs.

"Dismal," he chuckles against my shoulder. "But I can make it up to you in other ways?"

His fingers slip into my panties and I'm already breathless, waiting. His other hand finds the curve of my breast and squeezes. "Oh god, no bra? You're going to kill me."

I push on his lower hand until he's touching me where I need him most. I rock back, his erection hard against my butt. I'm gripping the edge of the desk so hard, I'm worried I'll break something else. I rest my cast on the flat surface and lean forward, giving him easier access but the angle is all wrong. My panties are in the way. The desk is in the way. The chair arms are in the way.

"Damn it," I swear.

He laughs and bites me gently on the shoulder through my dress. "Why don't we get this done and then move this party somewhere else?"

"My place?"

"Mine is closer," he says, circling the pad of his forefinger against me until I have to bite my lower lip.

It's my turn to murmur incoherently.

"Two hours and the bar will be closed." He growls. "The things I want to do to you."

I swear softly because I want him to do all of those things to me too but we're adults with responsibilities and he has a bar to run. When he removes his hands, I get up but I only turn around. I sink back down on his lap like I did when I first arrived. I kiss him like he kisses me. Long and drugging, ravenous and urgent. When I can't breathe and my insides are combustible, I get up again, lick my lips and then tell him to get up. "You close up, I'll do the invite, then we get naked? Yeah?"

He takes the hem of my dress and slowly lifts it so he can see what I'm wearing downstairs. He nods and says, "Naked sounds good."

Then I'm alone with his computer, in his office, making an invitation for a Halloween bash, wondering how many ticks of the clock I have to endure before the naked part of the evening comes.

27

Every movie I've ever watched has prepared me for Nick's apartment. I didn't guess that he lives right above the bar. He says it's not something he tells people. He doesn't want to mix business with his personal life.

Exposed red brick gives the place an industrial feel but it's softened by greenery. He has plants in pots on the floor, on the kitchen counter, on the window sills. My cats would either eat them or go to the toilet in the dirt. A bright rug with greens and pinks and blues breaks up the monotony of the timber floorboards but his furniture is distinctly male. The sofa is dark leather, his TV is huge, there's no dining table but there are four high stools at the kitchen island. There's only one bedroom but we haven't made it that far yet.

There's not one item out of place. Not one dirty dish anywhere. No cat hair to brush from your clothes and no explosion of blankets and pillows to cover scratched furniture or fishy puke stains. He's a neat freak. "You must hate staying at my place," I comment.

He goes to the fridge and takes out two beers, twisting the tops off and offering me one. I take it even though I don't love beer. "Why do you say that?"

I gesture with the dark glass bottle to his abode. "Your place is perfect. Picture perfect in fact. My place is messy and probably smells like cat pee but you're too polite to point it out."

He shakes his head and swigs from his bottle before saying, "Your place smells like chai, actually. Not cat pee."

"That's a relief," I mutter under my breath. I stroll around the room, touching things, moving things to see if he cares.

"My place is like this because I don't spend much time here. And I have a cleaning lady."

I choke on the beer with a splutter. "I knew this couldn't be all you!"

He gives me a pointed stare and says, "She's here for an hour a fortnight to dust and do the floors. I like things tidy. I'm too tired to worry about mess when I get up those stairs."

That makes perfect sense and it's another reminder that we're two very different people. I've been ignoring these signs but they keep coming back to haunt me. He's employed, I'm not. He's a business owner who knows who he is and what he wants out of life. I'm completely lost. He owns the building (outright), drives a car (purchased in full), generally adults quite well all things considered. But as I get around the room, to the kitchen, I notice he's sprawled a date and address on a piece of paper.

Court, 1pm, November 7th.

"What's going to happen to you when you go to court next time?" I ask. I still don't know much about his anger management stuff. "Ooh, can I see the diary you're writing for the judge?"

Oh. My God. He blushes! His cheeks are fire engine red and I need to know where that diary is. I put my beer on the kitchen counter and take off towards what I assume is his bedroom. He catches me, puts his arms around my stomach and lifts me off my feet. I squeal but again, I let him manhandle me because I like it. I like this feminine feeling that he's strong and hard, this caveman ideal that I'm weak and soft which I'll never admit out loud because feminism.

Nick actually carries me back to the kitchen where he sits me on a stool and holds me captive in the circle of his arms. He spins the chair and traps me with a hand on the counter at my sides. "You are not reading that diary."

"How personal is it? Ooh, does it have feelings?" I've never seen a guy squirm like this!

"Of course it has feelings. If I don't take it seriously I'll be in huge trouble."

That sobers me. "How much trouble?"

"You do not need to worry about this."

But I can tell by his tone and the hard look in his eyes that he's worried. "Is there anything I can do to help? Provide a character witness? I could write a page in the diary for you."

"You are not reading my diary."

"What if I show you mine?" I offer.

He thinks about it for a split second but then shakes his head. "No thanks."

"Hey!" I playfully push at him. "My diary has embarrassing stuff in it."

"Not as embarrassing as mine," he confesses.

"Seriously, though. How much trouble are you looking at?"

He sighs and his forehead drops to my shoulder. "Right now my sentence is suspended, no conviction recorded. If the judge deems me to be unstable, I'm toast. Jail time likely since this isn't my first assault charge."

"Not your first assault charge?" He'd said something about this before but then changed the subject.

"The diary isn't attached to the fight I told you about. There was another one a few months later. With Matt."

"What happened?"

"I beat the shit out of him. He's a cheating dirt bag and he said a few things, wouldn't leave the bar. Things got out of hand."

"Didn't your sister stand up for you? Explain to the judge what happened?"

"My immediate family don't know about this. Only my uncle. He's the one who was here that first day you rocked up."

"But your sister could explain away most of it, couldn't she?"

"Maybe" Nicks shrugs. "But she could also damage my defense too."

"How so?"

"She thinks I shouldn't have done what I did. She accused me of overstepping my boundaries, that she could take care of her own business."

"She knew he was cheating though didn't she?"

"Can we please stop talking about this?" He kisses my cheek and his hands drop to my hips.

I have so many questions. So many! But it is very clear Nick doesn't want to talk about any of it and I have to respect that as his not-girlfriend. As his piece on the side I can't get involved. But damn, I want to read that diary!

I change the subject but only because it suits me, not because I don't want to pry. "I seem to remember you making some promises if I made your invitation?"

"I did," he says with a nod and kisses me until I'm panting and in so much need. "Do you want gentle or rough?"

My insides trill. I didn't even know that was possible. The human equivalent to a cat purr. "Let's start on the rougher side of gentle and see where we wind up?"

"I think I can work with that."

Dear Freddy,

That woman. I know this diary has turned into some sort of sexca-pades retelling but I think I found my center.

Jesus! Did he actually write that? And did he actually mean it? Nick's whole world was upside down and inside out. Imelda helped him with the invitation that he'd botched and promised to help with the actual party too.

Like a partner.

Like a girlfriend with mad event planning skills.

Or an unemployed person who was bored and needed something to do.

I know we're getting close to the pointy end of this thing and I promise, I've not had a mad thought this week. Even my most annoy-ing customers don't phase me. I know you're probably going to say that once the post-sex glow wears off, I'll be back to no good but you're wrong.

She makes me happy. God, that sounds so corny but it's true. I've got a plan to change her mind about the 'just having fun' thing.

I just have to get past this court thing first. A guy with no future has nothing to offer a girl with her whole life ahead of her.

As much as slugging his brother-in-law made him feel good at the time, he wished it never happened now. He wasn't sorry he punched Matt. He was only sorry he got involved in his sister's drama once again. It's not the first time she's fallen for the bad boy. It won't be the last. She comes from a long line of women who fall for assholes. He came from a long line of assholes himself. Did that make Imelda just like his sister?

Nope. No way.

If they were in a real relationship and he cheated, he could envision Imelda castrating him with a dull butter knife. She was fiery and bold and wouldn't take his shit. He was sure of that much.

28

I'm seriously losing my mind. It's been four weeks since the Denni episode. Four weeks of sleeping with Nick every chance I get. I'm so deliriously happy that some days I can't believe this is my life right now. I have a few interviews lined up but first, Nick's Halloween party. Jess, Amy and Candice are all coming along. The costumes we bought are outrageously skimpy, a witch, an Alice, a Dorothy and I'm going as Red Riding Hood. The adult version. A very adult version. Think obscenely short skirt and fishnet stockings.

Nick is even dressing up.

It took a lot of convincing but he finally got on board when I promised to be naughty if he did. I'm not sure if he's the wolf in my story or the savior, the woodsman. I'll find out when we get to the bar.

I've had more fun organizing this party than I've had in years. Nick handed over full control of the catering and decorations, even what kind of spooky cocktails to serve. Okay, for that he gave me a book of cocktails because we both know that's not in my wheel-house.

It's been invigorating to be given a budget and just go wild.

It's given me some ideas on what kind of job I might want and what I won't settle for. Pity there's no need for party planners in our part of the city but I'm working on it. I haven't told my family yet that I'm unemployed. I figure by the next family dinner I'll just tell them about my new job. I have to miss one but I enlist the help of my sister to lie with me and for me. She has her hands full with Jia but assures me she'll come up with the best excuse and that I should not answer my phone under any circumstances if my mother calls. A part of me is worried but what is my mother going to do? Really? I'm about to get started on the beginning of the rest of my life. I cannot be worried about upsetting my mother. My adult mother. She never calls anyway and I prefer the silent treatment to the disappointing daughter routine.

The excitement levels in my apartment are deafening and I'm expecting at a full week of complaints from at least two of my neighbors. My cats have also gone into hiding but they'll slink out from their hidey-holes later, after we're gone.

Candice stops behind me and meets my eyes with hers in the reflection of my bathroom mirror. "So, is this your couple thing with Nick?"

"He's putting on an event and needed help with it. It is not a couple thing."

She frowns. "So, he's paying you? The event coordinator, to help him coordinate his event?"

I shake my head and roll my eyes. "I know where you're going with this and we're still just seeing each other. We are not an official couple. Might never be."

Jess pokes her head around Candice, which is hard given that Candice is even taller in the thigh-high, black boots she bought to go with her costume. She and her dress and her tall pointy hat are almost taking up the entire doorway. "Not yet," Jess says with a smirk.

I get defensive. This is my default setting after all. "We've talked about this, guys. *We* are not a couple. *We* are happy with the arrangement the way it is. Just fun. Strictly no strings."

Amy joins in but I can't see her face. "And yet you're organizing a party for him. Getting involved in his business. You're probably going to be in couple's costumes tonight too? Am I right?"

The way she reiterates *business* makes my skin crawl. Like I'm all up in his business. All over him. Like I can't do without him. The couple's costume thing seemed like a bit of fun but when she says it, it feels dirty and it shouldn't.

"I happen to be unemployed. And bored." That's not true. Another little white lie. If I'm being honest with myself (and not my friends) I'm exhausted. I know I've had this thought, made this comment, but I am tired. I need a solid week of sleep to catch up. But I don't want to miss one experience with Nick. We might be strictly no strings on the surface, but my heart is starting to get attached. I like hanging out with him. I like seeing him, discussing the day or the night ahead. I wait for his texts and get all fluttery in my belly when he says nice things. Or naughty things.

I recall my promise to be naughty and my mind wanders to being naughty with Nick.

"Ugh, she has her sex look on," Candace complains and then backs out of the room, one hand on her hat so it doesn't get dislodged by the door frame.

"I do not have a sex look!"

Jess and Amy nod. "Yes, you do."

I look back in the mirror and only see me. Only, I'm different. No, there's no sex look. My makeup is heavy on account of the costume party but my eyes seem brighter. My smile is definitely wider. Somedays I find myself smiling so much my jaw hurts. Or maybe I'm clenching my teeth in my sleep? Who knows? I do not have a sex look. This I'm sure of.

"Why can't you all just be happy that I'm happy?" I ask them. I'm gentle with my tone but maybe I shouldn't be?

Candice tsks and Jess says, "We're happy for you. We are. You've found a guy who is treating you right and giving you orgasms and happiness but I for one am worried about you."

"You don't need to worry," I try to assure her but the words are somewhat hollow.

Amy says, "You're just not yourself. Your self wouldn't have quit your job without having another one to go to. If someone asked me if you'd ever quit that job, I'd say hell no! And yet, you did. Now you have no plan and no fall back and if things sour with Nick, you'll be alone again and I don't want to see you fall into a hole of your own making."

"I do have a fallback."

"What is it?" Amy asks.

They're not going to like it but things aren't going to sour with Nick, not anytime soon anyway. We're great. Not even a little argument or any nitpicking. No tense or awkward silences. My friends are not going to like what I'm about to say. "Nick says I can do a few shifts at the bar if I get stuck."

Total silence meets that statement. Until Candice yells from the other room, "You are so in a relationship!"

Amy nods. "Your boyfriend is going to help you out if you get stuck for cash. It's nice but you can't rely on it. Or him."

Now they're attacking Nick? "What is that supposed to mean? Nick is reliable."

Jess comes back with, "Isn't Nick going to court next week? For his anger management stuff?"

I should never have said anything to them about that. I never should have told them he was facing a criminal conviction. When I saw the appointment date written on a scrap of paper on his fridge at his apartment it was like a tiny prick to my bubble. What if he does get sent to prison to do real time? I've watched those shows. Everyone winds up joining a gang or getting bashed. Or worse. Even going to jail for something minor will ruin your life. And everyone else's around you.

I'm not worried though. He *is* a good guy. No volatile temper in sight. I have no doubt it's inside of him somewhere but he'd been pushed to action and it hadn't ended well. If my sister was dating a straight-up player, I'd kick his butt too!

"His brother-in-law was at his bar picking up women, cheating on his sister. I really can't blame him for what he did."

"I wouldn't put a guy in the hospital," Amy says.

"You've seen Nick!" I say. "He's big and just doesn't know his own strength."

Candice scoffs. "Spoken like a battered wife there, Mellow."

Jess puts down her makeup pallet with a solid swear word. "Has he ever hurt you?"

I am definitely not telling her about the tiny bruise I'm currently sporting on my backside or the minor carpet burn on my spine. We got carried away and little did I know, I do like it kind of rough. Am I supposed to feel dirty though, after? I just don't even know anymore. My feelings and emotions are all over the place. The best, hardest orgasm I've had to date came with a carpet burn. No warning, just hard and fast and intense. Nick's rug looks soft but it bites! I had to try so hard not to cry, but not from the burn, from the orgasm. It's happened twice now where I explode so hard I almost sob. I do not want to ask my friends about that just in case it is bad and I'm weird again. Or it's Nick's fault, something he's doing, or not doing, and my friends blame him.

Candice and Amy also put what they're holding down and all three circle me. We're about to start the Spanish inquisition. Again.

Amy. "Has he hurt you?"

I shake my head. "No, not at all."

Candice. "Why the silence?"

"Not silence," I say. "Just paused too long." My cheeks are burning.

Jess. "Spill. Now. We are not leaving until you're honest. If he's hurt you, we need to know."

I hold my palms to my face to end the burn, only my hands are sweaty and I'm probably about to break out into hives. But then words are spilling from my mouth and I can't stop the torrent. "God, this is so embarrassing and I don't know how to talk about it or if I even want to talk about it but Nick does get carried away. I do too. He has this caveman thing going and I know it's awful and anti-feminism but I like it. A lot. I like it so much!"

Candice smirks but then clears her throat and flips back to serious. "Explain. In more words."

Jess and Amy kind of 'ew' but they don't call a stop to it. In fact, they look like they want more details too. I'm dying. I'm going to die. In a red riding hood dress, fishnets and satin, hooded cape. I cannot be buried in this. My mother will never forgive me.

"Our relationship..." I've been hesitant to use the word but sex is still a relationship in a way. "Is different."

"Different how?" Jess asks.

"We don't always make it to a bed."

Amy looks confused. "We all have sex in weird places."

"I..." How the hell do I explain this? I know I don't have to but I don't want them going to Nick's party tonight thinking he's some kind of abusive deviant. "We kind of can't keep our hands off each other and just do it wherever we're standing. Or sitting. Or falling."

Candice's smirk is back and I start to laugh. "Stop looking at me like that. I'm enjoying myself."

She laughs too and says, "You go for it. Have fun."

Jess says, "But know that it won't last like this. The heat will wear off eventually."

"I realize that but we're just having fun and part of that is trying new things for me. New places, new positions, new everything. I feel like some kind of defective fairy who finally has her wings and I want to get the most out of my freedom."

My friends nod and then Amy says, "Just as long as you know these kinds of flings have expiration dates, Mellow."

Do they though? I'm almost at the point where I feel like what Nick and I have is worth exploring. He's certainly not slowing things down. The sex is just as hot now as a few weeks ago, and just as often. I'd have thought I'd get a little bored by now. Or at least want to talk more, fuck less.

One more miserable statement to add to the list comes from Jess, along with a pointed finger at my cast. "And remember there are guys out there who like to pull the wings from their creatures."

"I promise I'm in control. I am not going to get hurt. Emotionally or physically. Nick has his temper under control and for the very last time, we're just having sex. We're not setting a wedding date! It just happens to be very hot, out of this world sex."

They let it go and we finish getting ready and I'm a mess inside but I don't let them see. I can't let them see how attached I am already. Nick might very well go to jail next week and I am not interested in conjugal visits or waiting for a felon to walk free.

I smile and joke and make about as much small talk as I usually do but there's something heavy in my belly, replacing the glow Nick put there earlier in the day. This time next week I could be unemployed *and* all alone. I don't like the thought of it one bit.

· ♥ · ♥ · ♥ · ♥ · ♥ ·

Dear Freddy,

I'm writing in the diary now because I fully expect tonight to get wild and go late. Then I'll be with Imelda and she is not finding this notebook. I am not writing in it in front of her.

It's Halloween on the weekend and the party Imelda is throwing tonight at my bar is going to be huge. She's amazing at her job and has pulled together a much better plan than I've ever put together for an event. Maybe I need to take the bar to the next level and maximize on the holidays and other special times of the year?

I'm going to talk to Imelda and ask her to put some stuff together. She's amazing.

Her focus is amazing.

She's amazing.

Now he's rambling. And maybe gushing? Is that the word for it? He isn't sure. He just knows the lightness in his chest is still there after a few weeks and she's the reason. Tonight will be a smashing success and he'll end another day wrapped around her curves and he couldn't be happier. Now he just has to get through the final hearing. After that he'd hopefully be free to convince Imelda that he *is* boyfriend material.

From what she's said about her family, Nick knows they come from different worlds but he didn't buy into the bullshit that it won't work for that reason. He's from the other side of the tracks but he's pulled himself up from the stereotype and made something of his life. He can keep up with her world. He'd just never show her his...

29

I know it seems from the start of my story that I'm a big drinker but I'm not. A few yes, but too many? No. We get to *Johnnie's* and dive right into a martini glass filled with Witch's Heart, a blackberry flavored cocktail that looks awesome and tastes great. I'm limiting myself to three because there's nothing worse than being the drunkest person in the room and then going home with the most sober person from the same room. Nick isn't allowed to drink in the bar and I respect that. I also hate the hung-over feeling the next day so I try to avoid it.

This makes me feel more adult. More in control. Throw in the costume and being surrounded by my friends and I'm in the best mood.

There's fake spider webs, werewolves, vampires, loads of onesies and over the top costumes everywhere I look. I haven't seen Nick yet so I signal to my friends that I'm going to go find him.

He's not in his office so I follow the corridor right out to the back and then take the fire stairs carefully since I'm wearing heels that could kill me if I slip. When I get to his apartment above the bar, there's one light on and through the window I see Nick struggling with braces. He's got some growth on his cheeks that he's been growing for tonight instead of shaving it clean every day. Fitted black jeans suit him but the huge boots don't. The red flannel I like too.

"Need some help?" I ask as I push through the door. My heels are loud on his floor and his eyes go there first. But not for long. His gaze is slow to lift and I can practically feel it touching me as he takes in my outfit.

"That is not a costume," he says, his tone gruff, coarse, kind of cranky.

My heart sinks and my steps slow. "You don't like it? It doesn't go with my cast." Which I've colored in black with a sharpie but it's getting grosser by the day with bits hanging off it.

"I fucking love it." His touch isn't gentle and neither is our kiss. His whiskers tickle.

When he finally lets my body go from his death grip, he holds my good hand high while I turn for him. "But so will every other guy down there." He attempts to wrap me in my cloak, cover me up. I laugh.

"You're the hero tonight though," I tell him while fixing his braces, my finger in his pants to fasten the clip. His intake of breath makes me hot. Hotter. "Maybe if you were the villain, things might take a turn? Then again maybe not. My friends think I have a thing for bad boys all of a sudden."

I don't expect him to get serious but he does. "Imelda, next week is going to change everything one way or another. You know that don't you? Your friends are right that I am the bad boy."

I don't answer until the other clip is secure on the waistband of his jeans. I wrap my arms around his neck and wait until he circles my waist in return. I don't want to push these words out of my mouth but I also don't want to ruin the good times we have left either. "I know what this is, Nick. If it all ends next week, I've had fun. You've taught me things I never knew were possible." I also force a chuckle and it's hollow. A lie to how I'm feeling inside. "I still don't know how some are possible. Whatever happens, I don't regret a thing."

"God, you're amazing," he says, kissing me again, holding me tight. "I definitely don't deserve you."

I attempt to rub my lipstick transfer from his mouth with my thumbs. "What you don't deserve is to be in this position in the first place. If I thought you were a common criminal, I wouldn't be here."

He doesn't answer. Just kisses me again. And again. And again.

At some point I push away. "We have to get downstairs. The girls will send a search party and we do not want that."

"I don't want everyone to know I live up here."

"Don't worry. Your secret is my secret."

"Okay. You go ahead. I need a minute."

"Are you sure you're okay?" He's acting kind of weird but I guess with the hearing on his mind, that's to be expected.

He gestures with his head downwards and my attention goes to the bulge in his pants. He rakes a hand through his already mussed hair and groans. "You are going to kill me in that dress."

I make a show of readjusting everything that will readjust, and all with a wicked smile on my painted lips. I lift my boobs higher in the corset-waisted dress and then bend over and run my hands (and ugly cast) up the fishnets to my thighs. I finish with a finger to the outside of my lips to make sure I'm not all smudged. Which I totally am. "I'll see you downstairs."

"Unless you want to stay here? You could text your friends and tell them the woodsman has it hard for Red Riding Hood?"

"Downstairs, Nick. You have to see how much everyone is loving the party. I want to have some fun with you!"

I grip the stair rail hard on my way down, walk back into the bar the way I came and join my friends for another round. There's no way these heels are going back up there after another cocktail but it isn't long before Nick shows up behind the bar.

He's all business as he pours drinks. He's still business even as he laughs and jokes with patrons. Always the professional. This is why I know he's good for me and not the negative version of the bad boy. This thing with his brother-in-law Matt was a one off. Nick said it himself. A hazard of the job. Alcohol and hot tempers never go hand-in-hand.

As if just thinking of Matt conjures him, he walks through the front doors of *Johnnie's* and has a woman under his arm. She's wearing go-go boots and a very short, bright, flowery dress reminiscent of the 60s. He's big-noting himself by dressing as a gangster. He does look slick but he also looks kind of drunk, as does the woman. I turn to find Nick and he's seen them too, judging by the scowl he's wearing. I'm caught in the middle of wanting to do something but not quite knowing how to help. I leave my friends again and go to Nick.

"Do you need me to do anything?" I ask him, my hand on his arm to get his attention just in case he doesn't hear me over the music.

He looks at the floor and sighs. It lifts his entire body but then he smiles, kisses me, right in front of an entire room full of friends, patrons and strangers. "Leave them be. They'll move on soon enough." And then Nick tries to wrap my red riding hood around me again.

I like this. There's banter but there's also a deeper connection. We share something now and even if this isn't going anywhere beyond next week, it'll keep me warm on the lonely nights.

I dance with my girlfriends while they beat off unwelcome and welcome advances. Everyone is horny tonight it seems. Too many short skirts and too much liquid courage in the room. I've never been to a real Halloween party like this before and I'm pretty damn proud of it. I pull out my phone to get some pictures for a portfolio if I ever decide to build one, but before I've clicked off the first shot, a shadow blocks my light.

"Do you mind?" I call over the volume of the music. Michael Jackson's Thriller and it's getting people moving.

"You wanna dance?" is slurred in my direction.

"No thanks," I say and turn to head in the opposite direction.

Someone grabs my arms and I'm spun so fast on my platforms heels that I nearly topple. I reach out my good hand to find purchase but am forced to hold onto the stranger holding me. Only this is no stranger. "Hi Matt."

"Hello, beautiful," he croons.

The alcohol sours in my stomach. It isn't that he's not pretty to look at. He absolutely is. But he's ugly on the inside. Through and through. It's that he obviously did nothing to speak up for Nick after the fight that landed him in front of a magistrate.

"Where's your girlfriend?" It's a question but it's also a reminder that he didn't come alone.

"Wife," he corrects me.

"But..." I stammer and maybe splutter. That's Nick's sister? My brain is going a million miles an hour as my gaze tries to pick him out of the crowd, my eyes darting so quick it hurts.

"What are you doing here?" He's come to cause trouble. It's in the cocky grin he flashes me, in the way his hand tightens on my arm as he pulls me toward the dance floor.

"You don't want to do this, Matt."

"We're just dancing, honey. Just one dance and then I'll leave you alone."

I hope beyond all hope that when Nick sees us—not if but when—that he remembers that I can take care of myself and stays out of it. I'll dance one dance with the son of a bitch and then ask him to leave.

"Why do you torture him?" I say to Matt as he wraps his arms around my waist and begins to move to music only he must be able to hear. The beat thumping out of the sound system isn't slow at all.

"Cause it's fun!" he laughs.

"And his sister? What does she think about this whole mess?"

Matt shrugs and I long to wipe the smug wanker look from his face. I wonder how bad it will hurt if I punch him with my cast? And will it hurt me or just hurt him. Feeling violent should be bad. I should feel bad. But I don't. I just feel violent towards this man who ruins lives for the fun of it.

I see Amy's shocked face as Matt whirls me dangerously around the dance floor but I shake my head in her direction. Candice is about to interrupt but I hold up a hand over Matt's shoulder to stop her. I can dance one dance.

Jess slips away and I really hope it's for the lady's and not to find Nick.

That hope is short lived. One more turn and there's Nick and his sister on the edge of the crowd. He is pissed. She looks...smug. The exact kind of smugness that Matt is wearing on his face.

Shit.

30

I do the only thing I can think of and slip out of Matt's arms.

Nick looks me over as he reaches a hand out and asks, "Are you alright?"

I nod. Of course I'm alright. "Don't do anything you'll regret," I try to keep my voice low, pitched into his ear, but his sister is right next to him. She hears. She laughs and then joins her husband on the dance floor.

Nick grinds his teeth together. It shifts his entire jaw. Nicks turns away first and I go to follow but once again I'm pulled backwards. My first instinct is once again reach out to steady myself and I catch the back of Nick's shirt but I don't have enough to hold onto. Jess yells my name as I'm hauled against Matt's chest, his arms like a vice around my stomach.

"I think we're going to have a little fun," he slurs into my ear.

My skin is crawling and I'm working out how best to extricate myself when I remember the high-heel to the toe maneuver. But I don't get that far. I pull my leg up and the rest happens in a blur of shapes and movements and pain.

Nick grabs Matt by the throat but Matt still has a hold of me. I'm falling but then my friends are there to catch me. I think a little of my hair gets pulled out but as soon as I have my feet under me, my first thought is that Nick cannot do this. Matt is only here to cause trouble. To get Nick into trouble.

"Nick" I shout but he can't hear me. He has Matt up against a wall while at least two other men try to get him off but he won't be moved. He shoves them away roughly and everyone gets the hint to butt out. But I won't do it.

"Nick! Don't do this." I'm pulling on his arm trying to get him to relax his grip while Matt turns purple and claws at the hand around his throat.

"He deserves this!" Nick shouts.

Matt gets a second wind and pushes off against the wall.

One minute I'm standing. The next minute I'm on the floor and I can't breathe. Nick has landed on top of me, crushing my broken hand and cast between my chest and his back, Matt on top of him. Matt throws a punch at Nick but Nick moves his head and there's so much pain in my face, I don't know where it's all coming from. My nose? My cheek? My jaw?

I can't breathe and I can taste blood and I become this hysterical thing thrashing and screaming to get up.

My brothers would hold me down, one would sit on my chest while the other would tickle my feet but they didn't realize I couldn't breathe when they did it. I would scream and scream until I'd pass out.

Big hands cradle my face and I get wilder, more out of control. I'm screaming and lashing out and I just need to be on my feet and take a deep breath.

I'm scooped up and the cold air hits me everywhere, my legs, my arms, my chest. But not my face. I'm no longer wild but the sobs wracking my body still take all of my breath. My head is pushed forward and I think it's Jess who is telling me to calm down and breathe.

"Big breaths, Mellow, big breaths, in, out, in and out."

I focus on her voice and breathe in time to her instructions until everything starts to come back into stark reality. What the fuck just happened?

Two men behaving like children. Two men who can't control their tempers or their fists. Fighting over women. Fighting over women like we're possessions, or weak, or available to the strongest victor.

"Take me home," I beg my friends.

Nick's voice comes from behind me and I shrug off his hand when it touches my shoulder. He apologizes, over and over, he says he's sorry. Why did he have to get involved?

"Why couldn't you just leave him be?" I whisper, big, fat tears falling from my hurting face to my now ridiculous dress.

"Imelda, let me call the police, you can press charges."

And then Nick will be arrested because technically he started this fight. Nick and his temper. The temper I told my friends he had a handle on. If he called the police, he'd go straight to jail. No diary, no day in court, no freedom. They might already be on their way.

I let Amy get under my shoulder on one side and I reach my hand out to Candice on the other. "Take me home. Now. Please. I need to get out of here. No cops."

I take a few steps but then stop to take my shoes off but my stupid cast seems to be hanging in pieces around my wrist and my other hand hurts too. Something drips from my nose onto the street between my toes and I see the tinge of blood mixed with tears glisten in the pool of streetlight.

What had started out so perfectly ended in me being hurt. The one thing my friends had tried to warn me about but I'd bet even they didn't mean hurt like this. If Nick and I had stayed fuck buddies and not blurred the lines, I wouldn't have been at the bar tonight. I wouldn't have helped make his party a success. I wouldn't have been hurt...

"How bad is it?" I ask Jess as she finishes cleaning my face with cotton swabs and makeup remover. They won't let me look in the mirror. Probably for the best.

I got slightly better the closer we got to my apartment. A cup of tea and a blanket wrapped around me brings me peace and calm. My face throbs but it isn't so bad. I'm sure nothing is broken.

Apart from my stupid heart. I take a deep breath in through my mouth and will myself not to cry. Again.

"That's that then," I mumble, more to myself than my girlfriends.

Amy sighs. "It won't look good," she says. "An assault charge on top of what he's already facing and he's a goner for sure."

I nod and my eyes fill with tears. Again.

Amy leans in and hugs me. "I'm so sorry, Mellow. We tried to warn you this wouldn't end well."

I smile through the tears. "Really? An I told you so? Already? At least wait until I finish bleeding." But it isn't funny and I don't need I told you so's. Not now, not ever.

Candice paces in front of the dining room table, into the lounge and then back into the dining room. "I'm going to bloody kill him," she is muttering. Nick or Matt? I'm not sure. It doesn't matter though because they are right. Even Denni was right in a way.

I only needed a Mr. Right Now to prove something to my friends and to myself. The fact that my Mr. Right Now came with a rap sheet meant it was only a matter of time until he flipped out. I couldn't make a relationship work with a bad boy. Here for a good time, not for a long time. Isn't that what people say?

The sob that breaks through from my chest and out of my mouth is so pitiful it makes all three of my friends gather me up. They hold me while I cry. I get blood, snot and tears on Jess's dress but she doesn't seem to mind.

Once my tears dry up, they help me out of my stupid costume and into a pair of comfy pajamas with cats all over them. They're a Christmas set but they're the first ones Candice finds and I find I need the extra comfort. Since my friends had planned to stay at my apartment after the party, they all change into pjs too. It's like an old-fashioned slumber party.

Only about an hour has passed since we left the bar and the buzzing starts. Someone is leaning on my intercom. We know who it is. It's nearly one in the morning and everyone else in the building will be sleeping rather than expecting a visit from either the cops or a guy with baggage and a record.

"Make him stop," I complain and pull the blanket over my face.

Amy leans on the button and yells, "Go home, Nick. Come back tomorrow."

"Let me see her," his voice comes back, scratchy through the years old system.

"Not tonight. She'll call you when she's ready."

"Just tell me she's okay. How badly did he hurt her?"

"She's fine. Just a few bruises. It looks worse than it is. She's sleeping so go home and wait for her to call you."

Silence descends and I thought he'd go but then he says, "Tell her I'm sorry, okay. Can you do that? Tell her I am so sorry."

I clamp my good hand over my mouth so he won't hear me crying. I should have stayed away from Nick. I should have accepted where my life was at and not looked for anything more. Then none of this would have happened.

I wouldn't have found satisfaction in his hands.

I wouldn't have needed the kind of completion I hadn't known existed until he gave it to me.

I wouldn't know the feeling of a shattered heart if only I'd just stayed the hell away from Nick.

Now he was going to go to jail and one of my friends' predictions would come true. I'm unemployed, broke and broken. And now I'm alone too.

Dear Freddy,

Something terrible happened tonight. Matt and Dahlia showed up at the party and Matt wouldn't leave Imelda alone. When I saw that arsehole put his hands on my girl, I saw red.

But once again she grounded me. When she told me to calm down, I did. But then Matt came back again and seeing him with his arms around Imelda, throwing her around, I had to step in. I had to. Once I had him, I didn't want to let him go. Maybe I do have a problem. But it's not with anger. It's with my sister and her dead-shit husband. It's like they only exist to upset me...

Nick had thought his temper on the boil before, when he'd seen his sister's husband in a booth, his hands and mouth all over another woman. He'd punched Matt so many times he'd lost count. He'd protected his sister and had been charged with assault for his trouble.

After the first hit, Matt hadn't been able to fight back. Nick had been in such a furious haze, he hadn't noticed his brother-in-law didn't lift a hand to defend himself, the first punch had half knocked him out.

Nick's lawyer had argued that Nick had raged out, blacked out while still fighting. That he wasn't in control of his actions and in a way he hadn't been, but in another way, this guy had messed with his sister. Not only was he cheating, he was doing it in Nick's bar, right in front of everyone!

Only, Dahlia hadn't cared at all and it wasn't the first time Nick had got in a fight over her. She was the epitome of a train wreck and he'd come to her rescue time and again but no more. Not after she testified against him. Testified against her own brother about his wicked temper and how her own husband had only made one tiny little mistake.

Nick wrote his sister off after that. He didn't even know she'd gone back to Matt. Last he'd heard, they were separated. That's when Matt had come to the bar a few weeks back for his first attempt at Imelda. He should have known the rat bastard would try again. Nick had shown his interest in Imelda and shouldn't have. She became the toy Matt just had to take away.

Nick knew exactly what was at stake this time and he had zero plans to get involved. The fact that Dahlia was back with the piece of shit, and at his bar, pricked his anger. But he'd been prepared to let them have their fun, wait until they were bored, and then piss off.

Until they literally dragged Imelda into their games. Until Matt had physically taken a hold of Imelda and tossed her around like she was a puppet. He'd only meant to make Matt let go. He was only going to squeeze his throat until Imelda was clear but then they'd all fallen over in a tangle and he couldn't move.

His reaction was to duck to avoid the punch but the sound as Matt's knuckles connected not with the floor but with Imelda's face... He'd never forget that sound. Not ever. His stomach turned and he worried he might be sick.

Thank God someone had recorded the whole exchange and Matt was the only one arrested. Despite Nick being technically on bail, the witnesses had all given statements that he had simply tried to break up an altercation as the bar owner. No more. No less. He passed the breath test and didn't get taken in.

I know you're likely not going to believe this but I wasn't going to hit him. I didn't hit him. I just wanted him to let Imelda go so I could kick his ass out of my bar. When Matt hit her, I couldn't do a god-damned thing about it. I couldn't hit back, I couldn't protect her. I couldn't even

look her in the eye. What does she think of me now? Probably that I'm
gutless and nothing but trouble...

The judge was going to throw him in jail anyway. It's not like he
was a simple bystander to the mess. He had four days to get his affairs
in order, put the bar on the market or hire a manager and clean up
his books, put some measures in place while he was away.

Nick couldn't help but think it was a cruel blessing in disguise,
what had happened that night. People like him didn't get girls like
Imelda. It was probably only a matter of time until it all blew up
anyway. Better for her if it was a clean break. If he'd kept his hands
to himself from the get-go, she would still be working her nice job,
living her nice life with her nice friends and her sweet little cats.

He was a fool to think he'd be good for her. Selfish to hold onto
her when she was far too good for the likes of him.

31

As much as I want to hide my head in the sand until the bruising on my face goes down, there's only so long a girl can be silent and off the radar. The police have been my only visitors besides Candice, Amy and Jess. A junior officer came by with a camera and no matter how much I protested, insisted that they collect evidence. When his partner threatened to arrest me and take me downtown so they could have the photos forever on my mug shot, I had no choice but to agree. They did tell me that Nick wasn't in trouble for this altercation. They didn't have to tell me it would still look bad for his case though.

I've had two days since then to wallow. If only someone would pay me to do it. I'm getting really good at it.

A knock at my door comes early in the morning three days after the incident. No calls from Nick. No texts or visits either. But my phone is broken. I must have landed on it. Still, he has my address, he knows where I live.

"Imelda? Imelda open the door this instant."

"Oh, fuck me," I mumble into a pillow. I don't get up.

"I know you're in there, Imelda, your nice neighbor told me you haven't left your apartment in days. Let me in right now."

Nosy neighbor more like it. I get to my feet and shuffle over to the door. I don't care that my hair looks like rats have nested in it. I don't care that I'm still wearing the same cat pajamas or that my cast is literally falling off my hand in crooked pieces of blackened green. I open the door. "Hello, Mother."

"Jesus, Imelda, what happened to you?"

I'd be touched by her concern if she wasn't trying to shove me back into the room so she could shut the door. So no one would see me.

"Did that boy do this to you?" she asked, taking stock.

The bruises really aren't so bad today. More green than purple. My nose isn't broken, thank God. I do not need another hospital visit.

There is a tiny split in the skin above my eyebrow which, with my squashed nose, bled like I was dying.

"Nick did not do this to me."

"Who did? What has happened to you? What are they going to say when you miss all of these days at the hotel? What will they say when they see you like this? You'll lose your job."

I just don't care anymore. I think this is what rock bottom looks like so I decide to test the theory that the only way from rock bottom is up. "I don't have a job."

My mother clasps her hands over her heart with a theatrical gasp. "They fired you?"

"I quit."

Silence. But not for long. "Why did you quit? When? This is not a game, child."

I meet her shocked, questioning gaze with my own flat stare. "No, it's not, mother. It's my life. *My life*. I quit my job because I'd rather be unemployed than face the coworker every day who set me up to be sexually assaulted. I'd rather be broke and homeless and living on the street than give into the sexist arsehole boss who partially blamed *me* for the whole mess because, ya know, bro's before hoes! There are worse situations in this life than to be unemployed."

"Why are you taking that tone with me?"

Just like my mother to turn it all around. Where is the hug for her daughter who'd literally been in a bar fight? Where is the concern for her child's suffering? "Do you even care that I've been hurt?"

"Of course I do. No mother wants to see her daughter like this."

The way she gestures *at* me doesn't make me angry. It makes me sad. I've been toeing this line with my mother my whole life. Nothing is ever right for her. Nothing I do is ever good enough, not like my medical profession siblings. "No, Mother. *You* don't want to see me like this."

"What is that supposed to mean?"

"Do you know this is only the second time you've ever been to my apartment?"

When she flounders like a fish out of water, I smile. It's terrifying to realize that her acceptance isn't really my problem anymore. That I don't care if I'm the disappointment in the family. Someone has to be. From the times I refused to hug or be kissed on the cheeks by her friends, to when she was extracting me from her skirts to making me stand up straight, smile, make small talk, even though she must have known how much it would kill me, I hid in shame, withdrew into myself until university where I finally found a measure of freedom. It's been ten years and I'd rather hide from her still.

"I'm not doing this anymore with you," I say into the heavy tension that's settled in the room.

"Doing what? Imelda, speak up and try to make sense."

"Everything I have done in my life has been to make you proud. At first. But then nothing worked." I raise the tone of my voice until I'm perfectly mimicking her. "Your grades aren't good enough to get into medical school. Look at what your sister has been through and her SATs were almost perfect. Your brothers managed, why can't you?"

"I have never said those things to you."

"No," I say with a sad shake of my head. "You didn't have to say them. I could see it in your eyes."

"You're being awfully dramatic, Imelda. Maybe I should come back when you're feeling better."

"Please don't bother," I tell her and follow her to the door. "I'll see you at dinner."

"Yes, well." She sniffs and nods. "We can talk about it then. You're too overset right now and you're making no sense."

"See you in a few weeks, Mother."

As she walks down the corridor with the cat pee stains in the carpet, careful not to touch anything, using her arm to open the door so only her sleeve touches the glass and not her skin, I wonder if I was born into the wrong family. I am literally the black sheep.

I'm wistful as I head back into my apartment. I pat Harry when he comes out of hiding. Move Matilda over on my bed so I can sit down next to her on the comforter and then laugh as Missy comes flying through the open window as if another cat is chasing her.

This is exactly where I belong. With my cats. As soon as I get a job, everything can go back to normal again.

I don't want to think about Nick. About his hearing tomorrow. About the fact he hasn't come by to see me. It's a clean break but it has edges so jagged, it's like I've been sliced open and left raw.

The girls have been by every day to see me. Candice said *Johnnie's* has been closed up since that night which tells me Nick is in trouble. I do wonder if there's anything I can do for him? Testify on his behalf that Matt was there to annoy him and the best way to do that was through me?

But would Nick welcome my interference? There has to be a reason for his staying away these last few days. I get that he feels bad but he hasn't been by once other than that one time a few hours after the incident. Maybe he's decided I'm too much hassle after all? If Matt hadn't set his sights on me, Nick wouldn't have been forced to action. Or maybe he still would. I'm so fucking confused!

The only clear, and very loud, factor here is that he's a bad boy and I'm a good girl.

We're too different. It doesn't matter how much I let loose and give in to my inner she-devil, it never feels one hundred percent right. Don't get me wrong, it's always good in the moment but life is more than those moments. I have to turn my energy to finding a job first and sometime down the track, I can hunt for Mr. Right.

There has to be a good guy version of Nick out there somewhere. Doesn't there?

The smell of camphor, wax and old books can't be hidden by air fresheners and carpet cleaner and it all serves to make Nick's head ache even more than it did yesterday. The law chambers he was summoned to for his hearing is intimate and small but the weight of the day carries a piano and it's sitting painfully on his chest. The only fact he'd come to terms with is that he had no control over his life anymore. It's all up to the judge. He'd stood before her as she'd clucked her tongue over the most recent turn of events, reading from the police report on her desk. He'd handed over the diary, seriously considering burning the bloody thing since it was unlikely to make much difference now anyway.

Then he's told to sit while she reads each and every entry.

The ticking clock is the only sound in the room besides the turn of each page.

"Dahlia?" the judge asked. "Your sister. Matt's wife?"

Nick nods.

"Say it out loud, for the record, Mr. Russo."

"Yes, Dahlia is my sister. Matt's wife."

"Is he the one you were fighting with when you were arrested this time?"

She says *this time* like my one and only stint in jail brands me a loser for life. "Yes, ma'am."

"And your first assault charge?" She consults my file and then looks back at me. "At nineteen? For the record, what was that for?"

"Dahlia again," I remind her, not that it makes a hell of a difference anyway.

"Your sister sounds like she still has the same lousy taste in the company she keeps."

I nod and then remember the court secretary silently typing in the corner. "Yes, ma'am."

"Why do you keep fighting for her?"

"She's my sister."

"She's an adult. If she gets into these messes, surely she can get herself out?"

That's the problem. She can't. "Yes ma'am."

"Stop all the yes ma'ams and talk to me, Nick. I'm trying to help you."

Tracy had been his court appointed lawyer at nineteen. She'd worked as a public defender and had helped him not only avoid more than three months in jail but she'd picked him up and put him in the straight and narrow, set him up with an uncle he hadn't known about and made sure his life got better.

His mistake, as he saw it, was staying in contact with his sister.

"Dahlia and Matt came into the bar to cause trouble. There's video evidence. I only held him back. He's the one who pushed me over and then he punched Imelda in the face."

"And how is the young lady?"

"I don't know," Nick mumbled.

"You haven't checked on her?"

"Her friends tell me she's fine. Just a few bruises."

"I have the police photographs if you want to see them?"

His heart thumps against his ribs. "I don't want to see them."

Tracy asks the secretary to take a coffee break and then waits for her to leave the room before she goes on. "Nick, I gave you the diary sentence because I couldn't just let you off after the last time and now you're in trouble again. I just don't know what to do."

I look to the bailiff standing guard at the door but he might as well be at Buckingham palace standing guard over the queen. He doesn't move a muscle.

"It won't happen again," Nick assures her through clenched teeth. It sure as hell won't. Dahlia can fight her own battles from here on out. Unless she asks for help. Specifically.

"I think you should sell the bar."

That gets my full and complete attention. "You what? Is that your sentence? You're going to make me sell the bar?"

She raises one brow. "Don't be dumb. I can't make you do that. I'm offering you a piece of advice. Sell the bar, get your girl, settle somewhere away from your family. Away from your sister."

"Imelda isn't my girl. We were just hanging out."

"So, hang out in another city. Take a long vacation. Start over."

"She doesn't want a convicted felon as a boyfriend."

"Did she say that?"

"No, of course she didn't say it." She doesn't know about the previous conviction, just the weight of this one hanging over his head.

"But she knows about the diary? About your temper?"

Nick was feeling about three inches tall. "Yeah."

"And she didn't care. Take what you started with her and show her you're secure. That you're worth taking a chance on."

"But I'm not secure. I wanted to hit Matt so bad."

"You can't tell me that, Nick."

"I think you have to lock me up. For my own good. For the sake of Dahlia and Matt. If they come back to my bar, I'm going to lose it. Not tomorrow, but one day."

"Matt's going away for a long stint, Nick. The footage shows he broke at least three laws, one a felony. He's being sentenced tomorrow but he's not getting out for a minimum of seven years."

"Make sure we don't go to the same prison." Wouldn't that be the icing on the shit sandwich? If they wound up in the same cell?

Tracy swears under her breath. "You're not going to prison." She clicks her fingers at the bailiff and asks him to bring Lucy, the secretary, back into the room.

Twenty minutes later, all charges against him are dropped and Nick emerges out into the sunshine of a new afternoon. His head is spinning but in a good way. He's free.

Tracy has been trying for ten or more years to tell him that just because he's a bit of a brawler doesn't necessarily make him a criminal. "Protecting your sister is noble," she'd said. But she also told him he had to draw the line on someone who didn't want to be saved.

"Stop fighting her fights until she comes to you and asks for your help. Even then, you call someone else. You're bigger and you're stronger than most of those other boys and it's going to land you in the shit every time."

He nods and agrees on the outside but on the inside, he'll always put family first. Whether his deserved it or not.

Shaking off the sentence hanging over his head is exhilarating and there's only one person he wants to celebrate with. He heads straight to Imelda's but is intercepted on the stoop by her friend Amy.

"What are you doing here, Nick?"

"I really need to see Imelda. I've got news for her."

"She doesn't need you in her life, Nick."

"Did she say that?" he asks, the bottom falling out of his day once again.

"She didn't have to. You've got to know that she's been playing at being someone else with you but it's over. She has to get a job and get back to her real life."

"I think she can tell me that herself."

Amy shakes her head. "She can't see past your big blue eyes so do her a favor and allow her to move on. Since you came into the picture, she's been all over the place and we don't like it. Imelda doesn't like it. She's someone who needs stability. A stable job, a stable partner, a stable life."

"I can give that to her," he protests. As he squeezes his hands into fists, the edge of the diary bites into his palm.

"If you really believe that, at least give her a little time to sort it out in her own head. Two weeks. Maybe four?"

She's right. Her friends know her better than anyone else, better than him. "Can you at least tell her I stopped by? That I... I... Never mind. Just tell her I'll call in a few weeks."

She looks as though she'll tell him no but then she nods and enters the building.

He considers following and demanding that Imelda tell him herself but if she truly wants to see him, she knows where to find him. He wouldn't open the bar but he would be home.

His heart is heavy again as he walks away. He looks back once but her curtains are drawn.

She knows where to find him.

32

I really hate family dinners. I really disliked them before but that dislike has morphed into a hate so primal that I have to keep unclenching my fists. And my jaw.

Tonight I have my petulant panties on. My skirt is short so if I drop something and have to pick it up, there'll be flashing. I'm wearing my knee high boots off season and a skimpy, transparent blouse completes my childish ensemble. It's not that my clothes are childish, it's my attitude. I've decided that my mother and my family are going to have to accept me the way I am right now or not at all. It won't be hard to miss these lovely events. I can catch up with my sister whenever I venture to her part of town and my brothers can keep ignoring me like they usually do until there's an issue they get dragged into.

Being unemployed means it's still early in the day when I walk slowly down the sidewalk on my mother's street. I wave to her neighbors and stop to talk to Luke's parents a few doors down. Mr. Mason mentions how grown up I'm looking these days but his eyes stray lower and lower until Mrs. Mason bumps her elbow into his and clears her throat loudly.

I wave them goodbye and flounce down the street like a teenager rather than a nearly thirty-year-old. I know it lifts my skirt when I bounce on my knee highs. I stop in front of my mother's house and lift my face to the weak sunshine while I get my mental battle props in a line. Tonight I'm going to tell them all what I really think of them and either they'll love me and respect me for speaking up for myself or I'll be uninvited, disinherited and truly on my own.

I'm okay with any outcome but I can't for one more day be looked down upon by members of my own family.

The door opens behind me but I don't move. I hear a giggle and a sshhh.

"Imelda," is hissed at me. Twice.

"Hello, Mother." I don't turn.

"What in God's name are you doing, child?"

I grit my teeth. "Just enjoying the sunshine."

"Will you get inside before the neighbors notice you?"

I finally turn and strut into the house, my heels decently loud on the floorboards. "Mr. and Mrs. Mason pass on their regards."

"You went by their house? Wearing that?"

I ignore her frown and look down at my outfit. It's a bit much but I'm feeling a bit much, like I'm going to burst out of my own skin. I miss Nick. I miss the sex, the banter, the laughter. I miss doing my own thing and knowing it's the right thing for me because it's my choice to make. I miss the voice I was given, the freedom to say and do whatever the hell I want. I miss the Imelda I was on my way to being.

It seems too silly to think it but the only person holding her back is me. I've been told my whole life that my behavior reflects on my parents and the upbringing they gave me. I was told as a little girl that if I didn't say hello and hug people that I was being rude and disrespectful to their friends and other members of our family. I was told people would think there was something wrong with me. And there bloody was! I was told as a teen to sit quietly and only speak when spoken to, then instead of people thinking I was rude, they would simply think me well-mannered and polite. There's no fucking difference! Quiet is quiet. For whatever reason. I was never intentionally being rude. I was a terrified child. Terrified of everything and everyone.

Not anymore!

I walk into the dining room and take three deep breaths. "I'm glad everyone is here. I have something to say."

My mother lets out an audible sigh. "Can we eat before there is drama please?"

I can't eat. There's a rock lodged in my throat already. My tongue is dry and my pulse is racing. "You're all going to want to sit down for this."

Another sigh and then, "You're already unemployed, how much worse could it get?" A gasp. "You're pregnant aren't you? To the man who beat you?"

"He did not beat me. I was in the wrong place at the wrong time and I got punched in the face. That man is in jail and I am not pregnant." I want to add, *that's what birth control is for,* but don't.

I breathe in again but this time the breath is shaky and my anxiety is off the charts high. I've been rehearsing the words in my head but we all know they never come out right. "I'm sure you're all aware of the recent changes I've made in my life, including the fact that I quit my job." Clearly news to my brothers. They both shake their heads with confused but bored, expressions. "I am sick and tired of being the butt of all the jokes in this house. I am, was, good at my job and I enjoyed it."

Tanay chimes in with, "If you loved it so much, why'd do you quit?"

"The reasons are none of your business, or anyone else's. But I was bored. It doesn't matter, what matters is that from now on I don't want to hear any negativity towards my life choices-"

"You're gay?" my mother cries out as though it's the answer she's been searching for all my life.

"For fuck's sake, I am not gay."

Aadive says, "It'd be okay if you are gay."

"I'm not bloody gay! I have been sleeping with a man, with a penis! A big, strong man with a big strong penis!" *Jesus.* I need to calm down.

Tanay mutters under his breath and it sounds like, "Me thinks she doth protest too much."

"My sex life is off limits to all of you, and that includes you, mother. My career is also off limits from now on. You lot have made my life so miserable for so long and I'm done feeling like the black sheep in the room." I pin my two brothers with a glare and add, "Literally."

"Alice is the only one who doesn't make fun of me, my job, my skin, my looks, my apartment."

My mother is shocked by it all. I wait for her to turn it all around, back to her, back to something she must have done wrong. Like drinking a single glass of champagne when she was pregnant with me, a story I've heard so many times before. She says, "What has brought all of this about? Is it this because of the boy you've been seeing?"

"Why does it have to about the boy? Nick is a really great guy but it has nothing to do with him." My eyes burn but I will not cry. Not here. I start pacing the dining room. "My friends made me realize there is something missing from my life and I thought it was a boyfriend, a husband, a relationship. But it isn't. It's the fact that I've lived up until now trying to please you lot. Trying to do whatever it takes to get a congratulations, or just one jot of praise. My grades were good enough to get in medical school but I didn't want to! I don't want to run a hotel or a hospital or even a drugstore. I want to plan parties and weddings and see the smiles on the faces of the people I help. I don't want to save the world or lives or money. I just want to be happy. Why isn't that good enough for any of you?"

Silence descends but predictably it doesn't last long and the matriarch exerts her authority once again. "You can't make a career out of being a party planner, Imelda."

"Who says?" I challenge her. "You?"

"There's no money in it, no stability. You don't know what it's like to be poor. To have to sell something to make the rent."

"Neither do you!" I explode.

Her face falls and she sits. "Before you were born, before Alice and Aadive, when I fell pregnant with Tanay, your father and I were living in a house we shared with another family because none of us were making enough money to get by. Your father was still studying and I was taking classes but we had nothing. Nothing to bring a baby home to. We had to live like that for three years until we scraped money together to buy a home. I push you all because I never want to see you in that place we were."

This is a new story. And it made so much sense. The keeping up with the neighborhood, the friends with money. Always making the best impression. "You never said."

She shakes her head. "And I wish I didn't tell you now either. You must make something of yourself to be financially secure in this world."

I look at her. Really look at her. I know she believes this to be the only truth but I have another one. "Have you ever heard the one that goes, money doesn't buy you happiness? Dad worked all the time. He was never home. You were never happy and neither was he. Maybe if we needed less money, we would have had him more. *You* would have had him more..."

This time when she shakes her head it's as if she's shaking the reality out and returning to nonsense. "You know absolutely nothing, Imelda. About your father and me. About living in poverty. About raising children. Take my advice and get a good job that pays well. Marry a man who has everything already. You'll be well taken care of."

"If he has everything then what does he need me for?" I hate that she's clinging onto these antiquated notions of being a good and proper little wife.

"Don't be a smarty pants, Imelda. I think we've had just about enough of this kind of conversation."

My siblings have been quiet and I didn't expect any less. They won't stand up to her either. "I've lost my appetite." I stand to leave and no one stops me.

Alice looks as though there's something she wants to say but she bites down on it. The boys look away and my mother's lips are compressed to a thin, disapproving line.

I pick up my purse from the hallstand and slam the door on my way out. My eyes no longer burn. I don't even want to cry anymore. I just want to be happy. Not rich. Not famous. Not even infamous.

Why is that too much to accept?

33

Another week passes and I have my appointment to get my cast reset but the doctor tells me there's little point and fits me for a brace instead. I still have to wear it all day every day, except in the shower, but it's more manageable. More comfortable. Not green. Because the break was only very minor, there's no bones shifting together, no chances of doing further damage really.

He did tell me not to hit anyone else. Said I'm lucky.

I don't feel lucky. I'm still out of sorts. Restless and wandering. I've had a total of five interviews. Four for hotel work and one for a convention center but none excite me. There's no thrill for a new challenge. The jobs are the same. Exactly the same. The same work, the same politics, the same crap in and out. Isn't that what I'd just left?

An advertisement in the paper catches my eye and I pull my cell straight out of my pocket and dial the number.

"Is this Peter? As in the Party Man?"

"It sure is, how can I help you?"

"I just saw your ad in the paper and wondered if we might be able to make a time to sit and talk about business opportunities."

"Are you in the market for a franchise?" he asks.

"I don't really know what I'm in the market for, to be honest. I've just wound up a job as an events coordinator of a major hotel and I only know that's the type of job I don't want."

"I'm free in an hour?"

I say the name of a café a few blocks from my apartment and he agrees. Just like that.

I tear the square out of the paper with the relevant details and then head to my closet. I won't be needing interview gear for this. I take out a soft pair of worn skinny jeans, nice boots with a low heel and a blouse and blazer combo. Professional yes. Armor? No.

I have a list of resolutions now.

No hiding. Behind anything.

Be myself.

Only reach for what I want, not what others want for me.

Do only good things for good reasons.

That's it and I may have had some help from a few new-age, life coach type websites, but this sits well with me. I have some savings but they're dwindling. I need a job and I'll need it soon but I also need to take a job that fulfills my soul, not one guaranteed to destroy it.

Yes, I have been reading. And watching too much affirmation TV.

Today is actually one of those rare days in the life of an unemployed person where I have two events to get dressed up for. First is the meeting with the party guy and the next is a date with an ex. Well, not a date. I don't think. He found my profile on Facebook and asked if I want to catch up. I couldn't think of a good excuse to say no. I have no job to get up early for. I'm not working late. I'm not tired. I say yes.

My meeting with the party guy goes well. Really well. When I shake his hand I feel comfortable and energized. I put forward a plan to him. At first he's disappointed because his ad was to sell his business so he can retire. I convince him to take me on as an apprentice of sorts, teach me the ropes, and then in twelve months, I buy him out. Unless he has other offers?

He doesn't.

He needs twenty-four hours to think on it and I agree. You can't make hasty decisions. Unless you're me.

I need to call someone to tell them, to share in my excitement. But I have no one to call.

Nick is probably in prison, my friends are probably sick of my drama and I don't know if my sister is talking to me or not.

I try Alice and she picks up on the first ring. "Hi," she whispers.

"Where are you?" I ask.

"At home. I just finally got Jia to lie down for a nap."

"You're looking after her again, how's that all going?"

Alice groans. "I think she's the devil. She was up all night, happy, playing, wouldn't go to sleep, but then she got cranky and I didn't know what to do. Babies are loud! Anyway, what's up?"

I can't help it. I have to ask. "How was dinner after I left?"

"Quiet. No one was very hungry."

"Are you very angry with me?"

"Why would I be angry with you?" she asks. "You said what you needed to. Mum's story made a little sense but it sounded like an excuse rather than a reason. Nothing is going to change her mind. She said you'll be back next dinner."

Oh, she did, did she?

Alice goes on. "Listen, the offer to live at my loft still stands. I know you're in a lease but if you get stuck, I have a spare room. I can pay out the end of your time and you can come live with me? Find a good job on this side of the city?"

"I know you're trying to help but I'm okay. Really I am. I just had a meeting with a party planner. I've offered to buy his business from him."

Silence. I'm beginning to hate the fact no one wants to give their honest opinion straight away. "Um. You did? Aren't you kind of broke?"

"I have some savings. Where did this idea come from that just because I work a normal job in a normal tax bracket, that I can't put something away for a rainy day?"

"How much do you have?" Alice asks.

"Not enough," I admit. "But I've asked that he trains me for twelve months and then I'll buy him out."

"And he said yes to this? How do you know you can trust him?"

"He hasn't said anything yet. But he didn't say no."

"I hope you know what you're doing," she says down the line. "We're all really worried about you right now, Mellow. This is not like you. Those clothes you wore to dinner? Quitting your job with nothing to go to? What's going on with you and Nick?"

I wish I never told her about Nick. "Nothing is going on. We haven't spoken for a few weeks." Twenty-six days to be exact.

"Did you break it off or did he?"

I know I walked away from him. I didn't answer the intercom or let him in that night when he tried to apologize as if it was all his fault when it wasn't. He hadn't been back and *Johnnie's* had been shut every time I passed it.

My phone has been replaced but all my contacts were lost. I considered visiting him at his place above the bar but it didn't feel right. That's his space and if he wanted me in it, he could have called or stopped in.

He's probably thinking that if he hadn't got involved with me, Matt likely wouldn't have shown up. I'm trouble when he didn't want any. Didn't need any.

Turns out I was the one with the temper anyway. I broke my hand on a guy's face. I quit my job and then had it out with my mother in what pretty much amounted to a tantrum.

And I don't regret any of it. Not one bit.

· ♥ · ♥ · ♥ · ♥ · ♥ ·

At nine o'clock I'm still wearing my jeans and blazer from the interview figuring it's a just a drink with an ex. I don't need to impress anyone. I don't need to dress up and put on a show. I just need to be myself. My new mantra.

When Paul arrives at the little Italian restaurant, I'm nervous and I don't know why. It's not a date, I keep telling myself. But he looks good! We met in college and he still looks the same. Same chinos and blazer. Same citrus scent on his navy collar when we hug hello.

It's nostalgic. But not in a way that reaches anything overly sentimental in me.

We make small talk through the meal and reminisce. "What are you doing with yourself these days?" I ask him.

"Lead architect on the bridge reconstruction," he says proudly.

"Oh? Good for you." I try to sound happy but really I'm just bored.

"What about you? What are you up to now?"

Instead of telling him the sordid story of how I wound up unemployed, I ask, "What did you think of our sex life? When we were together?"

Paul chokes on his garlic bread and I go back to eating the best lasagna I've ever had as if I haven't just dropped a dirty bomb on his lap.

"I'm sorry? What?"

"Were you bored? It was never fireworks and passion but tell me what you really thought at the time? I broke up with you if I remember correctly, but you couldn't have been happy? No, not happy. Satisfied?" I nod and meet his gaze. His eyes are watering from coughing and he gulps three big slurps of red wine from an oversized glass. "Were you satisfied?" I ask.

"Were you?" he comes back with as though I just took a hammer to his masculinity. He's defensive and leans in low over the table, pitching his voice to a whisper so no one overhears. "Where's this coming from, Imelda?"

God, how I wish people would stop asking me that. It's such a dumb question. "I just want to know. If I hadn't broken up with you, would you have broken up with me?"

He considers me over the table and I'm not regretting asking the question. This might help me understand something. He says, "We were both so busy. How long were we together? Four months? Over mid-terms? I was so distracted by doing well on my exams that I don't even really remember much about it."

"About *it*? About our relationship?"

"We didn't have much of a relationship. We were hanging out. Having sex and having fun."

"We were definitely in a relationship, Paul. What do you remember about me?"

He shifts uncomfortably in his seat. "What do you mean?"

"Was I fun? What drew you to me?"

"I guess it was how serious you were all the time. I wasn't looking for a giggly coed who spent more time on her nails and hair than studying. I was looking for someone who was as serious about college as I was."

"I was serious, wasn't I?" I was still fighting my shyness and wanted to connect with someone, anyone. I had my girlfriends but they were always with boys and I was either the third wheel or left behind. Paul had made me feel like I was given a second look by someone.

"Are you having some kind of crisis, Imelda?"

I laugh. "No. No crisis."

He tilts his glass in my direction and says, "I like it when you laugh. You should do it more often."

Cheesy but my cheeks warm and I eat another bite of lasagna. Drink another glass of wine even though I really don't like a red.

"Can I walk you home?" Paul asks as he helps me with my jacket.

"I'm over on Gardener," I tell him.

"I'll see you home and then get a cab. If you want?"

Did I want? After being attacked by Ted and then Matt, having someone walk me home would be nice. Nick had walked me home a couple of times. Denni once said I didn't want a gentleman. I wanted a man who would bend me over the hood of his Mercedes and make me forget my own name. Not surprisingly he was wrong about that too. I did want a gentleman. Someone to walk me to my door and kiss me goodnight.

Oh, God, would Paul want a goodnight kiss? Did I?

As we stroll in the chilly night, the small talk dies and it leaves me to wonder why I can't have a gentleman who will bend me over his hood? I bet Nick would if the situation warrants it. And he has a Mercedes too. I could imagine being cheek to the polished metal, my dress flicked up in the dark driveway to his building, panties around my ankles, Nick behind me, his big, strong hands bruising my hips as he holds on to stop me sliding across his paintwork.

A thought pops into my mind so suddenly that I stop dead in the middle of the sidewalk.

Paul stops as well and turns to look at me. "Everything okay?" he asks. "Did you leave something behind?"

"No. I...I just realized something. Sorry. I'm a bit distracted."

"You're not really yourself."

I frown as we walk. His words irritate me. "How do you know I'm not myself?"

"You're different."

"A fair bit of time has passed since school," I point out.

"Yeah, but do any of us really change? I went to a reunion last year and everyone was still the same. Sure, different hairstyles, different careers, different situations, but at the heart of it, everyone was still the same personality. You can't change that."

"Bullshit."

"I beg your pardon?"

It's no wonder he's confused. I have been too. "You don't know who a person is from a few hours. You can't possibly know any more than the exterior they show you at the time."

"I took a few semesters in psych and it's been proven. The leopard cannot change his spots."

"But people can change anything they want. Eyes, skin, face, size, shape. Why not personality? Three months ago I was a doormat who did everything everyone wanted me to do. I said the things they wanted me to say and acted correctly at all times."

"And now?"

"Now I want to be swept off my feet. I want a job that doesn't require me to say yes all day every day. I want my family and friends to see me for me and accept who I am becoming. I guess I want to be *seen* and still loved."

"That's pretty deep for a catchup meal."

I begin to laugh and the load I've been carrying lifts. What I really want is to have my cake and eat it too. I want to be wild in the bedroom, let my hair down and be uninhibited. I want to look forward to the possibility of being bent over the hood of a guy's car but have the choice if it goes that far or not. I want my intelligence acknowledged rather than questioned. I've been running that hotel for years but without the acknowledgement that I was doing it and doing it well. My family see me as wasting my time. My girlfriends see me as lonely and isolated. And I let them. I let them all believe what they want to about me without showing them they're wrong.

I gave it a good crack with the confrontation over dinner, but I need to prove to them all I can stand on my own two feet. That they don't have to worry about me.

"This is me," I say, coming to a stop on the third step of my building.

"Nice place," Paul says with a nod.

He does want to kiss me. He lingers and I actually for once in my life get the body language cue. I lean in and press my lips to his. He cradles my face with his cold, lean fingers and touches his tongue to mine. His mouth is also cold. And wet. I don't like it. I pull away and attempt a smile.

A throat being cleared gets our attention and I assume it's one of my cranky neighbors wanting to pass to the door. It isn't.

"Nick?" What the hell is he doing here?

"Uh, hi. Bad time?"

My cheeks are on fire as is the rest of my body and it's nothing to do with the wet, cold kiss. It's like I've been caught out doing something I shouldn't be doing but he never called or came around. We weren't boyfriend and girlfriend.

"You didn't go to jail?"

"All the charges were dropped, particularly after what Matt did to you."

I nod as if I understand. "What do you want, Nick?"

He looks from me to Paul and then back to me again. "I...It's stupid. I shouldn't have come."

He's holding something in his hand. It has brown wrapping and a ribbon tied in a clumsy yellow bow.

I step down one step and then another. "No, you should have come. Last week. Or the week before that. You didn't even have the decency to check to see how I was going after being punched in the face by your crazy brother-in-law." I don't know why I'm yelling but my voice gets louder with every word. I want to hit him over the head with every accusation, with every day he didn't make contact, with every hour he wasn't touching me and telling me everything would be all right.

He doesn't yell. He doesn't need to. "I did come by. That night. I also came a few days later after the court hearing too. Your friend told me not to come back for a few weeks. To give you time to sort your shit out and find yourself again." He indicates Paul with a finger pointed in his direction. "I see you found something. Someone."

"You didn't call or text or anything."

"Neither did you."

"I fell on my phone. It broke."

"You know where I live. You could have come by."

This is getting us nowhere, this blame game. I've blamed everyone for everything happening in my life and now I'm at a point of owning it. I'm aware of Paul watching the entire exchange. I'm angry but I can't tell if it's with Nick or myself. I was too scared to approach him in case I embarrassed myself. In case he'd had enough of me. The me he thinks he knows.

He sighs and rakes a hand through his hair. "Anyway, I was going to give you this. You wanted to read it last time you were at my apartment."

He passes it to me and I take it. Humiliation burns my stomach and I don't know what else to say. I'm angry and sad and confused and God, he looks so good. I want to push him away but also I want to jump him.

He doesn't say goodbye or goodnight. He nods towards Paul and then he turns and walks back down the street, back towards *Johnnie's*.

Paul comes to stand beside me and says, "That was intense."

I just nod and tears burn my eyes even though I've never cried this much in my entire, stupid life.

"I'm going to go," he says. "Have a nice life, Imelda." He looks like he wants to kiss me on the cheek but instead takes my hand and squeezes it.

What a mess.

34

I'm staring at a moleskin journal. Dark grey flecked with black with gold writing on the front that says, GET SHIT DONE.

I wasn't going to unwrap it but curiosity is dangerous and irresistible to someone with not much left to lose.

My fingers shake as I flip the cover open and read the first page. It's Nick's anger management diary. It's invasive to read a person's diary. Isn't it?

But he gave it to me. I read on. By the time I get to the last entry I can barely see through my tears.

He thinks I'm amazing.

He really likes me.

My stomach sinks and the lump in my throat is back as my tears fall. He likes the me I've shown him. The me who drops my underwear to have sex on a desk. The me who can't get enough of his hands on my body and puts out every time. The me who wears heels and dresses and gets her hair done sometimes but not all the time.

I slam my good hand down on the surface of the dining table and it stings my palm. How can he like me when he doesn't know who I am? When I don't fucking know who I am? Am I the violence I felt when I hit Ted and launched myself at two men fighting each other? Am I the passion I feel when Nick is inside me? Am I the scared little girl when my mother gives me her disappointed face? Am I the woman being scolded by her boss for something outside of her control?

I lean back on the couch and sob and feel sorry for myself because I don't know. The realization I'd had when Paul and I were walking earlier was that maybe it doesn't matter who I am, who Nick thinks I am, who the world thinks I am. I'm happy when I'm with Nick. I stop thinking about expectations and responsibilities and have fun. I smile and I laugh.

Because of Nick.

He's the first person in my life who hasn't got caught up with titles or salaries or letters after a person's name. He's a barman for God's sake. And he's happy doing it. He also doesn't need to save lives or run the world. He just does what he does because he likes doing it.

And he likes me.

I open a new page and grab a pen from a cup on my kitchen counter.

Dear Freddy...

35

What if he doesn't want to see me? It's late. It's dark. He just caught me being kissed by another guy.

His light is on as I climb the narrow stairs from the base of the building at the rear where he parks his car. I hesitate but then I knock. We need to have this out. I need to see where we stand.

The door opens and Nick stands there with a beer in his hand, sweats on the bottom and an old gym tank on the top. He's had a shave in the few hours since I saw him. His hair is wet and he smells of soap and water and everything clean and bright.

"Hi."

"Hi," he says back but he's wary.

"I don't know where to start. I'm sorry I didn't come see you. I was waiting for you to come and see me and when you didn't, I thought you didn't want to have anything to do with me or that you were locked up maybe."

"Your friend obviously didn't tell you I came by."

"No, she didn't. I didn't know. I was trying to start over without you."

"With that guy you were with tonight? Are you seeing him?"

"He's an old boyfriend. From uni. We caught up for dinner."

"And kissing."

My cheeks burn and I wish I didn't blush so easily. "He kissed me goodnight. I thought I was supposed to... or something. I don't know. Fucking hell, Nick, I don't know where we are or how we got here. We were supposed to be having fun and now it's so messy."

"Did you read my diary?" he asks.

I take it out of my purse and drop it on the couch. I sink down next to it with a nod. "I did."

"And?"

I'm too scared to think about this going wrong. I shake my head.

"Are you saying no, Imelda?"

I can't tear my gaze from my lap and I'm completely combustible. My insides are in hot knots and my tongue is stuck to the roof of my mouth. Anxiety makes me want to vomit.

I shake my head again and try to speak. On the third attempt I finally push out the words. "I added an entry."

"In my diary?"

He drops his beer on the coffee table as he sits and snatches the diary up without a second's hesitation, flipping the pages noisily.

I close my eyes because I don't want to try to read his expression as he reads.

It's too quiet.

There's no ticking clock here.

After what seems an eternity, he says softly, "Do you really mean this? All of it?"

I nod and for sure I'm going to explode in a mess of embarrassment, wanting, needing, confusion, and all the rest.

"I'm not a bad boy, Imelda."

"And I'm not a sex driven vixen, Nick."

"All the charges were dropped against me but the cop out is true. I don't know my own strength and when I'm angry, really angry, I snap."

I open my eyes and look into his. "So do I." I hold up my hand still in the brace. "I spent so many years quiet that I think all my noise came out in a few weeks. But I'm not that person any more than you are. My mother has always wanted me to be a good little girl, quiet and respectful at all times. Good in all things. I nearly was. Until I met you. You challenge me and let me be loud. You encourage me to be loud." I smile and twist my fingers in my lap. He's still so quiet. "Can you say something? Please."

"I like you loud. I like it when you shout at me and hit things. It makes you a real person, Imelda. If I'm going to settle down with someone, it has to be someone who meets me on every level, in bed and out of it."

"If?" This is it. This is where he tells me I'm too chaotic and it's bad for his life.

"If we're going to do this, you can't kiss other men."

I shake my head so hard my hair tosses around.

He goes on, coming to kneel in front of me on the couch his hands on the outside of my denim clad thighs. "If we're going to do this, we have to talk. About everything and anything and nothing. Tell me when you want to be bad, tell me when you want to be good. It doesn't make you any less if you ask for what you want."

I take a deep breath. "I want to be your girlfriend."

His eyes twinkle as he smiles. "And I want to be your boyfriend, if you can accept my past and possibly that I'll fuck up again in the future."

I shrug and lean forward, closer. "As we long as we fuck it up together. No one's perfect."

We laugh so hard it's difficult to kiss and make up.

The diary sits discarded on the couch, the pages open...

DEAR FREDDY

Dear Freddy...

I recently discovered I have a temper. I took bad advice from a colleague and things got out of hand real quick. I yelled, I got violent, I said things I shouldn't have said, did things I shouldn't have done.

In my quest to find Mr. Right Now, I found a bucket load of trouble instead.

But. I regret nothing.

That bad advice led me directly into the path of a man who has a wicked tongue and an overly inflated sense of protection towards those he loves. Bad boy, good guy, I don't even care anymore.

Nick is everything I've been taught to avoid in this life but they're wrong about him. He's hardworking, he's courageous and strong and sexy.

He likes cats.

He likes me.

I think I love him.

Consider this my penance for not believing in him, for not letting him have a chance at being my Mr. Right when I thought I was only looking for a good time and not a long time.

I'll write you every day until I can convince him that maybe I am his type after all.

That maybe he loves me too.

Imelda.

THIS MESS WE MADE (PEEK)

Callum West had zero problems with self-medicating. He was still a doctor with a prescription pad after all, but when a high-powered engine sped past his houseboat at the crack of dawn, the sound broke through his sleeping pill haze and he came to with a start.

He waited for the inevitable rocking to begin, sitting bolt upright in bed, the sheets bunched around his hips, and then swore. "Fucking moron." What was it about losers and their pleasure crafts who thought it was okay to wake people before- He swore again. Half past ten?

Rubbing the sleep from his eyes, he stood and stretched. Then he performed his only homage to the OCD gods, tapping his left arm, then his right. His left leg and then the right. He flexed his fingers and curled his toes, rolled his head and cracked his neck. Yep. All of his limbs were still there, still working, still whole.

What had started as a joke between he and his buddies in Afghanistan had become a religious practice for Callum all these years later. He'd seen too many men wake up after the crude anaesthesia had worn off and reach for something only to remember the IED that wiped out half their patrol had also taken their hand, their arm, their legs. They were the unlucky ones. To Callum, the lucky ones never woke up to reach for anything.

This is usually how he woke up after a week of insomnia and then giving into the sleeping tablets in the early hours. Cranky. Wound up. Glad he lived alone and didn't have to face a smiling, bouncy bundle of female over the breakfast table talking about happily ever afters and squealing about her plans for the day.

Damn. He needed coffee and a shower. In that order. Padding around his ancient houseboat in nothing but a worn pair of board shorts, he turned on the percolator and then went outside in an attempt to greet the day. It was going to be a hot one which was probably why the moron from earlier thought it was okay to speed around on the river and make a nuisance of himself. Ten years ago that would have been Callum and his mates, blowing off steam in their down-time. Summer didn't last long so hot weekends were at a premium and packed with water skiing and tubing from sunup to sundown.

How nice it would be to return to that state of naivety. No more worry than what to have for breakfast to cure the hangover. Before he knew the realities of war. Back when he'd been a stupid intern with stupid ideals. Before he knew more than he wanted to about meatball surgery in the middle of the desert. The stuff he'd seen in his years in the Australian Army made M*A*S*H look like a friggin' Hawaiian vacation.

Callum barely tasted the coffee but he knew it was strong and bitter, a lot like him. Maybe his godmother had been right when she'd warned him he'd need a hobby if he wanted to be *so* alone. He'd laughed then but as the months rolled by after her death, he'd come to realise she was right. That bloody woman was always right. Drunker than two skunks most of the time but she always knew what was going on with the people around her.

He missed Mavis and wondered for the billionth time in his life if there was a heaven for the special ones.

"Jesus," he cursed, the sound echoing across the still-as-glass water and bouncing back off the towering red cliff face on the other side of the Murray River. He was in bad shape and possibly even in need of some human company.

He looked through his cupboard searching for something appropriate to wear to town, or what passed for a town in Jupiter Creek, and decided he had to shop for food anyway. He might even make a day of it and head into Mannum or Murray Bridge. He hated crowds but sometimes he had to test the edges of his self-imposed limits just to make sure he hadn't died and was living in stunning purgatory for his half-sins.

When he had all he needed, he jumped from the back of the houseboat to the landing, his bare feet sinking into the thick carpet of cool grass before he walked up to the house.

Mavis's house.

Sure, he had a shower on the boat but it only dripped water on the back of his neck. He liked the hard spray of her shower. Before her death, she'd liked him to come inside so she knew he was okay. That's what she said anyway. He knew she craved the company and he liked to make sure she'd survived the night and her own personal demons.

When he stepped through the back door, he inhaled the earthy scent of Mavis's kitchen. Even though she was gone, the house still smelled like her. Not like ten-day old gin but like cloves and spices and home. It's why he'd stayed after the funeral. No one had come to kick him out and when the bills arrived at Jupiter Creek's post office, Nancy gave them to him and he just paid them and kept going on.

He had the words on a bumper sticker on his ute, *Just Keep On Keeping On*. Not his motto but when he'd bought the workhorse, he hadn't wanted to take it off just in case it left a mark.

Ignoring the sad memories and the calls of a dead woman, he headed for the bathroom. He left the door open like he always did now. He didn't mind his houseboat with its walls of windows and open plan but he didn't like to be shut in small dark spaces. It reminded him of army tents and hastily hung shelters, heavy camo covers blocking out the intensity of the sun but not the sand or the fear.

Both antique copper taps turned on full blast to the sounds of groaning pipes. Callum didn't care if the water was scalding hot or freezing cold as he stripped off his shorts and stepped under the spray, letting it wash away the residues of the demon sleeping tablets.

When he felt a little more human and a little less walking dead, he shut off the water and turned to reach for his towel. But that's as far as he got.

In the open doorway stood...someone. An almost naked someone. She was yawning, one hand in the air, the other near her ear, her elbow bent. Her blonde hair was everywhere that was up and matted like she hadn't brushed it this year. She looked like a hobo in designer undies. No fear, no fury, just a little brow raise when her eyes lowered to his package which was followed by a bored shrug.

She moaned something, swayed a little, and then ran for the toilet, heaving what had to be half her guts up into the porcelain bowl.

"What. The. Fuck?" was about all he could muster.

· ♥ · ♥ · ♥ · ♥ · ♥ ·

Audrey Hobson didn't remember much about the last few hours, or days. In her mind she saw loads of little clear bottles of vodka. She remembered a shiny black stretch limo with twinkling stars reflected off the roof and doors. She hoped she tipped the driver after she'd thrown up in the back. She remembered sleeping after the rocking car had stopped spinning around her. What she didn't know was where she was. That information was grainy at best, like the reception on the old-style televisions as a kid when a plane flew over or the day was windy.

The hot naked guy in the shower said something but she had only enough energy to get rid of whatever was left in her stomach. She couldn't even raise her arms to get her hair out of the way. Had she gone on a date? Blacked out again? She groaned. Had she had sex with hot naked guy and couldn't remember? God, it was all so blurry.

"Are you okay?" Hot naked guy asked from somewhere behind her.

More retching was about all she had. A cool flannel hit the back of her neck as her hair was pulled gently back.

"Are you sick?" he asked.

Are you a rocket scientist? she wanted to come back with but only more retching. She didn't think there was anything left to come up but her stomach just wouldn't stop heaving. She tried to take a deep breath, anything to calm her body, but a chunky hiccup left her coughing and shaking. She was used to the hangovers and the morning chuck, but this was different. Through the haze of unpleasantness she suddenly felt cold and just could not stop the shivers.

There was a rustle of plastic and the stranger who might not have been a stranger pulled her back from the rim and handed her a small bin to hold. "How long have you been sick like this?"

That was a good question. "About three months. I think," she managed to whisper. As she spoke, she actually felt her dry lips stretch and then split, tasting blood on her tongue. Where was her gloss? Where was her handbag? Where was *she*?

He snatched something from the top of the vanity and held her wrist while he looked at it. A watch. He had nice hands, she noticed. They were big and warm. Like a hug but not.

"Who are you?" she mumbled. He looked familiar so she must know him. *Please don't just be a random.*

"I live here. Did you get lost? Break in?"

Little glimpses flashed in her hurting brain. She didn't break in. She'd had a key. The limo driver had carried her to the front door but it wasn't locked. He'd put her on the couch and then she'd lost consciousness. She woke up in the dark, her jeans riding up and her ridiculous disguise hat still on her head. She kind of remembered throwing off her clothes and pulling a blanket from the back of the sofa but then it all went black again once she'd warmed up.

"Where are we?" Panic edged in and for a moment she felt too close to the looming stranger.

"Jupiter Creek," he said, giving her a kind of strange look mingled with wariness.

Her stomach started up again but there really was nothing left. Nothing left of Audrey Hobson. Nothing left of her career or her life. She tried to open her eyes again to tell the stranger she couldn't be back in Jupiter Creek. She lived a world away in Los Angeles. She was a star. Or at least she had been.

Jupiter Creek? "Are you sure?" she managed to murmur but she didn't hear his answer. Darkness swamped her and for a moment the pain and panic just...went away.

(this book is available in print and ebook at online book stores)

ABOUT THE AUTHOR

Thank you so much for reading my book and making it all the way to the end! I hope you enjoyed Nick and Imelda's story! It would be really helpful for me if you could leave a review at your place of purchase but don't give away all the plot points.

You can find more novels by me at Amazon and other online bookstores in print and ebook and Kindle Unlimited.

I also write Historical Romance a la Bridgerton (but sexier) and erotic short stories under the Club Never brand (which you can link to from my Amazon Author page). I also have a series set in tropical Queensland in a tattoo studio if you like it hot, flawed and fun.

If you found spelling errors in this novel or you want to reach out to me, I'm at bronwyn@bronwynstuart.com

www.ingramcontent.com/pod-product-compliance
Lightning Source LLC
Chambersburg PA
CBHW021454240626
47154CB00002B/368